k

the due

SLICK

SLICK

M.M. VAUGHAN

ALMA BOOKS

ALMA BOOKS LTD
3 Castle Yard
Richmond
Surrey TW10 6TF
United Kingdom
www.almabooks.com

Slick first published in the US as *Frendroid* by Margaret K. McElderry
Books in 2019
This edition first published in the UK by Alma Books Limited in 2019

© Monica Meira, 2019

Cover design: Leo Nickolls Design

Printed in Great Britain by CPI Group (UK) Ltd, Croydon CR0 4YY

ISBN: 978-1-84688-459-7

"Tiger father begets tiger son."
Chinese proverb

For Eli Maverick,
in memory of his tiger father
Eric Seagraves.

And for Emilia. Always.

SLICK

DEAR PERSON READING THIS,

My name is Danny, and I need your help. First off, I should tell you that this isn't my story – it's Eric's. Well, the name he was given was Eric, but I called him Slick, and he was my best friend. I say *was* because he died six months ago.

Before you start reading Slick's story, I want to tell you about him. I need you to like him, and you probably won't after reading the first few pages, unless all you care about is the kind of shoes you wear and how many friends you have on Kudos. I definitely didn't think much of him when I first got to know him. See, when I met Slick, he was *obsessed* with brands and being popular. Me: I didn't care about the brand of anything I wore or owned – not that I had ever had much choice about that.

But none of those things matter when you're friends. And that's what we became: friends. Best friends.

And then he was gone. And when I say gone, I mean he was killed. And the next day, it was like nothing had ever happened.

But it *did* happen, and there's no way I'm letting *them* get away with it. They think there's nothing I can do, because I'm just a dumb twelve-year-old kid. I guess they forgot that even a dumb twelve-year-old can use a computer.

So here's my plan:

1) Publish Slick's journal.
2) The whole world reads it.
3) The people who killed him spend the rest of *their* dumb lives rotting in a jail cell.

That's basically it. You wouldn't believe it took me four months to come up with that.

Anyway, before you start reading Slick's journal, there are a couple of things I need to tell you:

One, I've taken out some stuff. You're not missing anything. The first month of Slick's journal is kind of like reading a dictionary:

A duck pond is a pond with ducks in it.

That kind of thing. Also, I added some stuff – the parts where it made more sense if I explained what happened. I think it's obvious which parts are mine and which are Slick's – I'm the one who doesn't list every single thing a person is wearing. And I'm funnier. Which isn't as braggy as it sounds – my mum tells better jokes than Slick, and that's really saying something.

Two, and this is kind of important: Slick was a robot.

Actually, he was an android – a robot that looks and sounds like a human being. You've probably heard of them, but until the Canny Valley androids were built, the only ones that really looked or sounded like humans were the ones in movies. There are already sixty thousand Canny Valley androids in the world, including Slick's parents. They're everywhere. They live around us, acting like normal humans living normal lives, doing normal jobs and making normal – human – friends. But Slick was special. Slick was the first child android. He didn't know that, though. He thought he was just a normal kid moving to a new town, because that's what they'd programmed him to think. And we all thought that too, until a pillow fight changed everything. I'll get to that later.

So here it is – Slick's journal. And after you read it, please tell everyone you know. If word gets out, then they'll have to pay for what they did. I know this could get me into trouble, but I have to do something. You'd do the same if it was your best friend, wouldn't you?

OK, I'm done, and now I'd like to introduce you to my best friend, Slick. He was awesome – I'm sorry you didn't get to meet him.

– Danny

```
bool isAngry(Human human)
{
if(human.lips.getState() ==
HUMANLIPSSTATE.TIGHT && human.mouth.
getState() == HUMANMOUTHSTATE.CLOSED &&
human.eyes.getState() == HUMANEYESSTATE.
NARROWED &&
human.eyeBrows.getState() ==
HUMANEYEBROWSSTATE.LOW)
{
return true;
}
else
{
return false;
}
}
```

1
SLICK

Today was the day I found out that I had made my first real friend. I was seventy-five per cent certain Harry was my friend before this morning, but it wasn't until I got an invitation to his birthday party that I knew for sure. When he gave me the invitation, he looked annoyed. At first I thought this might mean that he didn't really want me to come and that he'd been made to ask me because I was new, but then he apologized for the lame invite. He said his mother had made him give them out so that she could keep track of the numbers coming. That's when I understood that feeling angry can look a lot like feeling embarrassed.

I don't know why it bothered him so much. I like the invitation – it has skateboards all around it. I love skateboarding. At the top it says "Let's Sk8 to Celebrate", and then a list of all the information: date, time and place. It was very clear, and I could see his mother's point: it must be hard to organize a party if you don't know how many people will be coming. I couldn't see Harry's problem with it.

Harry is just one of my friends. I have twenty.

- One is 100 per cent confirmed: Harry. See above.
- Two of these are 75 per cent confirmed friends: Luke and Tyler. These are the people who invite me to sit at their table at lunch and pick me for their teams, and who I have seen outside of school.
- Three of these are 65 per cent confirmed friends: Mateo, Jake and Theo. These are the people who invite me to sit at their table at lunch and pick me for their teams.
- Fourteen are 50 per cent confirmed friends. These are the people that I have had more than two conversations with (not schoolwork-related) since I got here.

I don't have a best friend. Maybe when I've been here longer I'll have one, but I think a month is probably not long enough to choose a best friend yet.

Notes:
- I now have 457 friends on Kudos. I had 320 when I arrived, but I don't remember any of them. It's weird how quickly you forget about your old life when it's gone.
- Of the 137 friends that I've made since we moved to Ashland, only eighteen are Real World Friends (RWFs). The rest are Virtual Friends (VFs), which are the same as RWFs, except you've only met them on the Internet. Most of my new VFs are friends of friends, so they will probably become RWFs at some point.
- Luke: 438,118 Kudos friends. Harry: 640 Kudos friends. Mateo: 509 Kudos friends. Tyler: 383 Kudos friends.
- Luke has the most Kudos friends because he is a singer and has his own video channel (LuckyLuke7). The last song he uploaded, 'In Your Dreams', has 2,004,833 likes.
- Harry said that nobody says "rad" any more. I will stop saying "rad".
- Two girls commented on my profile picture today. One said, "Cute!" The other wrote three heart emojis. I replied, "Thank

you very much," as I haven't met either of them and didn't know what else to write. They don't go to my school.
- My profile picture is cool. That's what Harry said, and the others agreed. It's of me mid-air on my Baltic Wave skateboard, and I'm looking straight ahead at the sea. I put it up before we moved to Ashland. I don't remember who took it.
- Mum and Dad do not have Kudos accounts. This is because they are adults, so they only count their RWFs. Mum has thirty-nine RWFs. Five of these are 100 per cent confirmed as they have invited her out to do something more than once. Dad has twelve RWFs, but none of these are 100 per cent confirmed. Dad said that this is because men make friends in a different way to women and kids.

2
SLICK

TUESDAY 9TH OCTOBER

I told my parents about Harry's party this morning before school. Dad said I can't go. He said I have to be at the fund-raiser.

A fund-raiser is an event that's held to raise money for a cause.

I asked my dad what the cause was. "It's for your sister," he said, which made no sense at all as my sister is dead.

My sister died before we moved here. I don't really remember her much, because she was in the hospital most of my life, but I know what she looked like, because there are pictures of her everywhere in our house. People say I look like her, which is a strange thing to say about a girl and a boy. I think they probably mean that she had blond hair and blue eyes like I have. Everyone who sees her picture says how pretty she was. She died a year ago. It was Mum's idea to hold a fund-raiser for the local hospital, even though my sister was never treated there. Mum said it's the perfect opportunity to meet our new neighbours properly and to do something good for the community. I think it's more important for me to make new friends, but I can't drive yet, and children have to do what their parents tell them, so there was no point in arguing. I don't know how this will affect my friendship with Harry, as this hasn't happened to me before.

I think Harry is still my friend. I told him that I couldn't go to his party because my parents were having a fund-raiser for my dead sister. His cheeks turned red and he said, "That's cool." Then everyone at the table went silent for a while, and I thought maybe things weren't cool at all. Sometimes people don't say how they're feeling, and I find it confusing. But then Harry told me that he'd asked for a Baltic skateboard for his birthday, and we started talking about that. So I think we must still be friends, because it would be strange to start a conversation with someone you didn't like any more.

Harry asked his parents for the Baltic Flame skateboard. I have the Wave version, which is the same design, just different artwork. They're both cool. Luke said he's going to ask for one too for his birthday. His birthday is in December. I wonder if I'll be invited to his party.

Notes:
- I changed my profile picture to one I took today. It's of me, Tyler, Harry, Luke and Mateo, with our arms around each other, laughing after football practice. I got Theo to take it with my Hexam R3 as the camera on it has better picture quality than Theo's. It also comes with over 120 filters to use. I chose the Woodstock filter. Luke and Theo also have Hexams, but the R2, not the R3.

3
SLICK

SATURDAY 13TH OCTOBER

Today I spent the day going around the neighbourhood with Mum and Dad to give out the flyers for the fund-raiser. Dad and Mum already know quite a few of our neighbours, as Mum is a member of the gardening club, the book club and the bridge club, and Dad is a member of the golf club and the bridge club. They like clubs.

It took us six hours to deliver eighty-five flyers, because we kept getting invited into people's houses.

After the fifth glass of lemonade, I said it would be much quicker if we just posted the flyers, but Dad said that speaking to people would make it more likely that they would come.

Notes:
- People say "please excuse the mess" a lot, even when their house is tidy.
- A lot of people didn't look happy to see us when they answered the door, even though they hadn't met us before.

- After we told them that we were raising money in memory of my dead sister, everyone was nice.
- Two people cried.
- The lady at 24 Holland Road opened the door in a towel. Her face turned bright red and she slammed the door closed without saying anything. We waited, but she never came back, so we put the flyer under the door.
- Harry answered the door at his house wearing a new pair of Slick trainers. He invited me to his house last week after school, and he didn't have any Slicks. I know this because his shoes were all lined up on a rack in his room. I told him that he should get a pair of Slicks as they're really comfortable and you can jump much higher in them (Harry likes to play basketball). I also told him that Brad "Slipstream" Brooks is wearing them in the new Slick ad. And now Harry has a pair. I told him they were awesome, and I said it would be cool if all our group wore Slicks. He agreed.
- I like Harry.

4

SLICK

TUESDAY 16TH OCTOBER

A delivery driver came to our house today with three boxes
– one for Mum, one for Dad and one for me. Dad's
was the biggest. Dad said the parcels were from Uncle
Martin. Uncle Martin works for a magazine in London. He
gets stuff to review and then sends it to us to keep when he's
finished. I have never met Uncle Martin, even though we
lived in London too before we moved here. He's probably
always busy with his magazine work.

My box contained:

- A poster of Justin Peterson. He's the new striker for the Ashland
  Wanderers. The Ashers are my team, so it's good that we moved
  here. My grandfather was an Ashers fan and passed it down
  to my dad and then to me. My grandfather died when I was
  little, but I have a nice memory of him showing me how to kick
  a ball. It's my only memory of him.
- Two pairs of Slicks from the new collection. They're not available
  in shops yet. The first pair are green and yellow. The second
  pair are red and orange.

- Four pairs of Oldean trousers, ten Oldean T-shirts, three Oldean jackets, three Oldean jumpers, two Oldean belts, one pair of Oldean sunglasses, six pairs of Oldean socks. I only wear Graves, so I won't be wearing any of this. But it is very thoughtful of Uncle Martin to send it anyway.

5

SLICK

FRIDAY 19TH OCTOBER

We went to see Dr Kilaman after school today. She is my dentist. Mum went in first at 7 p.m. Dad went in at 7.30 p.m. I went in at 8 p.m. While I waited for Mum and Dad, I played *Land X* on my phone.

Land X has over fifteen million active players every day. I only started playing when we moved to Ashland, so I am behind everybody else at school, but I'm catching up. I'm level twenty-one now. My avatar's name is Baltic_Slick. I picked this name because I like Baltic skateboards and Slick trainers.

We visit Dr Kilaman every Friday, but I am mentioning it today because Dr Kilaman wasn't there. Instead, we were seen by Dr Newmouth. When it was my turn to go in, I asked him if he became a dentist because his name was Newmouth, and he laughed and then stopped and stared at me.

"Did you just make a joke, Eric?"

The way he asked the question made me think that I had done something wrong.

"No."

"So you weren't trying to be funny?"

"No – I'm sorry if that was rude. It's just that Dr Newmouth, is like Dr New Mouth. And dentists make people's mouths like new."

"So you were just stating a fact?"

"Yes."

Then Dr Newmouth smiled and shook his head. "For a moment…"

Then he didn't say anything else except to ask me to close my eyes. I was asleep after that, so we didn't talk any more until my appointment was over. He said it had been a real pleasure to meet me at last. I don't know why he said "at last", but I didn't want to ask the wrong question again, so I didn't say anything about that. Instead, I asked him if he was my new dentist. He said that he was only covering for Dr Kilaman while she was on holiday, and that she would be back next week.

"Now *that's* a name to strike fear into the hearts of patients," he said, and then he started laughing. I smiled even though I didn't understand what he meant.

I found the things that Dr Newmouth said today confusing. That's why I'm thinking about them now.

When we got home it was 10 p.m. We spent the next two hours getting ready for the fund-raiser tomorrow. I am going to wear my new Oldean clothes. I hadn't really looked at them when they arrived yesterday, but now I realize how cool they are. I don't think I'm going to wear my Graves stuff any more.

It's midnight. I have to go to sleep now.

6

DANNY

SATURDAY 20TH OCTOBER

I met Slick on Saturday the 20th of October at the fundraiser for his dead sister. Slick didn't have a dead sister, or even a live one, but he didn't know this at the time, and neither did I.

Anyway, I wasn't supposed to go. I was meant to be spending the day with my dad. My cousin Vito calls him "the person who made a biological donation to my existence", which is kind of a mouthful but way more accurate. I'm supposed to see "Dad" every other weekend, but in the last year he's only shown up three times, so I wasn't exactly surprised when Mum called him to see where he was and he told her he wasn't going to be able to make it. I knew that's what he was saying, because Mum always walks away and starts whispering on the phone when she's cross with him. After a couple of minutes, she came back and passed the phone to me.

"Hey, sorry, son. I'm on my way to the races. A friend of mine got a good tip on a horse, and I couldn't pass it up."

My dad likes to gamble on horses. He's terrible at it. You'd think he'd have worked that out by now.

"Sure," I said.

"I'll make it up to you."

"Whatever."

"Watch your mouth." He paused. "How have you been?"

"Fine. You forgot my birthday."

"I did? Oh... I'll get you whatever you want after my big win."

"I won't hold my breath."

I heard something being slammed down hard. I hoped it was his head on a brick wall. "You little..." he started saying.

I hung up.

Mum came over and tried to give me a hug, but I shook her off me and went down to the basement to work on the computer I was building. I felt bad – I know it's not Mum's fault that he's such a loser, but then again, she did choose to have a child with the man, so it kind of is.

Mum said she didn't want to leave me home alone when I was upset, so she made me come with her to the fund-raiser. She wanted to go because it was raising money for Ashland Hospital – which is where she works as a nurse – and because her friend Annie had asked her to go. Annie also works at the hospital. I told Mum that a) I wasn't upset, and b) I didn't work at the hospital, so there was no need for me to go, but then she gave me one of her looks – the one that means *shut your mouth, put your jacket on and get in the car*. Mum has a whole language she can speak with just her face. Vito says it's a mum thing – apparently they're all fluent in Face.

"*Amore*, come on, cheer up. It'll be fun," said Mum as I sulked in the back seat of the car. The car stopped at a red light, and she turned to look at me. "Who knows? Maybe there'll be some kids your age there."

I rolled my eyes and put my hood over my head. Mum sighed.

Mum is always trying to get me to make friends with other kids. Vito says to chill out about it and that it's a mum's job to worry. I get that, but it doesn't make it any less annoying.

We got to the fund-raiser early, as Mum told Annie that she'd help set up, even though she didn't know Slick's parents.

"Remember, be polite," whispered Mum as we walked into the church hall. "This must be very hard for the family."

I nodded. "OK, OK," I said.

"You're a good boy," she said. She kissed me on the top of my head and walked over to join a group of adults. As I made my way over to the side of the room to find a spot to hide, I saw Slick. We'd never spoken, but I recognized him – he was the newest kid in my year. I'd seen him hanging out with Luke and Tyler, which said everything I needed to know about him. I put my hood over my head and went to sit down in a corner, as far away from him as I could.

I took out my phone to play *Land X*. I was close to completing the Stone-Cold Slayer quest and had found the last thing I needed that morning – a gold-mirrored shield. Now all I had to do was find Gorgon Gaia and destroy her, but Mum had other ideas.

"I want you to meet someone," said Mum, taking the phone out of my hand before I could stop her.

I was so angry. "MUM! I'm about to kill Gorgon Gaia!"

"Looks like it's Gordon's lucky day, then," she said. She switched my phone off and handed it back to me.

"*Gorgon*, Mum, not Gordon," I said.

She ignored me and pointed to Slick on the other side of the room. He was laying a stack of posters onto a table. "His name's Eric. His mum told me he's just started at your school. Do you know him?"

I nodded. "He's in my year." I knew where this was going. "*Mum*... I don't want to make friends with him. I'm fine. I'm happy. I have friends on here."

I held up my phone.

Mum sighed loudly. "Those are not real friends. Now get up, or I'll go and get him and bring him over."

I knew she'd do it too.

"You don't know what he's like," I said, but she was already walking away.

"I'm ignoring you," she said in a kind of singing voice.

I kind of hated my mum at that point.

She was already introducing herself by the time I caught up with her.

"...so lovely to meet you. I'm Maria Lazio, and this is my son, Danny. I think you and Danny are in the same year at school."

"Yes, we are," said Eric/Slick. "It's a pleasure to meet you, Mrs Lazio." Slick shook my mum's hand, and then he turned and smiled at me.

"Hi, Danny."

I nodded. "Hey."

"I'm so sorry about your sister," said Mum. Until that point, I hadn't realized that he was the brother of the girl who had died. I felt kind of bad then.

Slick smiled. "Thank you," he said.

"I was thinking you two might want to hang out today before the fund-raiser starts," said Mum.

I rolled my eyes.

"I'm sorry, but I have to help get things ready," said Slick.

"Danny would love to help, wouldn't you?" said Mum.

"I have a system," said Slick. He pointed over to the table.

"I'm sure Danny can pick it up quickly," said Mum. "If you don't mind?"

"He *said* he has a system," I said. I knew that my help wasn't wanted, but, apparently, my mum didn't pick up on that.

"I don't mind," said Slick. "I'll show you, Danny."

"What a sweetheart," said Mum. She put her hands around my face and gave me a loud kiss on the cheek. "Have fun!"

"Mum!" I said. I couldn't believe she had kissed me in front of another kid.

Mum laughed. "I'm going, I'm going," she said.

"My mum is so embarrassing," I said when she was gone. I wiped my cheek. "She always does that."

"Does what?" asked Slick.

"Gives me kisses in front of people."

"Oh," said Slick.

"It's an Italian thing," I explained quickly. "Everybody kisses each other in Italy."

Slick nodded. "That makes sense – we're not Italian, and my parents have never kissed me."

And that right there is when my weirdo counter started on Slick. It went up pretty quickly after that.

Slick showed me his "system" for putting up the posters, which was basically put tape on the four corners, stick poster on wall. Slick seemed surprised that I picked up how to do it so quickly. It took us about ten minutes. We didn't talk the whole time, which was just fine by me – I'm not the best at small talk.

Slick pressed down on the corner of the last poster and then smiled at me. "Cool – that was quick. You can help me with the next job if you want."

Mum was watching me from the other side of the room. There was no way I was going to get away with playing *Land X* while I was here, so I nodded.

"Awesome," said Slick.

I followed him over to a table full of plastic boxes filled with food. Slick grabbed a plastic carrier bag from underneath it and pulled out two large bags of balloons. He handed one to me, and then he walked away. I followed him.

"What brand are your shoes?" he asked as we sat down in the same corner I'd been sitting in earlier.

I looked down at the white trainers that Mum had bought me over the summer.

"They're not any brand," I said.

"But you must have got them somewhere," said Slick.

I didn't know where this was going, but I knew I didn't like it. I had a flashback to year four, when I had come to school wearing a jacket that Mum had been given by someone in the family. I wear a lot of hand-me-downs. Anyway, turns out this jacket was the same one that Luke's sister had, and he told everyone, so they all started calling me Daniella. I told my teacher and she laughed. She said it was just a joke and not to take everything so seriously. Easier said than done, in my opinion, and one day – during lunchtime – Tyler Bowdry called me Daniella one too many times and something snapped. I punched him in the face. I was probably as surprised about that as Tyler was. I'd never done anything like that before. It got me suspended, but at least nobody ever called me Daniella again.

"Danny? Where did you get them?" Slick asked again.

I shook my head to get rid of the memory and glared at Slick. "We're not all swimming in money," I said.

"What do you mean?"

"Not everyone's parents can buy them everything."

"My parents don't buy me everything. My uncle Martin sends me things."

It was like talking to a five-year-old. "Fine," I said. "I don't have an Uncle Martin. Get it?"

Slick looked at me blankly for a moment.

"Do you mean you don't have much money, and you don't have somebody in your family to send you new shoes?"

"Wow. You're smart," I said.

"Thank you," said Slick. He didn't look like he was joking. I stared at him. Before I could say anything, though, he changed the subject to another one of my least favourite topics. "Are you on Kudos?"

"Why are you asking?"

"Because I looked everyone up before I started school. You were the only person in the whole year without an account."

"That's kinda creepy. And maybe I don't use my real name."

"*Ohhh*," he said, ignoring the creepy thing. "Do you use the name Danny?"

I was confused. "Danny *is* my real name," I said.

"I thought it was Daniel."

"Are you serious?"

There was a long pause. Way too long.

"So what name *do* you use on Kudos?" he asked finally.

"I don't."

"But you said—"

"I said *maybe* I don't use my real name. I didn't say definitely."

"What do you mean?"

"I mean I'm not on Kudos, OK? Can we leave it now?"

"I thought everybody was on Kudos."

"I'm not. What's so great about it anyway?"

"Because you can share things with your friends" – Slick smiled – "like photos and videos, and you can send each other messages. How do you talk to your friends, then?"

"I don't."

"Oh," said Slick. "Why? Don't you have any friends?"

I didn't say anything. I was really starting to dislike this kid.

"But at school, you must have friends there, right?"

Look, I know this whole thing makes me sound like the biggest loser, and I guess I kind of was. I don't know why things went the way they did at school… I was kinda messed up after my dad left – I was only six. Anyway, I started to worry about stuff – like something happening to Mum, that kind of thing. So I'd try to run out of school to go home, and then cry when the teacher would stop me. Kids made fun of me, I got angry, and so on and so on.

"Are you not saying anything because you don't have any friends?" asked Slick.

I know now that Slick wasn't being mean – just confused – but at the time, I didn't read it that way.

"What's your problem?" I asked.

"What do you mean?"

That's when I decided I was done with the conversation. "You're an idiot," I said, and started to walk off.

I heard Slick running up behind me. I put my hood back up and kept walking.

"Hey, Danny, I'm sorry."

I kept walking. Slick grabbed my shoulder to stop me.

"*Get your hands off—*"

"Wait, Danny. I'm really sorry. Sometimes I say the wrong thing, but I didn't mean anything."

I looked up at Slick, and, as I did, I saw one of the posters of his dead sister over his shoulder, and I suddenly felt really bad. I mean, if I were at my dead sister's fund-raiser, I'd probably act a bit weird too.

I shrugged. "It's fine. Whatever."

Slick smiled. "Cool. You want to help me with these?"

He held up the bag of balloons. "We have to blow up three hundred."

"*Three hundred?!*"

Slick nodded. "We'll be twice as quick if we do it together."

Slick was wrong. I can't be bothered to work out the maths, but I blew up eight in the time it took Slick to blow up the rest of them.

I stared at Slick. "Don't you ever run out of breath?"

Slick shook his head, then began to tie the balloons up with thread. I had no clue what I was supposed to be doing, so I just watched as Slick twisted and tied the balloons together. He worked quickly – not robot quickly, but like somebody who had done this hundreds of times before.

"Hold this," said Slick. He passed me the end of the string, then went over to the other end of the balloon pile and called out for me to pull. I pulled back and a loud *ooh* filled the room as a huge arch of perfectly twisted balloons lifted up into the air. I'm not really a balloon person, but I have to say that this arch thing *was* kind of awesome.

I stared up at it. "How did you know how to make it?" I asked.

Slick took the string from me and tied it to the leg of a nearby table.

"I don't know," he said. "I've always known."

"Always?! You must have been a weird baby."

Slick gave me a serious look. "I don't remember being a baby."

"It was a joke," I said. "A lame one, admittedly," I added.

"Oh. OK. That's funny." He pretend-smiled.

"They had jokes back in London, right?"

"Sure."

I was curious. "Go on then. Hit me."

"I don't want to hit you."

"Wow," I said. I couldn't work him out at all. "Hit me – as in tell me a joke."

"Do you like skateboarding?"

"That's your joke?"

"No. I just…"

"You don't know any jokes, do you?"

Slick shook his head. "Do you?"

I shrugged. "Nah, not really. Not any good ones."

"What's a bad joke?" he asked.

I thought for a moment. "OK, but it's lame – my mum told it to me when I was like four. Ready?"

Slick nodded.

"Where do cows like to go at the weekend?"

"I don't know," Slick said.

"The mooooovies."

Slick stared at me for a few seconds, and then he started laughing. Hard.

"It's not *that* funny," I said.

Slick was still laughing. "Nah, it's funny! Because cows say moo. And it's the movies."

"You are seriously weird," I said, but I couldn't help smiling.

Slick stopped laughing. "Why do you think I'm weird?"

I was going to answer, but then I remembered the reason we were here and that I should cut him some slack, so I just shook my head. "Forget it," I said. "I was just joking… So, do you have anything else you need help with?"

"No, that's it."

"OK. Cool. Well, nice to meet you, Eric."

"Where are you going?"

"It's just that I'm right at the end of a quest in *Land X*, and I was—"

"You play *Land X*?" asked Slick.

I nodded.

"I'm level twenty-two. What level are you?"

"Sixty-four," I replied.

Slick's mouth dropped open. "That's crazy good. Harry is the highest level of anyone I know, and he's only level thirty-seven."

I shrugged. "What can I say? I put in the hours."

"How? Don't you have to wait twenty-four hours for quartz?"

Quartz is the stuff you need to travel in *Land X*. If you can't travel, you can't do quests. I smiled.

"I'll show you something. What's your avatar name?"

"Baltic_Slick. Because I like Baltic skateboards and Slick trainers."

"Right, whatever. I'm Binarius_X. I'll add you now."

Slick and I sat in the corner and took out our mobile phones. I showed him how to change the date settings on his phone so he wouldn't have to wait twenty-four hours to harvest more quartz, and then I took him to where the Harp of Discord was so that he could complete the quest he'd been stuck on.

Slick and I had found something we had in common.

We played for an hour, until his dad came to get him when the fund-raiser was about to start.

"Thanks, Danny. That was awesome," said Slick as he stood up. "See you Monday?"

"Yeah, sure," I said.

I had to admit I was glad Mum had made me come, though maybe not as glad as Mum was. She actually called my aunt and my grandmother to tell them about my new friend when we got home. But whatever – I didn't make a big deal out of it. Truth was, I liked Slick. I mean, sure, he was weird, but I never did think that was such a bad character trait anyway.

7

SLICK

MONDAY 22ND OCTOBER

Miss Lake asked me to stay after class today. Tyler whispered, "Man, you are so lucky," and punched me in the arm. It was a friendly punch. I know this because he was smiling when he did it. Tyler said this because he likes Miss Lake in a girlfriend way. He is not the only one who likes her like this – all of my new friends were talking at lunch the other day about how hot she is. It took me a while to work out that they weren't talking about her temperature. I don't understand why a kid would think an adult is hot, but it's important to agree with your friends, or they may not stay your friends, so I agreed with them.

After everybody left the classroom, I went up to Miss Lake's desk. She was wearing a Blise top – that's my mother's favourite brand of clothes. My mum only wears Blise clothes, which is how I know the collection so well.

Miss Lake asked me how it went at the fund-raiser. I told her it was fine and that my mother was very pleased with the bids on the Freshen containers.

"I heard you spent some time with a boy at the fund-raiser – Daniel Lazio."

"Yes," I said, "but his name is actually Danny."

"Danny is a short way of saying Daniel. It's called a nickname."

"Oh," I said. This made sense now.

"Did you make friends with Danny?"

"I don't think so. I don't think he likes me much."

"That's good. He's not a very popular child, and you don't want to associate yourself with the unpopular kids – it wouldn't make you look good. You should focus your time on making friends with Luke and the other boys you've been spending time with at school. Luke in particular."

"Yes, Miss Lake."

I wasn't certain why Miss Lake cared who I was friends with, but my guess was that she was looking out for me as I'm new at the school, so this was very nice of her.

"Also, I think you should consider making friends with Ethan Schwartz. Do you know him?"

"Yes. But he isn't that popular." I was confused. Miss Lake was telling me to make friends with the popular kids, but Ethan only has 135 friends on Kudos, so this makes him average in popularity.

"That's true," said Miss Lake. "But his father is very important and knows a lot of people. I think your parents would like it if you made friends with him."

"Yes, Miss Lake."

"Good. See how it goes, and if you need any help, let me know. I can arrange for the two of you to sit together in our next lesson if you haven't managed to talk to him before then."

"Yes, Miss Lake," I said.

"That's all," said Miss Lake. She smiled, and I smiled back, and then I left the room.

8

DANNY

MONDAY 22ND OCTOBER

lick and I aren't in any classes together, and I didn't see him until lunchtime. I was standing by my locker, and he was walking by himself. He didn't see me until I said "hi". He looked at me for a moment, then looked back ahead and kept walking. I joined him.

"So you going to lunch?" I asked.

"Yep." He didn't slow down. I should have got the hint then and there, but I knew he was kind of a weirdo, so I didn't read anything into it.

"Did you find the safe?"

Slick stopped and turned to look at me.

"Safe?"

"Yeah, it's behind the painting of the battleship in Dame Vickers's house."

Slick's eyes opened wide. "I *knew* there had to be something there. I went there yesterday, but I couldn't find anything."

"You're going to need the code to open it."

"OK. What is it?"

"It took me hours to get it, and you want me just to tell you?"

Slick nodded. "Yeah."

I rolled my eyes, but I wasn't really cross. "It's her date of birth."

Slick thought for a moment, and then he grinned. "It's on her birth certificate in the drawer. Two seven oh five five oh. Awesome!"

I shrugged. "No big deal. If you want I can show—"

I was interrupted by the most annoying sound in the world – Tyler Bowdry's voice.

"Hey, Eric!"

Slick and I both looked up. Tyler was standing with Luke, Harry and Mateo.

"I have to go," mumbled Slick.

He didn't look at me, and I knew why – he didn't want to be seen talking to me.

I felt my whole body fill up with anger as Slick walked away. I wasn't sure who I was more angry with: Slick for being one of them, or me for thinking he might not be.

I kicked the door of a locker – hard enough to make everyone around me stop and stare at me, but I didn't even care. I heard Tyler's stupid donkey laugh and then the others joining in – probably Slick, too, but I didn't look back to see. I put my hood up and walked off in the other direction. I made a promise to myself right then that I would never talk to Slick again.

9

SLICK

MONDAY 22ND OCTOBER (II)

While we were waiting to get our lunch, Luke asked me if I was best friends with Danny now. I told him we weren't friends at all. Tyler said he was the biggest loser in the school and that he cried like a baby all the time. Harry said that he didn't really do that now, and Tyler asked him why he was sticking up for someone who had punched him in the nose. Harry shrugged, and Luke said that anyway, he was a total freak, and Harry nodded. Then they all laughed, and I laughed too, because they're my friends. It was strange, though: even though Luke, Harry and Tyler are my friends, and I don't want to be friends with someone who is as unpopular as Danny, I still felt bad laughing about him. I don't know why.

On our way to sit down, I saw that Ethan Schwartz was sitting at a table. We sat at an empty table two tables away. Everyone started talking about Harry's party that I didn't go to. I couldn't join in, so I spent the time trying to work out how to make friends with Ethan.

So far, I haven't had to try to make friends with anyone – it has just happened. This is how:

On my third day at my new school, I failed my first assignment. It was creative writing, and we had to make up a story about the sea. I decided to use a few scenes from a book I read once called *Moby Dick*, but the teacher didn't like that.

It was not a good start. I knew this because my teacher wrote on my paper: "*This is not a good start, Eric.*"

On the plus side, I heard a teacher telling a kid in the hall the other day that nobody likes a smart-arse. I guess it's true, because, after class, Tyler, who is the third most popular boy in my year, came over to me and said hi. I could see the *F* on the paper in his hand, which I guessed meant he was no smart-arse either.

Friends are made by finding the things you have in common. At first the only thing we had in common was that we had both handed in a bad assignment, but then we started talking and found out that we both like skateboarding and that we are both fans of the Ashland Wanderers. I think he didn't believe that I was a fan at first, because he wrinkled his nose and said, "Yeah, right. Didn't you move here like two days ago?" I explained that, even though I lived in London before moving here, my grandfather was a fan, and he made my dad a fan, who made me a fan. Then Tyler asked me two questions about the Ashers (that's what fans call them – they don't use the whole name). I think these were a test, but I answered them easily, as I know everything about the team. I am glad he asked these questions, because Tyler was standing with Harry and Luke, and they were the boys I wanted to make friends with as they are the two most popular boys in our year.

When I answered both questions correctly, all three of them smiled, and Harry gave me a pat on the back. Then they asked if I wanted to join them for lunch.

That was it. That's how I made friends with this group. I was finding it hard to see how I would repeat this with Ethan, as I hadn't seen him fail any assignments yet, but then I looked down at his feet and saw that he was wearing Slick trainers. They are my favourite kind of shoes. So now we have something in common.

Notes:
- I decided not to tell my friends about the safe in Dame Vickers's house. I used to think that friends told each other everything, but I've started to think that maybe I can keep a few things to myself. I don't think they really care that much about *Land X*, even though they all play it. They only talk about what level they're on, and so I think they only play because they want to be the best one in the group. But I think Danny plays it because he likes playing. He gets excited about it, like when he told me about the safe, or like when he told me at the fund-raiser that he works out strategies for solving quests and beating new enemies. And anyway, Danny definitely can't be playing it because all his friends play it, because Danny doesn't have any friends.
- When I started to play *Land X*, I did it because everyone else did, but now I play it because I like finding new ways of doing quests and unlocking new levels. This is one thing that I think I have in common with Danny. This doesn't mean I want to be friends with him – I am just observing a fact.
- I told Ethan I liked his shoes when I walked past him to put my lunch tray away. He looked surprised for a moment, but then he said thanks and smiled. That's all, but I think it's a start. I will follow this up somehow tomorrow. I think Miss Lake will be pleased.
- I didn't see Danny at lunch. Maybe he wasn't hungry.
- I didn't see Danny at all for the rest of the day. I'm glad, as I didn't want to have to ignore him again.

10

SLICK

WEDNESDAY 31ST OCTOBER

Today is Hallowe'en. I dressed as a zombie skateboarder. I wore:

- A white hooded zip-up top that had a black skeleton face across the front
- Ripped grey jeans
- Black knee pads
- Black Slick trainers
- A black baseball cap with white bats all over it.

The jeans and top were stained red to look like blood. The hooded top had a bag of fake blood sewn into it so that when you pressed on my stomach blood oozed out. It was a cool trick, but I got a spot of fake blood on my new pair of Slick trainers when I tried it out, so I decided not to do it again.

My uncle Martin sent me my costume. He sent my mum and dad vampire king and queen costumes. He also sent a woman to our house to do our make-up. She must have been very good at her job, because when I turned up at Harry's house his mum screamed and Harry's eyes opened really wide and he said, "Awesome."

Harry was dressed as a zombie prisoner. Luke and Tyler were already there.

Luke was dressed all in black and wore a skeleton mask. He was holding a long stick thing in his hand. I had to ask him what he was. He said he was dressed as Death. I didn't know Death was a person – I thought it was just a thing that happened to people when they were finished being alive.

Tyler was dressed as a clown. I didn't have to ask him what he was. Clowns are supposed to make people happy, and Hallowe'en costumes are supposed to be scary, so this did not seem like a good choice. I didn't say anything to Tyler about this as he might think I was being rude.

We had dinner at Harry's house. I ate, even though I don't normally eat dinner, because it is rude to turn down food when it is offered to you. Harry's mum said that the meal she had made was worms with blood and eyeballs. This was not true – it was spaghetti with tomato sauce, olives and cheese. I don't know why she lied.

We left the house at 6.12 p.m. to go trick-or-treating. I was carrying my Baltic Wave skateboard under one arm and a black bag with a skeleton on it to collect sweets in the other. I looked up what a zombie was this morning, and they are only interested in eating human flesh and organs, so I don't think they'd be carrying skateboards around, or bags to collect sweets. But as zombies are not real, I guess nobody can say that they definitely wouldn't. Even so, I thought other people might think it was weird, but nobody said anything, so maybe they didn't. Or maybe they were being polite, like how nobody mentioned that Tyler was dressed as an entertainer for little kids' parties.

I had never been trick-or-treating before, but it looked like everybody in Ashland did it. Harry's street was already full of kids when we went out. The younger kids had adults with them. We were old enough to trick or treat without an adult, so we went on our own.

The streets looked very different to how they normally look at night. This is because most people decorate their houses for Hallowe'en with lights, pumpkins, candles, spiders' webs, ghosts, bats and witches. Some people had put gravestones and dead bodies on their front lawns. Not real ones.

We did not decorate our house. I will tell Mum and Dad to decorate our house next year.

We went to thirty-two houses. Sometimes we had to wait a long time to get to the door as there were so many kids in front of us. Some of the houses ran out of sweets. The code for running out of sweets is to leave an unlit pumpkin outside your home.

One of the houses had a big basket filled with sweets on the front porch. The owners of the house were not there. The basket had a sign saying TAKE ONE. Harry, Luke and Tyler grabbed handfuls of the sweets, even though the sign was stuck on the handle of the basket and the words were written in large orange letters, so they couldn't have missed it.

I took one.

"Seriously?" asked Luke. He was looking at me.

"It says take one," I explained. Harry, Luke and Tyler all laughed. I think they were laughing at me.

"Don't be such a loser, Eric," said Tyler. "There's nobody here."

I laughed too. "Yeah, OK," I said. I put my hand in the basket and pretended to take more sweets and put them in my bag.

Everybody smiled, and Tyler grabbed another handful. Then we all walked away.

Luke, Harry and Tyler kept comparing how full their bags were. I did the same. Even though I didn't take those extra sweets from the basket, my bag was more full than Tyler's. This is because he kept eating his sweets as he walked.

My friends were very excited about trick-or-treating. I was also excited, because friends should be excited about the same things. Sometimes I don't feel excited about the same things as them, but I don't want them to know that, so I pretend. Sometimes I get it wrong, but then I learn and I don't do it again. Like at 42 Locke Road. The woman who answered the door was dressed as a doctor with blood on her white coat and on her face. She told us that sweets would rot our teeth and gave us an apple each. We all took one. As we walked away, I acted excited, just like Harry had done at the house before, but then I saw that Luke, Harry and Tyler were all frowning.

"You're being sarcastic, right?" asked Harry.

"Sarcastic" means you say one thing but mean the opposite.

"Yeah, of course," I said, just to agree with him. Harry, Tyler and Luke all nodded.

"So lame," said Tyler. He threw the apple onto the pavement.

As we walked to the next house, I thought about what had happened, and I decided that it was only OK to get excited about sweets.

We finished trick-or-treating at 8 p.m. On our way back to Harry's house, Luke said he had an idea.

"Your best friend's house is down there, Eric. Why don't we pay him a visit?"

I wasn't sure who Luke meant, as I don't have a best friend yet. I thought Luke, Harry and Tyler were the best friends that I had in Ashland.

"Who?" I asked.

They all laughed. "Danny, you idiot. His house is down there."

I didn't like that he called me an idiot. I didn't know why they wanted to go to Danny's house, as I knew they didn't like him, but I didn't want to say anything else in case they called me an idiot again.

Danny's house was much smaller than mine. The front yard had some grass but no plants or flowers, and the outside of the house was painted dark green. The paint was peeling in a lot of places. There was a pumpkin with a ghost shape cut out of it on the front steps. It was not lit. The front door was shut, but the lights in the house were on. We stood on the pavement in front of the house, and nobody said anything for a moment.

"Any ideas?" asked Tyler. I didn't know what he meant.

Luke looked around. He walked over to the end of Danny's garden and bent down. He picked up a rock the size of his hand.

"Everyone get one of these. I'll count down from three. Then throw and run the hell out of here," said Luke. He was grinning.

I didn't know what we were doing. I guessed it was a Hallowe'en tradition that I didn't know about, but I didn't want to ask, so I just did what Harry and Tyler were doing and looked around until I found another rock the same size as Luke's.

We stood in a line next to each other.

"Seriously, are we doing this?" asked Harry. He didn't look happy.

"Shut up, Harry," said Tyler.

"But I—" began Harry.

"Quit stalling," said Luke. He raised his arm – the one holding the rock. Tyler did the same.

I had no clue what we were doing. Luke counted down.

"Three... two... one..."

I looked over at my friends and realized, from the way their arms were moving, that they were about to throw the rocks at Danny's house. In that split second, I knew that, the way they were about to throw those rocks, the rocks would likely hit Danny's house and cause damage. This is a criminal thing to do. I couldn't allow it to happen, even if I'm not friends with Danny. I didn't have time to think of an alternative solution, so I ran out in front of them to tell them to stop, but it was too late. I managed to reach out and grab the rock that was coming from Tyler, but I only had one free hand and couldn't do anything about catching Luke's or Harry's rocks. The last thing I remember is seeing Harry's rock heading straight in the direction of my head and thinking what a lousy shot Harry was – his rock would never have hit Danny's house, even if my head wasn't in the way.

After that, everything went black.

11

DANNY

WEDNESDAY 31ST OCTOBER

I didn't go trick-or-treating. Mum and I both pretended that it was because I was too old to go out collecting sweets, but I think we both knew that it was because I didn't have anyone to go with. By 8 p.m. the trick-or-treaters had all gone, and Mum and I sat down to watch TV. We were about twenty minutes into *Hallowe'en Harlem* when we heard a loud bang outside – right in the middle of a super-creepy scene. We both jumped about three feet off the sofa.

"What was that?!" asked Mum.

I shook my head. "I don't know – it sounded like it was right outside."

Mum ran over to the front door and opened it. There was nobody there. I followed Mum out onto our front porch, and we both looked around to see where the noise could have come from.

Mum shrugged and put her hand on my shoulder. "Must have been a car backfiring or something," she said, and then something caught her eye and she gasped.

Mum bent down and picked up a rock lying next to the front door. She stared at it for a moment and then looked up at me. I couldn't read her expression – I think she might have been scared. Or cross. Or both. "Who would do something like this?" she whispered, looking down at the rock in her hand.

That red rage that sometimes comes over me came over me. I didn't think about what I would do if I found whoever did it – I just knew I wanted to catch them. I ran down the front steps towards the pavement. There was no one around, but whoever it was couldn't have got far.

"Danny! Stop!" shouted Mum. I heard her running after me, but I kept going.

And then I heard her scream.

It was dark, but I saw Mum running onto our lawn. I ran over too, and that's when I saw the body lying on the ground. Mum rolled the body onto its back. The boy wasn't moving, but his eyes were wide open and there was blood running down the side of his face. To top it off, his face was painted like one of the Death Creepers in *Night of the Zombies*.

"He's just a child," whispered Mum. She pulled his hood back from his head. As soon as I saw the blond hair, perfectly gelled back, I knew exactly who it was.

"Mum! It's Eric!"

Mum was now in nurse mode – she had taken her jumper off and was pressing it to the side of his head. She looked up at me.

"Eric?" she asked.

"You know, from the fund-raiser. The one who I was talking to."

Mum's eyes widened, and then she looked down at Slick. "Eric, sweetie, you're going to be fine. We're going to get you help."

She looked up at me. "Danny, keep this pressed up against his head. I'm going to call an ambulance."

Before I could say anything, she jumped up. "Keep talking to him!" she said as she ran into the house.

I stared down at Slick. I wasn't sure he was breathing. And I really didn't think I had anything to say that would help, but I did what Mum told me to do.

"Hey, Eric – wake up," I said. He didn't move. I was starting to think he really might be dead.

Mum ran back out; she was talking on the phone, spelling out the name of our street.

"He's in bad shape – you need to…"

Before she could finish the sentence, an ambulance pulled up in front of our house and two female paramedics jumped out.

Mum stopped and stared at them as they dragged out a stretcher from the back, then remembered she was still on a call. "Yes, sorry, the paramedics just got here… yes… someone must have already called you… thank you."

I stood up to give the paramedics space to do whatever they needed to do.

"Did someone call you?" asked Mum. One of the paramedics nodded.

"Did they see what happened?" asked Mum. The paramedic now holding Slick's ankles looked up at Mum.

"We are not at liberty to share information about patients," she said.

"Do you need his details?" continued Mum.

"Excuse me, please step out of the way – we are dealing with a situation here."

"His name's Eric," I said.

"Thank you," said the paramedic. "We have all the details we need."

"Can we accompany him to the hospital?" asked Mum.

"No, it's all under control. He'll be fine."

"Is he dead?" I said. Mum fired one of her looks at me.

"No, he's not dead. He's fine," said the paramedic. "Now, if you could both step out of our way..."

Mum and I moved out of the way and watched as one paramedic gave the other a nod, and then they lifted Slick's body onto the stretcher. I saw something drop from Slick's hand. As the paramedics wheeled Slick away, I walked over to see what it was.

A rock.

I picked it up and turned it over in my head, piecing together what had happened. It didn't take me long – it had been Slick throwing rocks at my house.

By the time the shock had worn off – maybe a few seconds – and I looked up, the paramedics had already put Slick into the ambulance. I could see Mum getting more and more angry with one of the paramedics, who was ignoring her. Mum threw her hands in the air as the ambulance drove off.

"Grab your jacket," she said urgently as she walked past me back to the house. "We need to let Eric's parents know what happened."

I was going to say something about Slick and the rock, but she was gone before I had a chance to. When she came back, she was on the phone to her friend Annie, getting Slick's address, so I didn't have a chance to say anything until we were on our way. By that time I'd decided to shut up about it – I knew my mum wouldn't think this was important when Slick was lying unconscious on the way to hospital, but I disagreed. If Slick wasn't dead, I was going to kill him.*

---

* Not literally – I just mean that I was really angry.

47

12

DANNY

WEDNESDAY 31ST OCTOBER (II)

It turned out that Slick lived only about five minutes away from us, though it could have been a different world – all fancy houses and shiny cars. Slick's house stood out because it was the only one not decorated for Hallowe'en.

"Good, they're home," said Mum. She pulled up in front of the two brand-new cars in their driveway. I followed Mum as she rushed to the front door and rang the bell.

I stood next to Mum, feeling more and more nervous while Mum tapped her feet and jiggled her car keys. "Come on, come on," she muttered.

Slick's mum opened the door. She looked like a movie star – her hair wavy and to one side, bright-red lipstick, sparkly diamond earrings and a white silk shirt. Elegant: that's probably the best word to describe her. She was the exact opposite of my mum, who was in her big green overcoat with no make-up on and her curly hair pulled up and all over the place.

Slick's mum stared at us blankly for a split second, and then she smiled, showing us her perfect white teeth.

"Maria, what a lovely surprise," she said, then looked down at me. "And you must be Danny. We didn't get a chance to talk the other day."

I nodded.

Slick's mum turned back to Mum. "Please, come in."

Mum shook her head and took a deep breath. "Karen, I'm here because—"

Slick's mum interrupted her with a shake of her head. She was smiling.

"There's nothing so important that it can't wait for the best cup of coffee you've ever tried."

Mum's jaw dropped. I think she was going to say something, but Slick's mum had already walked away. We followed her in, through a hallway and into the kitchen. Slick's mum stood at a shiny red coffee machine in the corner of the room.

"Karen..." said Mum.

Slick's mum poured some coffee beans into the top of the machine and placed a sleek green metal cup under the tap.

"These Liscio machines are incredible," she said.

Mum tried again. "Karen, I need to—"

Slick's mum pressed a button on the top of the machine, and Mum's voice was drowned out by the machine's loud grinding. The hot coffee poured into the cup. Mum looked at me like she couldn't believe what was happening.

The grinding noise stopped, and Slick's mum took the steaming coffee and walked over to Mum. She handed her the cup.

"Tell me if this isn't the best—"

"Karen," Mum interrupted, taking the coffee and putting it down on the counter. "I need to tell you something."

Slick's mum just stared with a blank smile.

"Eric's had an accident," said Mum. "We found him on our lawn with an injury to his head. He's in an ambulance on the way to the hospital."

Slick's mum stopped smiling. "Oh dear. That's terrible news. How worrying."

Her words were right, but there was no panic, no emotion at all.

Mum put the coffee down on the counter and placed her hand on Slick's mum's arm.

"I'm sure he's going to be fine. Would you like me to drive you to the hospital?"

That's when Slick's dad appeared. He was smiling.

"What's going on here?" he asked. "It looks like somebody threw a party and forgot to invite me!"

He reached out and shook my mum's hand, and then shook mine.

"Frank, dear," said Slick's mum, "Maria was just telling me that Eric's been in an accident."

Slick's dad nodded. "Oh yes – I haven't had a chance to tell you. They called me from the ambulance and he's absolutely fine. He'll be home in the morning."

Slick's mum breathed a sigh of relief, and her smile returned. "Oh good."

Mum and I stared at them both.

There were an awkward few seconds when Slick's parents looked at Mum with smiles on their faces, and Mum and I stood in silence in the kitchen. Then Mum shook herself out of her shock.

"Oh," she said. "Right. I'm glad he's OK. Sorry to disturb you."

Slick's mum's smile widened. "Not at all. It was very thoughtful of you to come around."

"We should leave," said Mum. She grabbed me by the arm.

"But you haven't tried your coffee yet," said Slick's mum.

Mum mumbled something about dinner in the oven, and then we left.

Slick's parents stood at the door and waved as we got into the car, then closed the front door.

"Mum, was that as weird as I think it was?" I asked as we pulled away.

"Yes. Yes, it was," said Mum. She sounded distracted and was looking around as she drove slowly.

"Mum, what are you doing?"

Mum said nothing, then suddenly turned the car around and pulled up on the side of the road. She switched the engine off and slid down in her seat.

"Get down, Danny. I don't want them to see us."

I put my hood over my head and slid down in my seat too. I put my head against the bottom of the car window and looked down the street at Slick's house.

"Are we *spying* on them?" I asked.

"I just want to see if they're going to the hospital."

That question was answered about a half-hour later when the lights downstairs went out, then a light upstairs came on, then off. Slick's parents had gone to bed.

"Poor, poor boy," said Mum as we drove off. I felt bad for him too, but just for a moment, until I remembered what he had been doing to get hospitalized in the first place.

13

SLICK

THURSDAY 1ST NOVEMBER

I woke up naked in my bed. This is not unusual. What *was* unusual was that I normally remember getting undressed and going to bed the night before, and today I couldn't remember that at all. The last thing I could remember was a rock coming towards my head outside Danny's house.

My Hexam R3 was on my bedside table, but it had run out of battery. I plugged in the charger and waited for it to restart. There was a series of pings as my texts came through – four from Harry, one from Luke and one from Tyler. Luke and Tyler asked if I was OK. Harry said he was sorry they had left me, but they hadn't wanted to get into trouble. I understood why they had left – they didn't want to get caught throwing rocks at somebody's house. Even though they had left me on my own, I was happy – they didn't seem angry that I had stopped them from hitting Danny's house with rocks.

I got dressed and went downstairs. Mum and Dad had both already gone out. There was a note on the kitchen counter telling me not to go to school. I didn't understand, so I called Mum.

"Hello, Karen Young speaking."

"It's Eric."

"Oh. Hi, sweetie!" I knew that she must be with other people. She only calls me sweetie when she's with other people. "Everything OK?"

"Why is there a note in the kitchen telling me not to go to school?"

"The doctor said it's standard procedure to stay home the day after going to the hospital."

"But I'm fine."

"The doctor said it's standard procedure to stay home the day after going to the hospital," repeated Mum.

"OK," I said. "Did I go to a doctor?"

"You hit your head. Maria Lazio found you on her lawn. They called an ambulance."

"Mrs Lazio? Did you speak to her?"

"Yes – she came by with her son, Danny, to tell us you were going to the hospital. It was very thoughtful of her. I'm going to send her a gift basket to say thank you."

"Was she angry?"

"No. Why would she be angry?"

I ignored the question. "What happened at the hospital?"

"The doctor said they checked that you didn't have a concussion and you were fine, so they brought you back last night."

"Is that when you spoke to the doctor?"

"No – we were asleep when they brought you back. The doctor called me this morning. I have to go now – I'm having breakfast with my gardening friends and I'm being terribly rude talking to you all this time."

She hung up.

I spent the rest of the day doing my chores and homework and playing *Land X*. I got to level twenty-four. I would prob- ably have got to level twenty-five if I hadn't been interrupted. At 6 p.m. the doorbell rang. It was Mrs Lazio, Danny's mum. Danny was not with her.

"Hello, Mrs Lazio."

Mrs Lazio smiled and gave me a hug. This was unexpected, as I don't normally get hugs from people. I wondered if this was an Italian thing, like the kissing. I hugged her back.

"Oh my goodness," she said. She smiled as she pulled away from me. "You gave us a scare last night. Danny said you weren't at school today, so I thought I'd pop by on my way back from work to check on how you're doing."

"I'm fine. The doctor said it's standard procedure to stay home from school after going to the hospital."

"I should think so," said Mrs Lazio. "Your parents must have been worried sick?" She said this like it was a question, but I wasn't sure what to answer, so I just shrugged.

"Did you get stitches?"

"Stitches?"

Mrs Lazio reached out and ran her hand over my hair. She looked confused. "There's nothing there," she said.

"See, I'm fine." I smiled.

Mrs Lazio nodded slowly. "Are your parents home? I see their cars aren't here."

"Mum is at her book club, and Dad's out watching a football match with his golfing friends."

Mrs Lazio frowned. "What time will they be home?"

"I don't know, but they're always home before midnight."

"This happens a lot?"

"Most days. My parents have lots of clubs that they go to. They're making new friends."

Mrs Lazio pressed her lips very tightly together.

"Have you eaten?" she asked. She said this as she walked into my house. I thought that was kind of rude, as it's not her house, but I didn't want to say that to an adult.

She opened up our fridge. There was nothing in there except the bottle of milk that we keep in case anybody visits our house and wants coffee.

"There's nothing here."

"I wasn't hungry," I said.

Mrs Lazio put her hand to her mouth and stared at me.

"Are you OK, Mrs Lazio?"

"I'd like the number for your mum, please," she said. She put her purse on the kitchen table and started looking in it. She pulled out her phone. It was a Carmei.

"I'm really fine, Mrs Lazio. You don't need to be worried."

"Your mum's number, Eric."

I'm not supposed to argue with adults, so I gave her my mum's number.

"Hello, Karen? Yes, this is Maria Lazio... Yes, fine... I'm here with Eric at your house. I stopped by to see how he was... Yes, that's what he said. He hasn't eaten anything..."

There was a long pause.

"He says he didn't... Right, but there's no food here... I understand... Well, I hope you don't mind me saying that I don't think a twelve-year-old boy should be left on his own at home, especially after what happened last night..."

Mrs Lazio was now talking to my mum like she was a small child – very soothing and slow.

"Right. And I know you've all been through a lot... Yes, well I still think I should take Eric home with me. I'll give him dinner, and you can pick him up on your way home. Or he can stay the night."

"Oh!" I said. "I don't—"

Mrs Lazio put her hand up to tell me to stop talking. "That's fine, then," she said when my mum had finished whatever she was saying. "Whatever time. I'll send you my address now."

Mrs Lazio said goodbye to my mum, typed out a message and put the phone back in her purse.

"Eric, honey, go upstairs and get your pyjamas – your mum says she might be late."

"But, Mrs Lazio, I'm fine."

"I know you are, honey, but you shouldn't be home alone. And it will be nice for you and Danny to spend time together too, won't it?"

"Yes, Mrs Lazio," I said. I couldn't tell Mrs Lazio that I didn't want to be friends with her son, as this seemed like a rude thing to say to someone's mother.

"Now go get your pyjamas."

"I don't have any."

"You don't have any?" Mrs Lazio looked very surprised.

"I mean, I don't have any that are clean." This was not true, but I got the feeling that my first answer had made Mrs Lazio worry.

Mrs Lazio smiled and ruffled my hair. "No problem. I'm sure we can find you something."

I don't think Mrs Lazio knew that Tyler, Harry and Luke had thrown rocks at her house, because I think she would have mentioned it. Instead, Mrs Lazio asked me questions on the way back to her house. Some of these were easy:

Does your mum work? (No.)

Does your dad work? (Yes, for a computing company.)

How do you like Ashland? (I love it.)

But a couple of the questions were hard, because I didn't want Mrs Lazio to worry. So I lied about some of them.

Lying is OK when it would upset somebody to tell the truth. These are the questions I lied about:

Who cooks breakfast? (Mum.) Truth: We don't eat breakfast.

Did your parents stay out a lot back in London? (No.) Truth: I don't remember.

Mrs Lazio doesn't live too far from me, so she didn't get to ask any more hard questions. I was glad, because I don't like lying.

I followed Mrs Lazio up the steps to the front door. She opened the door and called out for Danny.

A man walked into the hallway. He had messy brown hair and was wearing a blue Oldean T-shirt that looked like it hadn't been washed in a long time and was too small for him. But it was Oldean, so it was still cool.

The man kissed Mrs Lazio on both cheeks and turned to me.

I put my hand out. He looked at my hand, smiled and then shook it.

"Old-school move. I like it."

"This is Eric," said Mrs Lazio. "A friend of Danny's."

The man opened his mouth like he was about to laugh, but stopped very suddenly after Mrs Lazio gave him a strange look. He coughed. "Hey, Eric, I'm Vito."

"Nice to meet you, sir," I said. "Are you Danny's dad?"

At this, both Mrs Lazio and Vito started laughing.

"Wow…" said Vito, still laughing.

"No," said Mrs Lazio. She put her hand to her mouth. I think she was trying not to laugh any more. "This is my nephew – Danny's cousin."

"Oh, I'm sorry," I said.

"It's cool," said Vito. "I mean, obviously I have to go kill myself now, but it's cool."

"Vito!" said Mrs Lazio.

"Kidding. Just kidding." Then he nodded to a door in the far corner. "He's downstairs being an antisocial weirdo," he said. He paused. "Urgh… he really *could* be my son. I am *never* having kids."

Mrs Lazio rolled her eyes.

Vito grinned. "Do you need me tomorrow?"

Mrs Lazio zipped up Vito's jacket for him. "No, thank you – I won't be home late tomorrow."

"OK," said Vito. He kissed Mrs Lazio on the cheek and nodded at me. "See you around." And then he left.

"Honestly, that boy," mumbled Mrs Lazio, smiling, as she walked over to the door and called out for Danny.

"I have a surprise visitor for you!"

There was a pause. Then Danny shouted up. "If it's the man who calls himself my dad, tell him I'm asleep." I thought this was strange, as his father would have known Danny wasn't asleep, because he was shouting. I didn't understand Danny.

"Now, Daniel!" said Mrs Lazio.

Mrs Lazio led me over to the kitchen. Everywhere I looked there was stuff. The fridge was covered with twenty-eight photographs, eleven postcards, five business cards and nineteen magnets. There were thirty-four recipe books and fourteen kitchen appliances along the counter and a radio, which was on and playing an advert for a mattress company. Everything looked old.

Mrs Lazio walked over to a pot sitting on the stove and lifted the lid. She sighed.

"Those boys," she said. "They've eaten everything."

"I'm really not hungry," I said.

Mrs Lazio did not reply to this. She opened up the fridge and pulled out a plastic container.

"Do you like lasagne?" she asked.

I didn't get a chance to answer, as this was when Danny walked into the room.

"Who's—" He stopped suddenly when he saw me. He frowned, then looked at his mum. "What's *he* doing here?" he asked.

Mrs Lazio's eyes opened very wide. "*Daniel Lazio!* Where are your manners?!"

I didn't realize Danny was being rude until his mum said that, and I wasn't sure what she meant.

"Mum! You don't know what he did… He—"

Mrs Lazio grabbed Danny by the arm before he could finish the sentence and dragged him out of the room. I didn't know what to do, so I just stood still and waited.

The radio started playing the Week's newest release, 'Ride or Fly'. The Week is the biggest band in the world at the moment. There are seven members. They are called Monday, Tuesday, Wednesday, Thursday, Friday, Saturday and Sunday. It must have been difficult to find singers that had the names of each day of the week, as I don't think these are very common. My favourite is Tuesday, as he is a skateboarder. I saw a picture of them on the front cover of a magazine yesterday, and Tuesday was holding a Baltic Wave skateboard. That's the same skateboard as the one I have. Harry likes Friday because Friday likes to play basketball. Luke is the only person I know who doesn't like the Week. He says there isn't anyone good in the charts at the moment, and that's why the industry needs a singer like him.

Mrs Lazio walked back into the room frowning.

"I'm sorry, Eric. Danny is just tired, I think, but it's no excuse for being so rude – especially after what you went through yesterday."

"That's OK," I said. I don't know why being tired would make Danny act rude.

"Eric…" Mrs Lazio paused. "You weren't throwing rocks at our house yesterday, were you?"

"No, Mrs Lazio – I would never do anything like that."

"Promise?"

"I promise. I wouldn't do something like that." I didn't tell Mrs Lazio who was throwing rocks, because I didn't want to get my friends in trouble.

Mrs Lazio smiled and shook her head. "No, of course not. That's what I said." She went over to the kitchen table, pushed aside a pile of books and papers and told me to sit down.

"Have something to eat, and then maybe you can tell Danny that after you finish – he should have calmed down by then."

14

DANNY

THURSDAY 1ST NOVEMBER

I don't know who I was more angry with – Slick for throwing rocks at my house, or my mum for not believing me. She asked me if I saw him doing it, I said no, and then – before I got to tell her about the rock I saw in his hand – she told me not to make accusations like that unless I was certain, that he had been through a lot, that I was being rude and other mum-lecture-type stuff. I waited for her to stop talking and stormed off. I didn't want anything to do with either of them. If Mum liked him so much, *she* could hang out with him.

I was down in the basement working on the computer I've been building for the last month when I heard footsteps coming down the stairs. I know what Mum's footsteps sound like, and it wasn't them, so it could only have been Slick. I didn't turn around.

"Your mum sent me down to see you," said Slick from behind me. I ignored him and kept on working. "She said you think I was throwing rocks at your house, but I wasn't. So you don't need to be angry with me."

I could feel my face turning red. He was a liar. I kept my head down and concentrated on installing the graphics card that Vito had given me.

"Did you hear me?" asked Slick.

"You're standing two feet from me. I heard you."

"OK – good. What are you doing?"

"None of your business."

"Are you angry with me?"

I spun my chair around and glared at him. "No, I think you're awesome. Now... GO... AWAY."

I spun my chair back, but the dramatic moment was ruined by the lever of my chair hitting a box and making me wobble. This did not help my mood. I kicked the box away, turned back to my desk and waited for Slick to leave.

He didn't leave.

"I don't think you're telling me the truth. I think you *are* still mad," said Slick.

I turned back again. A little more carefully this time.

"Wow – you worked that out all by yourself?" I said.

Slick nodded. "Yeah."

"Why are you even here? I know you don't like me."

"I haven't said I don't like you."

"So I guess it was just a coincidence that you walked off as soon as your buddies showed up the other day?" I asked.

"No. It wasn't a coincidence. They don't like you, and they wouldn't be friends with me any more if they thought we were friends."

I couldn't believe the words he was saying. "Wow," I said. "Nice friends you have."

"Thank you," said Slick.

I groaned at Slick's stupidity. "I was being sarcastic. I can see why you're friends with them. You're all as stupid as each other."

Slick frowned. "Hey, it's not nice to call people stupid. Maybe that's why you don't have any friends."

The anger that had been building up inside me erupted like a volcano. Before I could think about what I was doing, I jumped out of my chair, pushed Slick up against the wall and grabbed him by the throat. At that moment, it was like Slick had become every person I hated: Luke, Tyler, Harry, all the other kids at school, my gym teacher, my dad – *everyone*.

"*I hate you*," I said.

Slick opened his mouth, but he couldn't say anything. I think I was squeezing his throat too hard. I don't feel good about this – I wasn't thinking straight.

Slick grabbed my hand and pulled it away easily. I tried to pull my hand away, but Slick's arm didn't move at all. Turned out Slick was STRONG. The harder I tried to pull away, the harder he held on to my hand, until it really started hurting. I shouted out for him to let me go.

Slick released his grip. "I'm sorry I hurt you," he said, "but I couldn't talk when you were holding my throat. I want to explain about the other night…"

"Just go," I said, rubbing my wrist.

"I can't, your mum—"

"GET OUT!"

Slick didn't say anything else. He turned away and walked over to the stairs. Then he sat down on the bottom step. I turned back and pretended to work on my computer until his mum came to get him about an hour later. We didn't speak.

When I came up, after he'd gone, Mum asked me if we'd had a good time. I told her yes, to get her off my back. Plus I didn't want to get into the strangling-him thing with her. Truth is, I felt kind of bad about it. I always feel bad when I lose my temper like that.

15

SLICK

TUESDAY 6TH NOVEMBER

I was getting dressed this morning when Dad came into my bedroom. I don't normally see my parents in the morning – we are all too busy getting ready to go to work and school to talk.

"Mrs Lazio just called. You're to go to Danny's house after school. You'll walk with him. We'll come get you later."

"I don't think that's a good idea," I said. "If my friends find out that I'm going to Danny's house, they're not going to want to be my friends any more."

"Why?" asked Dad.

"They don't like him."

"Don't tell them," said Dad. "I've said yes now, so you'll have to go."

He left the room.

I decided not to tell my friends that I had to go to Danny's house after school. I didn't want them to think I was now friends with Danny.

At lunch we talked about the rock-throwing. We have been talking about it a lot since it happened. Today, Tyler brought it up because, he said, he had been thinking that maybe a neighbour of Danny's might have a security camera outside their house and would have seen what we had been doing.

"Nah," said Luke. "They'd have found it by now. It's cool. As long as Slick sticks to his story about being on his own and falling over and hitting his head, we're good."

Tyler, Harry and Luke all turned to me.

"What?" I asked.

"You're not going to say anything, right?"

"I told you already – I'd never snitch on my friends," I said.

Luke smiled and punched my arm. Then he laughed. "Anyway, we were doing him a favour. That place needs to be knocked down."

"Why?" I asked.

"Did you *see* it? I heard they have rats."

"Really?" I asked. I hadn't seen any rats when I was there, but I didn't want to say this, as I would have had to tell them I'd been to his house.

"And cockroaches," said Tyler. "I heard he opened his lunch box one day and about fifty of them crawled out."

Everyone made disgusted noises, including me.

"That's gross. So, why don't you like him?" I asked.

"Because he's covered in fleas," said Tyler. Everybody laughed.

"I heard his mum gets his clothes from the dump because she's too poor to buy him any."

I didn't understand why everybody was laughing about Danny being poor. Having to wear flea-covered clothes that your mum got from the dump didn't seem very funny.

Maths was right after lunch. Miss Lake had made a new seating chart, and she had placed me and Ethan together. Ethan smiled when I came over and sat with him. Miss Lake gave the class some problems to work on, but I noticed that she was standing next to our table most of the time. I think she was checking if I was trying to make friends with Ethan, but I was too busy thinking of the conversation about Danny at lunch. I was trying to work out why my friends were laughing, and that's when I realized that, most of the time since I met them, I had been laughing at their jokes only because they were laughing, not because I found the joke funny.

"Did you know that Danny Lazio gets his clothes from the dump?" I asked Ethan.

Ethan didn't laugh. "Why would you say that?" asked Ethan.

"That's what I heard. You don't think that's funny?"

Ethan shook his head. "*No*, I think it's mean. Who told you that?"

"Tyler. And he said that Danny's house has cockroaches and rats. And fleas."

"Tyler's an idiot – don't listen to him. He hates Danny. And he always lies."

"He does?

Ethan nodded.

"Why?"

"I told you – because he's an idiot."

"Do you like Danny?"

Ethan looked at me and thought for a moment. Then he shrugged. "I don't know. I don't really know him. He doesn't talk to anyone."

"Why?"

"I don't know. He used to get into trouble a lot – throwing stuff and running out of class. He got picked on a lot – maybe

66

that's why. Then last year, Tyler and Luke got caught putting Danny's clothes into the toilet when they were changing after gym, and they got suspended. After that, I think it all stopped. Now Danny just keeps to himself."

"I didn't know that," I said.

"Why would you? You're new."

I wanted to know more, but Miss Lake told us we had five minutes left to finish, and so we went back to our maths problem, and the conversation about Danny was over.

As we left the class, I thanked Ethan.

"No problem. You should be careful who you make friends with, though."

"I'm not friends with Danny."

"I didn't mean Danny."

I understood – he meant Luke, Tyler and Harry.

I was confused.

16

SLICK

TUESDAY 6TH NOVEMBER (II)

I didn't see Danny all day, so I didn't get to say anything to him about going to his house. I knew that he walked home, so as soon as I heard the school bell I said goodbye to my friends and rushed out to the gates. Danny showed up a few minutes after me, but I don't think he saw me, as he just walked straight past where I was standing.

"I'm coming to your house today," I said when I caught up with him. "I didn't have a choice."

"Me neither," said Danny. Then he stopped and stared at me. "My mum may think you're perfect or whatever, but that's only because she doesn't know the truth."

I didn't like that Danny was saying I was a liar.

"I'm not lying about what happened at Hallowe'en. I wasn't throwing rocks at your house."

"OK. Let's look at the facts: someone was throwing rocks at my house, and the only person there was you – WITH A ROCK IN YOUR HAND."

When Danny explained it like this, I understood why he might think I was lying.

"I see how that could be misunderstood," I said. "But I really didn't do it."

Danny rolled his eyes. "OK. Prove it."

I knew how to prove it. But not without breaking my promise to my friends. I didn't know what to do.

After a few seconds, Danny laughed without smiling.

"Thought so. Look, I don't know what the deal is with you, and I don't care. I'll tell my mum exactly what I saw, and then I don't ever have to see you in my house again. Deal?"

If Danny was going to tell his mum what he thought happened, then I might be arrested for committing a crime. This, I decided, was worse than breaking a promise to my friends. I took my Hexam R3 out of my Oldean jacket pocket and ran to catch up with Danny.

"Danny! Wait! I'll prove it. But don't say anything to anyone."

Danny looked at me suspiciously as I scrolled through my text messages to Luke, found the ones where Luke was asking why I had stopped them from throwing the rocks, then handed my Hexam R3 to Danny.

Danny took it and started reading.

I waited until he'd finished, and then I smiled. "See? I wasn't lying."

Danny shrugged. "Fine. You weren't lying. Doesn't change the fact that you're friends with people who throw rocks at my house."

"Sure, but you agree I wasn't lying."

"I agree that your friends are idiots."

"I didn't agree to that."

"Exactly," said Danny.

Danny walked off again, and I followed. He didn't talk to me the rest of the way, and that was fine by me – at least he knew I wasn't a liar now.

At his house, Danny let himself in, and we went to the basement, with me following a few feet behind. He went straight to his desk and picked up an instruction manual on how to build a computer. He closed it as soon as he saw that I was standing right next to him.

"What are you doing?" he asked.

"Standing here talking to you," I answered. "Why are you building a computer?"

"None of your business," he said.

Danny did not want to talk to me, so I just stepped back near the wall and watched him. I saw his eyes look quickly over to where I was standing, and then he went back to his project.

After eighteen minutes, I could see Danny was having difficulties, so I decided to speak.

"The I/O shield is in the wrong way," I said.

Danny turned to me. It was the first time he'd looked at me all day. "What?"

"The input/output shield – it's in the wrong way."

Danny turned back to his desk and picked up the motherboard he was working on.

"No it's not," he said.

"Yes it is," I said. "Check again."

Danny looked down and turned the motherboard one way and then the other. He put it down and slid the booklet he had hidden from me in front of him. He studied it for a while then turned to me, narrowed his eyes, turned back to his desk, removed the I/O shield and put it back the right way. Danny set it down and spun his chair around to face me.

"How did you know?"

"I saw the instructions when we came in."

"Yeah, but you couldn't have read them."

"Only the pages that were open."

"Do you have a photographic memory or something?"

"Sometimes."

"Sometimes?"

"If I'm reading something long, I don't remember all of it."

Danny picked up the piece of paper. "What was next? After putting in the I/O shield?"

He was testing me.

"Place the motherboard into the case so that the motherboard holes align with the standoffs on the case."

Danny looked up from his paper.

"Wow," he said. He opened his mouth as if he was going to speak, then closed it quickly and turned back to his desk. I think he remembered that he didn't want to talk to me.

A few minutes passed as Danny screwed in the motherboard and then turned the pages of his booklet. I couldn't see the whole page he was looking at, but it seemed to be a diagram of a computer. Danny ran his finger down one side of the page and then the other. Then he let out a groan.

"OK, genius, where does this go?"

I walked over to Danny and looked at the diagram for a few seconds.

"Here," I said, pointing.

He looked down at where my finger was. "Oh yeah," he said quietly.

I was walking back to the wall when I heard Danny's voice. "You can hold it if you want. It'll be easier for me to put the screws in."

Danny did not talk to me much over the next hour, but he kept handing me tools and pieces of his computer, so

I think he wanted me to stay. We worked together on the next fifteen steps of the instructions before his mum called down to tell us dinner would be ready in five minutes.

Danny stood up. For a minute, we both just stood there looking at the computer.

"Most people buy a computer from a shop," I said.

"I'm not most people," he said.

He was right. He wasn't like anybody else I had ever met.

"It's really cool," I said. I said it before I realized that one of the best ways to make a new friend is to pay them a compliment.

Danny shrugged. "I guess," he said. Danny looked down and turned to the next page of his computer instruction manual, but before we had a chance to do anything else, Mrs Lazio called down for us to come upstairs for pizza.

"COMING MUM!" said Danny. He looked at me and smiled. "Come on, let's go eat."

Notes:
- Danny was wearing a no-brand white T-shirt. I looked at it closely when we were working. I didn't see any fleas. I think Tyler was lying.
- Since I moved to Ashland, I have found out that I like playing computer games, and I like building computers. Doing these things is like solving a really hard puzzle, and it makes me feel good when I solve it. I like skateboarding and talking about sports with my friends, but none of those things feel as good as solving a puzzle.
- We did not finish the computer today. Danny invited me over after school on Friday to keep working on it. I said I couldn't, because Friday is the day I have my dentist appointment. He said "fine" quietly and then frowned.

- I liked working on the computer with him, so I said I could come on Saturday instead. Then he smiled and said that he would wait until then to do any more work on it.
- I think this means we might be friends.
- I am not supposed to be friends with him.
- I am not supposed to be friends with Danny, because he is not one of the popular kids.
- I have figured out how to fix this: I will make Danny popular.

17

SLICK

SATURDAY 10TH NOVEMBER

I didn't tell Danny about Operation Make Danny Popular when I got to his house on Saturday. There wasn't a good time to mention it, as he started talking about the computer right away and how it had been killing him to wait for me to come over.

"I got an even better graphics card after school yesterday," he said as we walked down the steps to his basement. "It's practically new."

"Where did you get it from?" I asked.

"My cousin Vito has a computer-repair shop in Clinton. He gives me parts if he doesn't need them."

We worked on Danny's computer for hours. Danny's mum came down with lunch for us so we wouldn't have to stop working. She was smiling a lot. Then she hugged us both. I guess that's an Italian thing too.

"Have you built a computer before?" asked Danny once his mum left.

I shook my head as I had my mouth full.

"How do you know so much, then?"

I swallowed my food. "I looked it up before I came over this morning."

"And that's it?" asked Danny. He didn't swallow his food before answering.

I nodded.

"So you learnt everything about building a computer by reading this morning?"

I nodded again.

"You know that's kind of strange, right?"

I didn't. Until I met Danny, I didn't think there was anything strange about me, but since I'd met him I'd started to feel like maybe I wasn't as normal as I thought. Except...

"Nobody else thinks I'm strange," I said.

"Maybe they do and they just don't tell you... Or maybe your friends are too dumb to notice."

"They're not dumb."

Danny shrugged. "Whatever."

"Why don't you like them?" I asked.

"Because they're ———."

I can't repeat the word. It was a curse word.

"I think they'd like you if they got to know you."

"Kids like them don't want to get to know kids like me."

I opened my mouth to tell him about Operation Make Danny Popular, but something strange happened – I couldn't say it. I couldn't say it because I knew Danny might not like my plan, and I didn't want Danny to be angry with me again. I think I was nervous. I don't remember feeling nervous before.

"Do you want to come to my house after we finish the computer? I want to show you something."

Danny gave me one of his looks again. "What?"

"You'll see. You want to come?"

Danny shrugged. "Sure."

At 1.45 p.m. Danny and I finished building his computer.

"OK – you turn it on," said Danny.

I shook my head. "It's your computer – you should do it."

Danny took a big breath. "I feel sick," he said as he reached out to press the button.

He pressed it. We watched as the blue light came on, the fan started whirring and the screen came to life. For a few seconds, we both stood in silence, staring at the welcome screen.

It worked.

"I can't believe it," said Danny.

I turned to look at him and saw that he was smiling. I'd never seen him smile like that. And then I realized that I was smiling too. Not because Danny was there, or because it was the right thing to do to make friends, or because smiling would be the polite thing to do. I was smiling because I was happy. It was a different kind of happy than I have felt before.

After we had set everything up, the first thing we did with the computer was load *Land X* onto it. I didn't even know you could get it on the computer, but it turned out that it was even better than playing it on my Hexam R3. *Land X* is more than just a game – it's an online world – but it never really feels like that on my phone (even though my Hexam R3 has the best graphics capability of any phone on the market), but on the computer it felt like that. Danny logged in and then typed in the coordinates of the Smuggler's Inn. We asked around for any new quests and then got sucked into the game – by the time Danny's mum came down two hours later, we had completed five new quests and earned twelve thousand quartz, and Danny had gone up two levels. This would have bothered me before – to spend that much time playing to level up somebody else's player, but – and I don't know why – today this didn't bother me at all.

"How are things going?" asked Mrs Lazio.

Mrs Lazio smiled and listened as we told her about everything we had had to do to make Danny's computer work: replacing the power cable, reinstalling the motherboard and all the other things. When we finished, she clapped and gave Danny a hug and kissed his head and told him how proud she was of him. And then she turned to me and hugged me too.

I don't know why she was so happy – I don't think she understood anything that we said.

18

DANNY

SATURDAY 10TH NOVEMBER

few nights earlier, I heard Mum on the phone talking to Auntie Loretta about Slick and how his parents left him alone all the time and didn't bother going to the hospital when he was hurt. She said they weren't fit to be parents, and other stuff in Italian that I didn't understand, but I got the general idea: Mum did not approve of Slick's parents. I knew this was the reason that Mum didn't look too happy when we told her we were going to Slick's house, and I knew that, as long as I stayed close to Slick and ignored her trying to get me to go to the other room to "show me something", she wouldn't say anything. There was no way she was going to bad-mouth Slick's parents in front of him – plus I think she was worried I might lose the only friend I had made in years. So, after a few minutes of Mum doing strange head motions towards the kitchen, Slick asking her if she was OK and me ignoring the whole thing, Mum agreed to drive us there.

"I'll come get you at six," said Mum on the way. "I have to take another night shift. Sorry, honey, I know it's the second one this week, but with Christmas coming…"

"It's OK, Mum," I said.

"I'll call Vito and see if he can babysit."

"MUM! He doesn't *babysit* me – we just hang out."

Mum laughed. "Fine. Whatever. I'll call him."

She continued. "I'll be home before you get up for school. And I washed Bertie, so you can cuddle up with him tonight. I left him on the—"

"MUM!"

"Who's Bertie?" asked Slick.

Mum looked at me in the rear-view mirror. I opened my eyes wide and shook my head to tell her to shut up.

"*Oops*," said Mum. "Never mind."

A five-minute drive – that's all it was – was long enough for Mum to totally embarrass me. We got out at Slick's, he said goodbye to Mum and I stormed off.

"Who's Bertie?" asked Slick as we walked up to his front door.

"Forget about it."

"I can't," he said. "Is he a pet? I haven't seen any pets."

I sighed. "He's a stupid teddy bear that I've had since I was a little kid, OK? I don't even sleep with him any more. I don't know why Mum said that."

"Oh. OK," said Slick, like it was the most normal thing ever. We walked up the steps to his front door, and Slick took his keys out.

"Why *did* you sleep with a teddy bear?" he asked as he opened the door.

"Eric, seriously, drop it."

"Drop what?" asked Slick.

I raised my eyebrows at him.

"You don't want to talk about your teddy bear?"

I shook my head.

Slick shrugged. "OK," he said. He opened the door and walked in, then stopped suddenly. He turned to me and put his finger to his mouth to tell me to be quiet.

Slick's mum was in the kitchen making a video. She was standing at the kitchen island in front of a camera on a tripod and two bright spotlights on black metal stands.

"…the great thing about these," she said to the camera as she took off her bright-pink oven gloves, "is you can make them the day before, and they'll keep perfectly for up to a week in an airtight container. As you know, I always use Freshen."

Slick and I stood silently and watched as his mum put some dinosaur-shaped pizzas into a lime-green container. She clicked the lid closed, said goodbye to the camera, then turned to us.

"Mum, this is Danny," said Slick. I guess he didn't know we'd met.

"Hi," I said.

Slick's mum smiled. "Danny! What a lovely surprise! How are you?" She picked up a container on the counter and came over to us. "Would you like one?" she said. "Freshly baked!"

"Thanks," I said, taking one that looked like a stegosaurus.

"Take two," she said, handing me a T-Rex. Then she closed the lid and put it on the far counter without offering one to Slick. I handed my second pizza to Slick, but he shook his head. I shrugged and took a bite of it. It was *good*.

"So what did you do today?" asked Slick's mum as I chewed.

"We built a computer," I said, trying not to sound like I was talking with my mouth full, which was exactly what I was doing.

"Oh, how unusual," she said. "You know you can buy them from shops."

"Um, yeah. I guess—"

"We're going to my room," interrupted Slick.

Slick's mum's smile didn't leave her face. "Right. Lovely to see you, Danny," she said. And then she turned her back to us and went over to the sink.

As we walked out of the kitchen and up the stairs to Slick's room, I thought about how Slick's mum hadn't said a single word to Slick the whole time. I think Mum was right about her.

If I'd had to guess what Slick's bedroom would look like before I actually saw it, I would have been one hundred per cent correct – skateboard against the wall, fancy laptop, a million posters of the Ashland Wanderers.

"I can't work it out – who's your favourite team?" I asked.

Slick looked at me looking at the posters. He looked confused. "The Ashland Wanderers. That's why I have their posters on my wall."

"I know – I can see. I was joking."

"Oh."

"You're really going to have to work on your sense of humour," I said. "Anyway, what did you want to show me?"

Slick walked over to the other side of his room and opened up the far-left door of his wardrobe. It was filled with clothes, and, no joke, they were arranged by colour. I watched as Slick knelt down and opened a long drawer at the bottom.

"So," said Slick. "You know my uncle Martin?"

"Not personally, but yeah."

"He sends me lots of stuff, and I don't need it all. I thought you could have some of it. If you want it."

"You want to give me your old clothes?" I asked.

"They're not old. I haven't even worn some of them."

I walked over and watched as Slick pulled out a pair of brand-new trainers.

"They're from last year's collection," said Slick, "but they're still in the shops, so they're still cool. What size shoe are you?"

"*What?* Why?" I asked.

"Because I want to know if they'll fit you. You look the same size, but—"

"No – I mean why do you want to give me this stuff?"

"You said you don't have an Uncle Martin, remember? And I do, so I thought you would like it. And I know your mum can't buy you this stuff."

"Who said that?" I felt my face start to burn up.

"People at school."

"Why are you talking about what my mum can't buy me at school?" My voice was getting louder.

"I asked them why they're not friends with you, and they said something about your clothes."

"*What* did they say about my clothes?"

"That your mum gets them from the dump. Is that true?"

I opened my mouth, but I was so surprised by what he was saying, and so angry, that for a moment I couldn't speak. But then I couldn't hold it any more. "WHO GETS CLOTHES FROM A DUMP?!" I shouted. "AND WHY WOULD YOU EVEN BELIEVE THAT?!"

"I wasn't sure," said Slick. He didn't raise his voice. "I didn't think it was true, but then I thought about how you said that you don't have an Uncle Martin to send you clothes, and I thought maybe it could be."

I turned to leave. I'd actually believed he wanted to be my friend. Slick jumped up and ran over to the door. He closed it.

"Get out of my way," I said. I tried to push Slick to the side, but he didn't move.

"But your mum isn't coming until six."

"I don't care," I said. I tried to push him again, but it was like pushing on a brick wall. "Let me go."

"No."

"No?"

"Danny, listen. Please. I want to be your friend. I like hanging out with you. And I want you to be friends with my friends too – I want to keep my other friends too. Right now, they don't like you, but I think if they get to know you, they will. They just need to see you in a different way."

I stared at Slick as I thought about what he was saying. He was totally serious.

And that's when I realized that Slick was not like other kids. I didn't think he was a robot – I mean, that's not the first thing you think of when you realize someone is a total weirdo, but I did think that maybe there was something different about the way he thought about things. That his brain didn't work things out in the same way as the rest of us. Sure, I thought his idea was the dumbest plan I'd ever heard, but I wasn't angry any more.

I took a deep breath and walked away from the door.

Slick sighed too.

"So – let me make sure I've got this right – you think that I'm going to magically become one of the popular kids if I put on a new pair of shoes?"

"Not just any shoes. Slicks are the coolest brand of trainers on the market right now. Did you see the Week talking about them in the new ad? Luke wears them. And Harry got a pair for his birthday. They're like the best trainers ever."

I rubbed my hand over my face. I was beginning to find this kind of funny. "I get it, Slick – you're into the stupid shoes."

Slick looked confused. "That's the name of the brand, not my name."

"It should be, seeing how much you love them."

And so Eric became Slick.

"You want to try them on?" asked Slick. "They're really comfortable. They have a gel insole."

"This is never going to work," I said. "I don't even want it to."

"You don't want to be popular?" I asked.

"No!" I said. "And even if I did, you can't just dress me in your clothes and think everyone will change their minds about me. I'm sorry, but it's a dumb idea."

Slick frowned.

"Sorry," I said, "I shouldn't have called it dumb. It's just that it won't work."

"But that's not the whole plan," said Slick. "There's more. I need your phone."

I raised my eyebrows, took my phone out anyway and handed it to him. I have to admit, I was kind of curious.

"I set up an account for you on Kudos," he said. I watched as he opened up the app store, downloaded the Kudos app and logged in. He turned the phone to show me. "I haven't put a picture up on there yet – I thought we could take one of you in your new clothes."

I stared at the phone with a sinking feeling in my stomach. Nothing about this seemed like a good idea.

"Look! See?!" said Slick. "You already have one friend. Me!" He smiled. "You'll get a lot more when you put your picture up."

Maybe there was a part of me that wanted it to work. So, whatever, I took the stupid clothes that Slick gave me and went to the bathroom to change.

"I feel stupid," I said when I came out.

Slick's eyes went really wide, and he grinned. "I think you mean you feel AWESOME!"

"No, that's definitely not what I mean." I looked in the mirror. "It looks like I've dressed up as you."

"Right! That's the whole point!" said Slick. "I just have to do your hair, and then we can take the pictures."

"Wait a minute. What are you going to do to my hair?"

"I'm just going to put some gel in it."

"Argh," I groaned. "Fine – let's just get it over with."

Slick looked super-excited as he dragged me over to the bathroom and put what seemed like a whole tub of gel into my hair. I looked like one of those dorky penguins with the middle bit of their hair sticking up, but I was too far in now. I let him take a picture of me by his window – one close up and one full length. Then he uploaded them to my account and wrote "Got my new Slicks. Awesome." He added an emoji of a pair of trainers and some stars, then got out his phone, logged into his account, liked my post and then shared it on his page. He turned back to me.

"And now," said Slick, "it's time for part three of my plan."

I rolled my eyes. "There's a part three?"

Slick nodded. "Yep – upload content to your VieVid channel."

"I don't have a VieVid channel."

"You do now. Open it up on your phone."

I gave Slick a look, but I did what he asked.

"Your username is Binarius underscore X," said Slick. "Same as your username on *Land X*. And your password is capital V, h, g, a, n, i, d, g, h, one, four, five, exclamation mark, four, two."

"Eh?"

Slick repeated it. Slower this time.

"Couldn't you have picked something easier to remember?" I asked.

"It's secure," said Slick. "Passwords should be a mix of letters, numbers and special characters, so that no one can guess them."

"Well, you definitely nailed that," I said as the account Slick had made for me opened. There was nothing on my channel except for a description that Slick had written for me. I read it, then looked up at Slick.

"Are you *serious*?" I asked. "You want me to make videos about *Land X*?"

Slick nodded and grinned like a little kid. "You know everything about it. I thought you could give other people tips. Tons of people would view that. I know I would."

I didn't know what I felt. I liked the idea – I just didn't like the idea of actually doing it.

"This isn't going to work," I said. "I'm not very good at talking and stuff in public. I wouldn't know what to say."

"You're fine at talking. You talk all the time. Just say what you know about *Land X*. It's not like you have to make anything up."

"I don't know."

"*Please*," said Slick. "Just try making one?"

I sighed and let Slick drag me over to his desk. He sat me down in front of his laptop, leant over me and logged into my account.

"Hey!" I said. "How do you know my password?"

"I saw you type it in the other day. You should use something more secure."

"What? Like *y, u, j, i, b, i, d, o, o, b, i, z, e, d, f, e, x*, one million, three thousand and eighteen?"

Slick nodded. "That would be a good one. Just remember to put a capital letter in there somewhere."

I laughed.

Slick set up the rest of the things we needed to make the video as we discussed what I would say.

19

SLICK

SATURDAY 10TH NOVEMBER (II)

We decided to make a video about finding the birth certificate in Dame Vickers's safe. It took Danny twenty-three attempts to make the video. This is because he kept making mistakes:

- Forgot what he was saying or messed up his words: eighteen times
- Danny's phone rang – both times it was Mrs Lazio to check if he was OK: two times
- Danny sneezed: one time
- Danny said his hair looked weird, and I had to fix it: one time.

I thought the final video was awesome, especially after we added the footage from *Land X* on a split screen and put in the text and a subscriber button. Danny did not seem as happy as I was.

"I look and sound stupid."

"But that's how you look and sound," I said.

"Wow, Slick, thanks."

I realized it sounded like I was saying he looked and sounded stupid. "I didn't mean that," I said. I didn't want Danny to get angry with me again. "I just meant that you don't—"

"It's cool," said Danny. "I know what you meant." He sighed. "OK, just put it up. No one's going to see it anyway."

"They will," I said. "It's all about the right links and hashtags." I made Danny stand up, and I filled in the information on the settings page. I put a link to every other *Land X* video I could find until Danny said that was enough. Then I got Danny to post it onto his Kudos page, and I shared it on mine. I didn't say anything about Danny being my friend – I just said that this was a really neat secret on *Land X* and people should check it out. I already had two likes on my post before I logged out.

Danny went home an hour later. By that time, his video already had forty-five views and four likes. This wasn't a lot, but it was his first post. Before he left, we agreed to make a video after school on Monday about how to get invited to join McKenzie's Quest on Signature Island.

Notes:
- Danny is coming to my house on Monday to make two more videos.
- Danny is 100 per cent confirmed as my friend.
- Even though he is not supposed to be my friend, I am happy about this.
- Danny's video now has seventy-five views and twelve likes. There was one comment on the video – the person posted anonymously. It said "Loser". That's all. I don't understand why somebody would do that. I logged into Danny's account, deleted the comment and then disabled comments so nobody else can write anything mean. I hope Danny didn't see it.

20

SLICK

MONDAY 12TH NOVEMBER

I woke up feeling excited about going in to school today. I don't normally feel excited. I act excited a lot, but this was different. I got dressed and unplugged my Hexam R3 from its charger. That's when I saw a message from Danny. Danny hasn't ever messaged me before. It said "Check out VieVid!" So I did, and I found out that Gamertropolis had picked up Danny's video about Dame Vickers's birth certificate this morning. Gamertropolis is the biggest game-review site. They shared his video, and it now had over 85,000 views and 1,172 likes. When I looked this morning, Danny already had 290 subscribers to his channel. And he only had one video!

Then I went on to check Danny's Kudos page. He still only had one friend – me. I would have thought he'd have more now. But still, 85,000 views was pretty awesome. We could work on the Kudos thing.

I was waiting for Danny when he came to school this morning. I wouldn't have waited for him by his locker before, but today was different. There was no way anybody could say he wasn't popular now that he had all those subscribers, so I didn't have to worry about being friends with him any more. Also, he was wearing the right kind of clothes now. Well, almost. He wasn't wearing everything I had given him, but he had put on his new Oldean T-shirt and his Slicks. We'd have to work on his hair.

"What are you doing here?" said Danny when he saw me. "Somebody might think we're friends." He was half smiling.

"It doesn't matter now – you're popular," I said. I smiled. "You have two hundred and ninety subscribers. And you're looking sharp."

Danny wrinkled his nose. "I don't know… I feel kind of weird. Everybody's going to notice I look different. Like I'm trying to be popular."

"You are."

"No, *you're* trying to make me popular. I'm quite happy to stay invisible."

"You're not invisible." I reached out and poked him on the shoulder.

"Ha ha," said Danny without smiling. "You know what I mean."

I shook my head. "No, I don't."

"I don't want people talking about me."

"They already do, but this way they'll talk about you in a good way."

Danny sighed. "You have no idea, Slick. I said it the other day – you can't just wear different clothes one day and suddenly become one of the popular kids."

"Why?"

"Just drop it, Slick…"

"OK, sorry," I said. "I just wanted you to sit with my other friends at lunch today, but I don't think they're going to change their mind about you if you don't look different."

"I don't want to sit with those idiots," said Danny. "I don't like them."

"You can't say that."

"I just did."

"I mean, you can't say that if you don't know them. And they shouldn't say things about you if they don't know you, either."

Danny just shrugged.

"Anyway, it doesn't matter now – you're popular." I smiled. "You have two hundred and ninety subscribers."

Danny's half-smile turned into a full smile. "I know! Can you believe it?! Gamertropolis!"

"So awesome," I said. "When are you going to put the next video up?" I asked.

"I already did it before school. Let's make another one today. You want to?"

"Sure. Maybe we could do one about stroking the Taxman's cat six times to get his healing powers? I don't think many people know about that."

Danny nodded. "That's a good one." He looked up at the clock on the wall. "I gotta go. See you after school?"

"What about lunchtime?"

Danny scrunched up his face. "I don't know. I feel kind of weird about it."

"It'll be cool," I said. "Things are different now."

Danny shook his head, rolled his eyes, then sighed and nodded. I wasn't sure what that meant.

"Fine, see you at lunch."

It meant yes.

I sat next to Luke in English. We had to take a test on a book we have been reading – the diary of a girl who hid in a secret part of a house during the Second World War. It was interesting as I didn't know anything about the Second

World War before I read this book, and I like learning new things. Luke had not read the book. He said he couldn't be bothered, so he just copied my answers. Luke says school is a waste of time for him as he is going to be a millionaire soon and he won't ever need to get a proper job. He said his mum is going to get him a tutor so that he can go on tour and be on television and not ever have to go to school again. This makes sense. I wonder if he will still be my friend when he isn't at my school any more. I guess I will find out when he leaves.

After English, I walked with Luke, Harry and Tyler to our next class. Luke talked the whole way about how his manager told him that he's about to hit the "big time". This is because Luke is going to sign a contract with a record company at the end of the week. I didn't mention Danny, as I would have had to interrupt Luke, and it's rude to interrupt your friends when they're talking.

* * *

When the bell rang for lunch, I was the first out of the door so I could go meet Danny as he was coming out of his class. I'm glad I did, because when I saw him he was walking the opposite way from the cafeteria. I ran to catch up with him.

"You're going the wrong way," I said.

"It's kind of creepy that you know my schedule," he answered.

"Why?"

"I need to go to the library."

"Why?"

"I hate it when you do your 'why' thing."

I stopped myself just as I was about to ask why again. "Come on," I said instead. "Come to lunch. It's all cool – you're a vlogger now."

Danny sighed, but he turned around and walked with me to the cafeteria. Danny didn't really talk all the way, and I think I've figured out why: I think he was nervous.

"It's going to be fine," I said as we walked into the cafeteria and lined up to get our lunches. "I told you – it's different now."

Danny still didn't say anything. We got our lunches, and I told Danny to follow me.

Luke, Harry, Tyler and Mateo were sitting at a table in the centre of the room. Harry was the only one facing in my direction. He smiled when he saw me. I went and sat next to him.

I was expecting Danny to sit next to me, but when I looked, Danny was still standing behind me with his tray in his hands. I nodded to him to sit down.

"What are you doing?" asked Luke. He was talking to me.

"Guys, you know Danny, right?"

Nobody said anything.

"He's cool now. He's got his own VieVid channel."

Danny smiled and shrugged.

"Oh yeah?" said Luke. "That's cool."

"Thanks," said Danny. He sat down next to me.

I smiled. This was going well.

"What are you making videos about?" continued Luke. "How to be a loser?"

Tyler let out a laugh so hard that his food flew out of his mouth. Then Mateo and Luke started laughing too.

"Nah, you got that covered on your channel, Luke," replied Danny without looking up from his food.

Harry burst out laughing, and Mateo and Tyler laughed even harder.

Danny, Luke and I were not laughing.

"It's cool, Luke," I said. "It's different now. Danny does videos about *Land X*. He's already got two hundred and ninety subscribers, and he only just set it up."

93

"Must have taken your mum a long time to make two hundred and ninety fake accounts," said Luke.

Tyler laughed.

Luke smiled and shrugged.

Danny stood up suddenly. "Told you these guys are losers."

"Takes one to know one," said Mateo. Luke laughed and thumped Mateo on the back.

Danny picked up his tray.

"Nobody wants you here," Luke said, looking at Danny. "Don't ever think about sitting down with us again, or you'll be sorry."

Danny started to walk off. I stood up.

"Why did you do that?" I asked Luke.

"Do what? I was just messing with him."

I looked behind me and saw Danny throwing his lunch into the bin.

"That was not cool," I said.

"Why are you being so weird?" asked Luke. "I thought you didn't like him either."

"I spent time with him," I said. "And he *is* cool."

"You should probably get some bug spray to get rid of the fleas," said Tyler.

"He *doesn't* have fleas!" I said. "You know that's a lie." I was almost shouting, and I didn't know why. I'd never shouted at a friend before.

"Chill, Eric," said Harry. "Just sit down."

"No!" I said. "You shouldn't have done that. None of you should have done that. If you were really my friends, you'd have given him a chance."

"What's wrong with you, Eric?" asked Luke. "Everybody knows Danny is a freak."

"He's not a freak – he's my friend," I said. I realized that everybody around us was staring at me. I didn't care.

94

Luke stood up and leant over the table. He stared at me with narrow eyes and a tight frown. "Well," he said slowly, "then I guess that makes you a freak too."

"A freak with fleas," said Tyler. He laughed. Nobody else did.

"Why are you obsessed with fleas?" I asked, turning to Tyler. "You know I don't have fleas. Danny doesn't have fleas. Your insults are dumb."

"Like your mum," said Tyler.

"That doesn't even make any sense," I said. "You've never even met my mum." I was confused and very agitated. I don't know how to describe it better. My body was shaking, and I wanted to do something to Tyler, but I didn't know what.

"Slick, leave it." It was Danny's voice. He'd come back. "Let's get out of here."

"If you go with him," said Luke, "we are never hanging out again."

In that moment, I realized I had to make a choice. It was Luke and his group of friends or Danny. I had worked hard to build up my friendships with Luke and the others. They were the most popular kids in my year, and being friends with them made me one of the most popular kids in my year too. It's what I had wanted. But I guess I'd changed.

I turned to Danny. "Let's go," I said.

"Loser," said Tyler as I walked away. I turned back to say something to him, but that was when I saw Luke put his leg out as Danny went to walk past him. Danny did not see this, and I did not have time to warn him. I couldn't do anything except watch as Danny fell forwards and landed on the floor. A few people laughed, but I didn't see who. All I saw was Luke smiling down at my friend as he tried to stand up, then I watched him kick Danny so that he fell back down again. I don't think that this is something any person should do to another person, even if they are not friends.

I saw Luke's leg go back. I think he was going to kick Danny again. Danny was scrambling to stand up. He looked very angry, and I think he might have been planning to hit Luke when he got up, but I didn't find out, because I got to Luke first. I grabbed him by his ugly Graves polo shirt and pushed him away from Danny.

"You shouldn't hurt other people," I said.

"Get your hands off me," said Luke.

"Apologize to my friend," I said.

"I'm not apologizing to anyone," said Luke.

"You should," I said.

"Make me," said Luke.

Luke punched me on my left cheek with his right hand. I didn't flinch. I grabbed his wrist and held it tight.

"Apologize to Danny."

Luke got his other hand and started punching me on the side of my body. I just stood there and let him do it, and the more I didn't move, the harder he tried to hit.

There was a crowd of people around us. I guess they must have hidden us from view, because there were no teachers to stop us. Even though they were supposed to be his friends, I noticed that Harry, Tyler and Mateo didn't come in to help him. They were just staring with wide eyes at what was happening. I think they were surprised.

Danny was standing up too. He was smiling. "Try grabbing him by the throat, Luke. See what happens."

I looked down at Luke as he swung his arm against my body. "I thought you'd be stronger," I said.

Luke was sweating and groaning, and he said some curse words, but I stayed calm.

"Are you going to apologize now?"

"NO! GET OFF ME!" shouted Luke. He was breathing very hard. I think he was tired, because he stopped hitting me. I let go of Luke's wrist and looked at him as he stood up straight. He was bright red, and the sweat was now pouring down his face.

"You are a bad person, Luke," I said. "You don't deserve any friends." I turned to Danny. "Let's go."

Danny smiled, and the two of us walked out.

I had picked my friend, and it felt good.

Notes:
- Ethan sat next to me in maths this afternoon. Miss Lake didn't tell him to sit with me. He said he thought that it was cool how I had stood up to Luke.
- Ethan said that Luke and the others are idiots. It is interesting – I thought Luke and his friends were the most popular kids in my year, but it seems a lot of people don't like them. Maybe popularity isn't measured only in Kudos friends.
- It turned out that Danny hadn't even checked his Kudos page. He wasn't used to doing it yet – that's what he told me when we got to his house that afternoon. He had 144 pending friend requests. He didn't know any of them, but he added them anyway.
- Danny now has 801 subscribers to his VieVid channel.
- Mrs Lazio brought us cookies that looked like computers. She said she saw them and couldn't *not* buy them. Mrs Lazio is very nice. I like being at Danny's house more than I like being at mine.

21
SLICK
FRIDAY 16TH NOVEMBER

I didn't speak to Luke, Harry, Tyler, Mateo or Theo until today. I haven't been avoiding them, but I haven't tried to speak to them either. Then, this morning, I walked by Luke, Harry and Tyler in the hall.

"Where's your boyfriend?" asked Luke.

I thought this was a strange question to ask me. I didn't have a boyfriend or a girlfriend the last time I spoke to Luke, which was only a few days ago.

"I don't have a boyfriend," I said. "Do you?"

Luke stared at me for a moment. "You're such a loser," he said, and walked off. Tyler followed him. Harry gave me a sort of smile, shrugged, then turned and followed Luke out too. I walked off to find Danny.

* * *

At lunch, Danny and I sat with Ethan and his friends Katie and Caleb. We have been sitting with them for the last few days. At first I thought it was kind of weird that Ethan was friends with a girl (Katie is a girl), but she's actually kind of cool. She even wears Slicks, which is awesome. Katie plays *Land X* too. In fact, she is level forty-one, which is higher than Luke and his friends.

Ethan, Katie and Caleb are not the most popular kids in the year (Ethan: 140 Kudos friends, Katie: 165 Kudos friends, Caleb: 108 Kudos friends), but they seem to be liked by a lot more people than my old group of friends. A lot of people come up and talk to Ethan, Katie and Caleb, but not a lot of people come up and talk to Luke and the others. Also, other kids come and join their table if there's space, and they don't turn anybody away. Nobody came and sat down at our table when I used to sit with Luke and Harry and their friends. If anybody tried to, they would be told to move.

I like Ethan and his friends. They don't like skateboarding much, but they are interesting. We talk a lot about science and computers.

I have been to Danny's house every day this week except today. We have been making videos for his VieVid channel and playing *Land X*. He has 1,031 subscribers! Even I am surprised, and it was my idea. I did not go to Danny's house today, because it's Friday and I had my appointment with Dr Kilaman. Danny asked me why I was going to the dentist again, and I said I wasn't sure. He said it's weird that I have to go so much, and then we started talking about something else. I will ask him more about this another time, as I hadn't ever thought going to the dentist was weird – I thought everybody had to go.

Notes:
- Three boxes arrived from Uncle Martin today. My box was full of packets of a new kind of fruit snack called Chewberries. I didn't eat any, because I don't eat when I'm at home.

- We went to see Dr Kilaman at the normal time. I asked Mum why we go to the dentist so much. She ignored me. I asked her again, and she said because it's good to look after our teeth.
- When we got back home, I ate a whole box of Chewberries. I don't know why I don't eat at home – maybe it's because I'd never tried Chewberries before. They taste really good, and they're good for you too – they have no artificial sugars or additives. Everyone at school eats Orchard Rolls, which are not very good for you. Maybe everyone will be eating Chewberries instead when they realize how good they are.
- Danny posted a new video tonight. It was about the hidden quartz-mine tunnel we found. You get to it by climbing the apple tree on Not Taken Road. It's the first video we haven't made together. I didn't like this very much. I'm not sure why.

23

SLICK

MONDAY 26TH NOVEMBER

Miss Lake was waiting at the school entrance this morning when I got in. She was wearing a green Blise jacket. It's the same one that my mum just received from Uncle Martin on Friday. She said she needed to speak to me.

"How are you, Eric?" asked Miss Lake after she had closed the door to her classroom.

"I'm very well, thank you, Miss Lake."

"Good. I just want to have a catch-up chat after our last talk."

She went over to one of the student seats and sat down. She pointed to the seat next to her. I didn't know what she was pointing at.

"Take a seat," she said.

I sat down.

"I hear that you are now friends with Danny Lazio."

"Yes, I know you said I shouldn't be, but I like him."

"I have changed my mind."

"You have?"

"Yes. I think what you have done for Danny is very impressive, Eric."

"What do you mean?"

"Before you met him, he was very unpopular. Now that he has met you, that has changed. It just goes to show what being friends with the right kind of person can do. Also, I see that you are now friends with Ethan too. I'm very pleased about that. I think these are going to be very good friends for you, as long as you keep helping them to become more popular."

"What do you mean, Miss Lake?"

"I mean that you should keep doing what you're doing – keep helping your new friends become more popular. This will be good for you, because you will be friends with other popular kids, and good for them, because everyone wants to be popular. Isn't that right?"

"I don't think everyone wants to be popular, Miss Lake."

Miss Lake smiled. She had a very shiny smile. "Of course they do. Everybody wants to be popular. The only people who say they don't want to be are the people who can't be. It's a defence mechanism."

"What's a defence mechanism?"

"It's when someone pretends they don't want to be popular so other people don't think that they want to be popular but can't do it."

"That's what it means?"

"In this situation, yes. OK, that's all. You just keep doing what you're doing: making more friends, enjoying your new school and helping your friends to be happier."

"By making them more popular?"

"Exactly!" said Miss Lake. She stood up. "Class is about to start – we both need to get going."

"Yes, Miss Lake. Thank you."

"You're welcome, Eric."

Miss Lake is very nice.

Ethan asked Danny and me if we wanted to come to his house after school on Friday. This makes him one hundred per cent confirmed as my friend, but I think I already knew that before he had asked me.

Notes:
- Danny now has 3,356 subscribers to his VieVid channel.
- When I got home, there was a package waiting for me from Uncle Martin. Except it wasn't for me – it was for Danny. There was a typed note on the top. It said: "Congratulations on all your success on VieVid! Any friend of Eric's is a friend of the Young family. Best wishes for your continued success. Uncle Martin." Inside the package was a pair of Slicks, four Oldean T-shirts, four Oldean tops and an Oldean baseball cap. I thought this was very nice of Uncle Martin.

24

SLICK

I went to Ethan's house today. It is at least twice the size of my house, and my house is quite big. It even has a lift! I didn't say it, because it would have been rude, but I think a lift in a house that only has three floors is kind of unnecessary. I suppose it would be helpful if you are carrying a lot of things up and down. Or if you are like my neighbour, Mr Beaker. Mr Beaker is eighty-three years old, and he can't walk very well any more as his spine is crumbling like a cookie in a pocket. That's how he explained it. He lives in a bungalow, so he doesn't actually need a lift, but I suppose he would if he lived in a house like this.

Everything is light-coloured, which makes it easy to see that it's also very clean. Ethan's mother met us at the door, took us into the kitchen and introduced me to Julia. I don't know who Julia is, but I guess she lives in the house too, because she was cooking. She gave each of us a freshly baked Danish pastry and a glass of orange juice. Then we went downstairs to the games room to play *Land X*. Turns out that "games room" is another way of saying basement.

Ethan's basement is very different to Danny's basement – it's bigger and tidier and has a carpet, and you can see right across it because there are no boxes or mess in the way. There are twelve colourful movie posters in frames hanging on the walls and a long bright-red sofa that faces the biggest TV screen I've ever seen. But I guess the reason they call it the games room is that it's filled with all sorts of different games, including ping-pong, table football and a pinball machine. I wanted to try out the pinball machine, but Danny and Ethan wanted to try to defeat the Maenadic Warrior in *Land X*. We really needed all three of us if we were going to have any chance of killing her, so I agreed. It's important to do the things that your friends want to do, plus I really did want to beat the Maenadic Warrior too.

Ethan had his laptop, and I had brought mine from my house, but Danny doesn't have one, so he borrowed Ethan's dad's. Ethan said his dad wouldn't mind. We all sat on brightly coloured beanbags and started playing.

Julia kept coming downstairs with more orange juice for me. I don't normally drink, but I always accept a drink when it is offered to me. The problem was that, whenever I drank the one she'd given me, Julia thought that meant I wanted another. It would have been rude to say no, so I just kept taking them, saying thank you and drinking them. After my fourth glass of orange juice, I needed to use the bathroom.

"It's upstairs," said Ethan without looking up from his laptop. "It's one of the doors down the hallway. You'll find it."

Ethan was right – I did find it, but only after I found the place where the coats are kept and a room that looked like a small office. I don't know why Ethan didn't just say "the third door on the left".

I was washing my hands after using the bathroom when someone started rattling the door handle.

"I'm coming," I called.

I quickly dried my hands and opened the door. Standing on the other side was a girl with long brown hair. I think she was probably around ten years old, but she might have been younger – it's hard to tell with girls. She was wearing pink jeans, a pair of silver shoes and a purple T-shirt with a unicorn on it. I didn't recognize the brand of clothes she was wearing, as I don't know much about girls' clothes.

"You can use the bathroom now," I said.

"I don't need it," she said. "I just went."

"Oh. Why were you trying to open the door?"

"To see who was there," she said. "Who are you?"

"Slick," I said. I decided to use my nickname. I prefer it. "Who are you?" I asked back.

"I'm Hope," said the girl. Then she gave me a hug. I hugged her back, but I have to say that I was very surprised. I can't remember ever hugging a girl. Or a boy, come to think of it.

"How old are you?" she asked.

"I'm twelve. How old are you?"

"I'm ten and a half. My birthday is on the 10th of August."

"That's cool," I said.

"Why are you called Slick?"

"Because that's my nickname. I like Slick trainers." I lifted up my foot to show her my red-and-orange Slicks.

"They're pretty," she said.

"Thank you. Why are you called Hope?"

"Because my parents called me that," she said.

"Are you Ethan's sister?" I asked.

"Yes. Do you like the Week?"

"They're my favourite band."

Hope smiled. "They're my favourite band too! I know all their songs."

"Who's your favourite?"

"Saturday. Who's yours?"

"Tuesday. He's a skateboarder like me. Why do you like Saturday?"

"Because he likes pink, and I like pink too."

"Cool," I said.

"Do you want to sing karaoke with me? I have all their songs on my karaoke machine in my room."

"I can't. I'm playing *Land X* downstairs. And I can't sing."

Hope frowned. "Everybody can sing. Copy me. *I'll paint you a rainbow with your tears...*" she sang. I recognized the lyrics from 'Masterpiece'. It's a song from the Week's latest album.

"You're a good singer," I said.

"Your turn," she said. She stared at me.

"I really can't..."

"Please?"

"OK... *Paint me a rainbow with your tears*," I sang.

She started clapping. "See? You can sing!"

I shrugged. "No I can't. It doesn't sound like the song. I'm not very good."

"You are not being very nice about yourself," she said. "You should be nicer."

"I guess. Hey, I have to go downstairs now," I said. "Ethan will be waiting for me."

"OK," said Hope. "It was nice to meet you, Slick."

"It was nice to meet you, too, Hope."

She gave me another hug, and then she skipped away down the hallway.

"What took you so long?" asked Danny. "We're going to get killed if we hang around this lake much longer."

I sat down on my beanbag and picked up my laptop.

"Sorry," I said. "I was just talking to your sister. She wanted me to sing."

"Let me guess," said Ethan. "The Week?"

"Yeah," I said. "She's really nice."

"Yeah, she is," said Ethan. "Annoying too, sometimes."

"Why isn't she at our school?" I asked.

"She's at another school that has a special unit," said Ethan.

"What's a special unit?" I asked. "That sounds awesome."

Ethan gave me one of the looks that Danny gives me all the time. "It's for kids that can't be in normal classes all the time."

"Why can't she be in normal classes?"

Then Danny and Ethan both turned and looked at me funny. I could tell I was saying something wrong, but I didn't know what that something was.

"Hope has Down syndrome. Didn't you notice?"

"Oh," I said. I had never heard of Down syndrome, so I couldn't have noticed that Hope had it.

"Right, yeah. I wasn't sure," I said. I decided it was a good time to change the subject. I opened up my laptop. "Let the battle commence," I said.

Notes:
- I looked up what Down syndrome is when I got home. Turns out it's something some people are born with and that it's genetic – like the colour of your skin or your eyes.
- I like Hope. She is very friendly and smiles a lot. And she likes the Week, and so do I. I think Hope could be my friend. Maybe I was wrong about boys not being friends with girls. We have a lot more in common than I used to think.
- Danny liked the new clothes from Uncle Martin. He wore his light-blue Oldean T-shirt for the new video we made so that

Uncle Martin would be able to see it if he looked on Danny's VieVid channel.

- I reached level fifty on *Land X* tonight. I am now Wise. Danny is level eighty-three. He is Enlightened. You become Enlightened after level eighty. I hope to catch up with Danny soon, but it's difficult because we both play a lot.

- While we were playing *Land X*, Danny said that he's making his mum a digital photo frame for Christmas. He is going to use pictures of him and his mum. He said his mum doesn't like him to spend money on presents for her, and that it means much more to her if she receives something that he has put time and effort into. Ethan said he hasn't got his parents anything for Christmas because he's Jewish. I don't think I have ever given my parents a present for Christmas, so maybe we are Jewish too. I will have to ask Mum and Dad when I see them.

25

SLICK

SUNDAY 9TH DECEMBER

I asked Dad if we are Jewish, and it turns out that we are not, so I asked Danny if he would help me make a digital photo frame for my parents for Christmas too. He said "Sure".

We spent the whole afternoon making my frame. I uploaded a couple of selfies that I took on my Hexam R3, but the only photos of me with my mum and dad are the framed ones hanging in our house. I will take pictures of them with my Hexam R3 and upload them to the frame when I get back. I didn't have any wrapping paper, so Danny gave me some that he had left over. It is silver with white snowflakes on it.

I'm so excited about giving Mum and Dad their Christmas present. Back in October, Mrs Okina gave Mum a pair of gardening gloves because Mum had said she didn't have any. When Mum opened the bag and saw the gloves, she couldn't stop smiling. She hugged Mrs Okina and kept saying how much she loved them. I'm pretty sure Mrs Okina didn't even make the gloves herself, so I think Mum will be even happier when she opens my gift.

Also, I decided tonight that I'm going to get Danny a gift, as he is my best friend. It's too late to give it to him, as we are going to visit Uncle Martin in London for Christmas, but I will give it to him after we get back. I don't know what it's going to be yet. I will have to think about it more tomorrow, as it's midnight now and I have to go to sleep.

26

SLICK

THURSDAY 27TH DECEMBER

We went away for Christmas to see Uncle Martin in London. We left on Christmas Eve and got back this morning. It was good. Everybody ate too much. Then we watched Christmas movies. I got eleven presents. This is what I got:

- Oldean winter jacket. Sea blue.
- Oldean wool hat. Fleece-lined. Grey.
- Oldean gloves. Fleece-lined. Grey.
- Chewberries. Forty packets.
- Baltic Monsoon skateboard. Limited edition. Artwork by the graffiti artist Reedsicks.
- Baltic Monsoon phone cover to fit my Hexam R3.
- BAM headphones. Silver.
- Slick trainers. Gold Stripe limited edition.
- Slick backpack. Gold Stripe limited edition.
- ShadowCloud drone.

Uncle Martin also gave me a present for Danny, which was very nice. It's wrapped, so I don't know what it is. I'll give it to Danny when I see him. We didn't talk while I was away. I don't know why I didn't text him either. I guess I was too busy at Uncle Martin's. I texted him as soon as I woke up this morning, though, and he called me straight back.

"Hey," he said. "You back?"

"Yeah, we got back in the night. I just woke up. How was your Christmas?"

"Christmassy. How about you?"

"It was good. Everybody ate too much. I got eleven presents. Then we watched Christmas movies."

"Ugh, you too? Did you see *One Last Kiss before Christmas*?"

"No," I said.

"You didn't miss out. Seriously – worst movie ever. My mum and aunt made everyone watch it, and they cried through the whole thing. It was painful. What did you watch?"

"I don't remember," I said, because I didn't.

"You don't remember?"

"Um, no. It was good, though. We ate too much. I got eleven presents. Then we—"

"Yeah, you said that already."

"Oh. Right. Sorry."

"Did you stay in your uncle's place? Bet he has some kind of cool London flat."

"Yeah."

"What's it like?"

"It's nice."

The truth was, I didn't really remember that, either. It was kind of weird. I remembered some things really well – like eating Christmas dinner – but I didn't remember what Uncle Martin's flat was like. I decided to change the subject.

"I got a ShadowCloud," I said.

"NO. WAY."

"Yep."

"Have you tried it yet? Does it actually follow you?"

I looked over at the box by my wardrobe. I don't know why I hadn't opened it.

"I haven't opened it yet. I was waiting for you." That wasn't really true, but I didn't want to sound ungrateful.

"Cool! When are you around?"

"Now?"

"OK. Come over. Bring the ShadowCloud."

"I will. Oh, and my uncle Martin got you a gift too."

"He did?"

"Yeah."

"Please say it's a ShadowCloud."

"I don't think it is – the box is a different shape."

"I was joking – those things are like five hundred quid. As long as it's not another home-made jumper – I'm all maxed out on those."

"I don't think so. I don't think my uncle Martin knits."

"I was… Oh never mind. Come over." Danny hung up.

I like that I'm back from London and that I get to hang out with Danny again.

I got dressed in my new clothes and put on my Gold Stripe limited-edition Slicks. I put my ShadowCloud and Danny's gift into my new Slick Gold Stripe limited-edition backpack and grabbed my Baltic Monsoon skateboard.

The front door was open when I came downstairs. Mum was putting stuff in the car, and Dad was by the door putting on his new Regent North coat. Regent North is my dad's favourite brand of clothing. He used to only wear clothes from QW's, but then he found Regent North, and now he only wears clothes from there.

"I'm going to Danny's," I said.

"OK," said Dad. He didn't say anything else. He went into the kitchen.

I put on my new Oldean jacket and was just about to leave when I saw my gift to Mum and Dad on the kitchen counter. It hadn't been opened. I can't believe I forgot to take it to London.

Dad came back from the kitchen carrying a crate of Kolding beer.

"What's that for?" I asked.

Dad stopped and looked at me. "Why?"

"Just asking."

Dad stared at me for a moment. "It's for Joe Prill. We're going to lunch there, and I thought I'd take him some of this beer I picked up in London."

"Cool," I said. "Hey, Dad?"

"Yes?"

"I got you and Mum a Christmas present. I forgot to take it to London."

"That's nice, Eric. Thanks." Dad smiled and picked up his keys.

Mum came into the house and picked up her red Blise jacket. Mum is the only one of us who didn't get a new coat this Christmas.

"I got you and Dad a Christmas present," I said to her.

"How lovely," said Mum. "Thank you, Eric."

She smiled and picked up a bag by the door. Mum and Dad turned to leave.

"Do you want to open it?" I asked.

Mum and Dad looked at each other.

"We're going out. We'll open it later."

"Can you open it now?"

Mum looked at her watch. "OK. We've got five minutes before we need to leave."

They followed me into the kitchen. I went over to the counter and picked up the present. I handed it to Mum. I was very excited and couldn't stop smiling.

Mum unwrapped my gift. Dad stood next to her and watched.

"Ohhh," she said when she saw the digital photo frame. "How lovely!"

"Wow – thanks so much," said Dad. "That's very thoughtful of you, Eric."

Mum put the digital photo frame down on the counter and stood up. "Let's go, Frank."

"Do you know what it is?" I asked.

"No," said Mum.

I picked up the frame and switched it on.

"Look," I said. "It's got pictures of us on it."

Dad and Mum stared at the slide show I had made. "They're the same pictures we have in the house," said Mum.

"Yes, but I made it."

"Why did you make it?" asked Mum.

"Because I thought it would mean more if I gave you something that I had put time and effort into," I said.

"But they sell these in shops," said Dad. "I'm pretty sure Electramart stocks a whole range of them. They're better quality than this."

"And you get a one-year warranty with every purchase there," added Mum.

"Right," I said. "I guess I just wanted to—"

"Frank, we have to go."

"Yes, Karen."

"Thank you for the lovely gift, Eric," said Mum. "You are too kind."

"Yes, thank you, Eric," said Dad.

They walked away and left me standing in the kitchen holding the frame. I don't think they liked it. I don't think I'll make them a gift next year.

27

DANNY

THURSDAY 27TH DECEMBER

I stopped asking Slick about his Christmas after I figured out that he didn't want to talk about it because it hadn't been a good time. I've met his parents, and they didn't care if he was in the hospital, so they probably ignored him the whole time. Maybe they didn't even do anything to celebrate. I guess even an Uncle Martin giving you crazy-good gifts wouldn't make up for that. I'm not saying I wouldn't have traded my new school backpack and jumpers for the gifts Slick got, but at least it was Christmas as it should be: too much food, my aunts arguing about how to cook the potatoes, my uncle Tony making everyone be silent while he sang Italian ballads for what seemed like for ever, Grandma pinching my cheeks too much, my little twin cousins over from the US making me give them piggybacks the whole day. And laughing – lots of laughing. I don't know for sure, but I don't think Slick's Christmas was anything like that.

I think Mum was as happy to see Slick as I was when he came over. I think she feels sorry for him. She hugged and kissed him, and I would have been embarrassed about it, except Slick didn't seem to mind at all.

"We've missed you so much!" said Mum after she'd released Slick. "How are you?"

"I'm good, Mrs Lazio," said Slick.

"How was your Christmas?"

"It was good," said Slick. "Everybody ate too much. I got eleven presents. Then we watched Christmas movies."

"Sounds like a perfect Christmas," said Mum. "And it's not finished yet. I have a gift for you too."

Slick and I both looked surprised.

I had no clue that Mum had got Slick anything. None. If I'd had, there's no way that Slick would ever have seen it.

"I made you a little something," said Mum, giving me my first clue that this wasn't going to be good. "I didn't get a chance to finish it before you left. I hope it fits."

I groaned, mortified, and put my hands over my face and listened as Slick unwrapped the gift. And then silence. After a few seconds, I looked out between my fingers and saw Slick staring at the gift that he was now holding out in front of him: a blue jumper with big white letters on the front that said "LAND X".

I wanted to die.

Mum was grinning, but the more Slick stared at it without saying anything, the more her smile began to disappear.

"Do you like it?" asked Mum.

Mum's voice seemed to snap Slick out of his (horrified, I thought) trance. He looked up at Mum, and he had the strangest look on his face – like he was about to cry.

"It's OK. I don't—" began Mum.

"I don't know what to say," interrupted Slick in a quiet voice. "It's the nicest gift that anybody's ever given me."

Mum's face melted. "Ah, honey, that's so sweet. Why don't you…"

She stopped mid-sentence as Slick walked over to her and threw his arms around her, the jumper still in his hands. Mum looked shocked for a second, then hugged him back. She kissed the top of his head, then looked up at me with a face I normally only see when she sees a newborn baby or a kitten. I think she was about to cry too.

And I felt like crying too. With AWKWARDNESS.

Mum pulled Slick away and dabbed her eyes. "Come on now, let's have a look to see if it fits."

I watched as Slick held his arms up and Mum tugged and tugged until she got the jumper over his head. Slick pulled it down over his body as far as it would go and tugged on the sleeves, which were nearer to his elbows than his wrists.

"Oh dear," said Mum. "It's a little small."

Slick shook his head. "No it's not," he said, running his hand over the lettering on the front. "It's perfect."

I waited until Mum left the room, then told Slick that he didn't have to pretend to like Mum's gift.

"What do you mean?" asked Slick, looking surprised. "I wasn't pretending. I think it's the nicest gift I've ever been given."

"Oh, *come on*," I said.

"You don't believe me?"

"I know you're not kidding, but, seriously, are you kidding?! A jumper… the best thing you've ever been given… when I know you got a ShadowCloud?!

Slick looked kind of annoyed. "Danny, you don't understand. Your mum *made* this for me. She spent a long time knitting it… for me. And she put LAND X on the front because she knows I like playing *Land X*, which is really nice. There are thousands of ShadowClouds, but there's only one of these."

I was about to get into a most pointless debate about whether ShadowClouds are better than jumpers when a picture flashed up in my mind of Slick sitting alone somewhere on Christmas Day being ignored by his parents. That's when I decided maybe I should just shut up and let Slick be happy with his badly fitting embarrassing jumper.

"Fine," I said. "I have like a hundred more if you ever want another. I might even have one that actually fits you."

Slick shook his head. "Thanks," he said, "but I'm happy with this one. Anyway..."

Slick turned around, walked over to his backpack and pulled out a small gift-wrapped box with a gold bow on the top. He handed it to me.

"From Uncle Martin."

Slick watched as I opened it. My mouth dropped when I saw what it was: a brand-new Hexam R3 mobile phone and a pair of BAM headphones. Seriously. I'm not even kidding.

"I think I'm actually going to die," I said, as I took the phone out and turned it over in my hands. I looked up to see that Slick was looking worried. "Chill. Not *actually*. But this is the coolest present. EVER."

I was about to go show Mum when Slick bent down and took something else out of his bag – a large, thin brown envelope. He handed it to me.

"I hope you like it," he said. He was looking nervous. I'd never seen Slick look nervous before.

I took the envelope from him and read what he had written on the front:

To My Best Friend Danny
Merry Christmas
From Slick

I wasn't sure what to think or say, so I just opened it. Slick came and stood beside me as I pulled out the single sheet of paper and turned it over.

"I went searching through our shared history on *Land X*," said Slick, "and printed out this picture of you and me – I mean, Baltic_Slick and Binarius_X."

I looked down at the picture of our avatars standing next to each other on top of a cliff. Around the picture was a large white border filled with hundreds, maybe even thousands, of tiny handwritten numbers.

"They're the coordinates of every place on *Land X* that we've been to together," explained Slick. "I had to go through our data logs to find them all, and then I went onto the map to get the coordinates of every one. It took me five hours."

I stared at it, not knowing what to say. I felt weird. Maybe kind of like Slick had felt when Mum gave him his jumper. Except worse. Much worse.

"Do you like it?" asked Slick.

"It's awesome," I said quietly. "Thank you."

"You seemed more excited about the Hexam R3," said Slick.

I shook my head. "It's just… well… it's just…" I looked up at Slick. "I'm really sorry, but I didn't get you anything. I didn't know we were giving each other gifts."

Slick smiled. "I don't care. Do you really like it?"

I wasn't good at this, but I knew how hurt he'd be if I didn't show him how much his gift meant to me. So I over-rode every awkward gene I have inside me and hugged him.

"It's the best gift that any friend has ever given me," I said.

I stood back and saw that Slick's smile had turned into a real one.

"Really?" he said, and then he frowned. "Wait… How many gifts have you ever been given by friends?"

"Not the point," I said. I smiled. "Come on – let's go put this up in my room, and then can we try out your ShadowCloud?"

Slick nodded. He looked really happy, even though I hadn't given him anything.

"When's your birthday?" I asked, as we walked off to my bedroom.

"The first of March. Why?"

"No reason," I said.

"You don't have to get me a gift," said Slick.

"I know," I said.

I was going to give him the best gift ever. I wasn't sure exactly what it was going to be, but at least I had a few months to think about it.

28

SLICK

THURSDAY 27TH DECEMBER (II)

"Come on – open it," said Danny. We were standing out on his porch with the unopened ShadowCloud box on the floor between us.

I knelt down and pulled out the tiny bird-shaped ShadowCloud. It was smaller than I was expecting – so small that if I closed my hand into a fist around it, you couldn't see it.

"How do you turn it on?" asked Danny.

I pulled out my Hexam R3 from the pocket of my Oldean jacket and unlocked it. "You have to pair it," I said. I opened up the ShadowCloud app and waited until the ShadowCloud beeped once to let me know it was linked to my phone. Then I pressed the green button in the centre of my screen. The ShadowCloud started humming quietly, and its sleek black wings began to vibrate until they were moving so fast that you couldn't see them. Three seconds later, it rose up in the air. Danny and I watched as it flew up vertically and then stopped ten feet above us, hovering silently.

"That is the coolest thing I've ever seen!" said Danny. "Is it recording?"

I held up my Hexam R3 and showed him the live feed in the corner of the screen. It was showing Danny and me looking down at the video playing.

"Ha!" said Danny. "That's crazy." He waved his arms around, and the Danny on the screen did the same.

"That *is* really cool," I said.

"Here," said Danny, handing me my Baltic Monsoon skateboard.

I took it and was about to hand Danny my phone when I had a better idea.

"You can follow my ShadowCloud if I approve you on my phone."

Danny smiled and took out his Hexam R3. He downloaded the app and put in the code I gave him, and then his screen came up with the same video feed as the one on my phone.

"OK, now go," said Danny.

* * *

I didn't understand why ShadowClouds were so cool until Danny and I tried mine out. The video of me skateboarding down Danny's street looked like an advert on TV – that's how good the picture was. I'm going to post it on my Kudos page. We went inside Danny's house, and the ShadowCloud followed us, adjusting its height whenever it was approaching an obstacle. It's very clever.

Danny hid behind the curtains in the kitchen and waited for Mrs Lazio to walk past. Then he jumped out and said boo. I didn't want to scare Mrs Lazio, so I didn't do it, but Danny told me to trust him, and it turned out that he was right – when Mrs Lazio watched the replay of her screaming and jumping backwards on my Hexam R3, she started laughing so hard she couldn't speak for a long time. The more we watched the video, the harder Mrs Lazio and Danny laughed, and then I started laughing too because it *was* funny to see Mrs Lazio wobbling around and screaming when it was just her son jumping out in front of her. After we all stopped laughing, Danny and I played *Land X* and made another video for Danny's VieVid channel.

I was supposed to leave at 4 p.m. because Danny's dad was coming to get him. I have never met Danny's dad. Danny said I haven't missed anything. Just before I was going to go, the phone rang and Mrs Lazio told Danny that his dad wasn't coming. Danny just shrugged, but I think he was sad. I don't know why, because he doesn't seem to like his dad very much. I asked him if he wanted me to stay and play some more *Land X*, and he said yes, so I did. Danny stopped looking sad when we found the red bandana of the Nelson Knight that we've been trying to find for two days.

I didn't like this morning at my house, but the rest of the day was one of the best I've ever had.

Notes:
- Danny has uploaded a total of sixteen videos. He now has 12,612 subscribers.
- Receiving gifts is very nice, but I think giving gifts to people who like what I give them makes me even happier.
- Mrs Lazio's digital photo frame was on the mantelpiece above the fireplace in the living room. The digital photo frame I made for Mum and Dad was still face-down on the kitchen counter where I left it when I got home tonight. I took it to my room and uploaded a video still of Danny, Mrs Lazio and me laughing in Danny's kitchen. I put it on my bedside table so that I can look at it. I don't think my parents will care.

29

SLICK

MONDAY 31ST DECEMBER

Today is the last day of the year, and I will be staying at Ethan's house with Danny.

I will be wearing the same clothes I wore to the fundraiser: a blue Argalio suit and white shirt, and a pair of brown leather shoes by LiFonti. I looked up what to wear to a New Year's Eve party yesterday, and all the men in the pictures were wearing bow ties. I don't have a bow tie, so I borrowed the Regent North one my dad has.

I have never been to a sleepover before, so I didn't know what to take apart from the Oldean pyjamas and the Chill & Smooth travel set that Uncle Martin sent me yesterday. Uncle Martin also sent me a note saying "Enjoy your sleepover, and don't forget to take your pillow". I don't remember telling Uncle Martin about my sleepover, but then again I don't really remember that much about Christmas, so maybe I did. It was very nice of him.

I didn't know what else to take, so I called Danny. He didn't answer the first time I tried, or the second, but he picked up on the third call.

"What?" he said. He was mumbling.

"What are you taking to Ethan's?" I asked.

"What?"

"The sleepover. What are you taking?"

Danny groaned. "I don't know. Just normal stuff. Why?"

"Are you taking your bed?"

"Ha ha. Funny."

I laughed because I didn't want him to think I hadn't been joking. "But seriously, what else are you taking?"

"Slick, I'm sleeping. It's five in the morning. I'll call you when I wake up."

He hung up.

Danny was not very helpful, so I went on the Internet to look up what to take on a sleepover. I found a lot of useful information. I even found a page that was about sleepovers for twelve-year-olds. It had an excellent checklist, though I did have to amend a couple of things.

Here is what I packed:

- **My pillow.** This was not on the checklist, but Uncle Martin told me to bring it.
- **Toiletries bag.** Plastic bag I found in the kitchen.
- **Toiletries.** Chill & Smooth travel set — includes shampoo, conditioner, shower gel, face moisturizer and deodorant.
- **Brush.** Comb. I have short hair.
- **Bobby pins and hair ties.** See above.
- **Hairspray.** Chill & Smooth hair gel. I don't use hairspray.
- **Sanitary products.** Eavings antibacterial hand wipes. Eavings hand sanitizer. I found these in Mum and Dad's bathroom.
- **PJs or nightie.** Oldean PJs.
- **Snacks.** Chewberries.
- **Book**. *Football Geek Stats & Facts Compendium 1920–50*.
- **Torch**. Dad has every type of portable light that Sharko makes, so I had plenty to choose from. I took the Sharko pocket pen-torch

as it is the smallest and I didn't have a lot of room left in my backpack.

- **Stuffed animal.** I don't have one. I know Danny has one, but I don't think he has any extra to lend me. Hopefully Ethan or Hope can lend me one. I'm not sure why I need it.
- **First-aid kit.** We had one of these under the sink in the kitchen. It was a small red box with a white cross on it. The website said that the parents would probably have medical supplies, but it was always better to be safe than sorry. I looked that up. It means you wouldn't want to need it and not have it.
- **Clean clothes and underwear.** Oldean hooded top. Oldean T-shirt. Oldean jeans. Oldean boxers. Oldean socks. Slicks Gold Stripe limited edition.
- **Entertainment.** There was a link in this section to a separate page about things everybody loves to do at sleepovers. Games and stuff. One is a pillow fight, and I already had a pillow. I managed to find the rest of the stuff I needed for the other games around my house. I couldn't fit them all into my new Slick Gold Stripe limited-edition backpack, though, so I used my old Slick backpack too. I hope Ethan doesn't mind that I'm bringing two bags.
- **Gift for your host's parents.** Case of Kolding beer. I wanted to take two – one for Mr Schwartz and one for Mrs Schwartz – but Dad said I could only take one as we only have two cases left, and he and Mum are taking one of them to Mr and Mrs Prill's house tonight. Then he asked me who I was going to give the beer to, as it would be a waste to give it to someone who wasn't going to appreciate it properly.

"I'm going to Ethan Schwartz's house, and I'm staying the night. I need a gift to take to his parents," I explained.

My parents both stopped and looked at me. "Schwartz?" asked Dad. "As in Mayor Michael Schwartz?"

"Yeah. That's Ethan's dad."

"Why are you spending the night there?" asked Dad.

"Because Ethan asked me to. His parents are having a New Year's Eve party, and they told Ethan he could invite some friends. He invited me and Danny."

Mum looked surprised. "He could invite two people and he chose you?" she asked. "I didn't think you were such good friends with him."

Mum turned to Dad. "I think we should go to the Schwartzes' tonight instead of the Prills'. What do you think, Frank?"

Dad nodded. "Yes, I agree. I've been wanting to meet Michael Schwartz since we arrived in Ashland. He's very well connected."

"But you're not invited," I said. "You can't just show up."

I didn't want my parents to come. I have been thinking about why I didn't want them to come. I think it was because they only wanted to go to the party because the Schwartzes were people who could help my parents get things they wanted – like membership to the Mapleworth Golf Club – and not because they actually liked them. This is like lying in a way, and I didn't want them to lie to the parents of my friend. I think this is why I didn't want them there.

"I'm sure they won't mind," said Mum. "Gail's a friend of mine."

"She's not your friend, Mum – you met her for five minutes when she picked me up."

"She asked me to lunch. People don't ask other people to a social lunch unless they consider them friends."

"Even so," I said, "you can't just show up if you haven't been invited. It would be rude."

"We'll drive you there," said Dad. "They'll have to invite us in if we do that."

"I was going to get a lift with Danny."

Mum smiled. "There's no need now. I'll give Mrs Lazio a call and tell her we're taking you."

I didn't like Mum and Dad's plan at all, but I don't argue with adults, so I didn't say anything more. Mum called Mrs Lazio and told her they were driving me to Ethan's, and Dad called the Prills and told them that Mum was sick and they wouldn't be able to make it. This was a lie. Then we got in the car and left.

Ethan's house has a driveway lined with trees, which were all covered in white lights. I think this was to help people find their way to the party as it was dark out. It seemed like a lot of work when people have headlights on their cars, and there are other forms of lighting that wouldn't have taken so long to install. The party hadn't started yet. I knew this because there were lorries in the driveway and people unloading flowers and tables and chairs from them.

"Are we early?" asked Mum. "You said you had to be here at six."

I nodded. "Yeah, that's when Ethan told me to come."

Dad stopped a man carrying a large glass vase of white flowers. "Do you know what time the party starts?" he asked.

"Eight," said the man.

Dad and Mum both turned to look at me.

"I know what Ethan said," I said.

My parents didn't say anything. We walked up the steps of Ethan's house, and Mum pressed the doorbell, even though the front door was open, as you can't walk into a person's house without being invited in. That's illegal.

I heard Mrs Schwartz's voice before I saw her. "Mind the piano! No… no… over there… beautiful!"

Then she appeared from a door on the right. She was wearing jeans and a white shirt. I didn't recognize the brands because they weren't Blise, and they're the only women's clothes I know.

"Eric! Oh my! Don't you look handsome," she said when she saw me. She came over and gave me a hug, then shook hands with my parents.

"I'm so sorry," said Mum. "Eric told us to come at six, but we've just been told the party begins at eight."

"No, no, that's right," said Mrs Schwartz, smiling. "The kids are having their own party downstairs. This way they're all set up before everyone arrives."

"Ah," said Mum. "Well, we could come back at eight?"

"Absolutely not," said Mrs Schwartz. "We plan to have Eric all night – you have the whole night off! We can bring him back to you about noon – I'm sure we'll all want to sleep in in the morning."

Dad and Mum looked at each other. I know they were trying to work out what to say that would get them invited to the party later, but before they could come up with anything, a woman dressed all in black came running into the hallway.

"The band needs to know when the sound system will be set up," she said to Mrs Schwartz.

Mrs Schwartz nodded and turned to my parents.

"I'm so sorry – I'm going to have to rush off. It's madness around here at the moment." She gave them both a hug. "Happy New Year! Have a wonderful evening!"

"Happy New Year!" I said to them too.

Mum and Dad were still standing on the front steps in silence as I left to go with Mrs Schwartz. I think I should have felt bad that they cancelled going to Mr and Mrs Prill's party and didn't get invited to the Schwartzes' party, but I didn't.

* * *

The games room at Ethan's house looked and sounded very different from the last time I visited:

- Strings of tiny lights were now covering all the walls.
- Two long tables had been placed against the wall, near the stairs. Both were covered in black tablecloths that had stars printed on them. One of them had lots of food and drinks on it. The other one had two Hexam tablets on it, a stack of white paper, markers, a stack of board games and a pack of cards. It was interesting, because none of these things were mentioned in the sleepover page that I had looked at.
- A pink machine with a small television screen on the top and two gold microphones attached was in the corner of the room. I guessed – because of the microphones – that this was the karaoke machine that Hope had told me about the other day.
- The table football and ping-pong table had been moved to make way for a large tent. Inside the tent were three sleeping bags and loads of brightly coloured pillows and cushions. I could see this because the side of the tent was open.
- Silver letters spelling out "HAPPY NEW YEAR" hung across the middle of the room. The lights in the ceiling were off, which made the string lights look like bright shining stars covering all the walls.
- There was music playing. It was the Week. I think I can guess who chose that: Hope.
- The television screen was on, but the sound was off. It was showing fireworks going off around the Eiffel Tower in France and lots of people cheering and hugging each other in the streets. I know that the new year begins at midnight, so I don't know why they were celebrating already. Maybe they do it differently in France.

Hope and Ethan were both in the room already. Danny was not. They were sitting on beanbags and playing on their

Hexam tablets when I came down the stairs. As soon as Hope saw me, she jumped up and ran over to me to give me a hug.

"Hi, Slick!" she said. "You look nice."

"Hi, Hope," I said. "Hey, Ethan."

Ethan smiled and waved. "Hey, Eric," he said.

"Why are you calling him Eric?" asked Hope. "His name is Slick."

I shrugged. "That's my nickname," I explained.

"You want me to call you Slick?" asked Ethan.

"Yeah. You don't have to, though. Only Danny calls me Slick."

"And me," said Hope. She stuck her bottom lip out and looked sad. It's the first time I hadn't seen her smiling.

"And you," I said. Hope smiled again.

"OK, then. Hey, Slick," said Ethan. "And, um, what are you wearing? You look like my dad."

Ethan was wearing jeans, a Graves jumper and a pair of Slicks. He looked cool. I think I might have made a mistake.

"I thought this is what people wore to New Year's Eve parties," I said. "I looked it up."

"You look nice," said Hope.

"You do too," I said. Hope was wearing a pink dress. I don't know much about girls' clothes, but it's polite to return a compliment.

I went over to where Ethan was sitting, dropped my Slick backpacks and sat down on the beanbag next to him. Ethan held up his Hexam tablet and showed me what was on his screen. It was *Land X*, but it wasn't a place I recognized.

"They've just opened up a New Year's quest," said Ethan. "It's only open for twenty-four hours."

"Cool," I said.

"Want to use a tablet? My dad brought two spare tablets from his work for us to use." He pointed to the table with the food on it.

I looked over and saw two latest-edition Hexam tablets next to each other. I nodded.

"I'll get it," said Hope, before I had a chance to stand up. She ran over and picked it up. She also picked up a gold cardboard hat and ran over. "But you have to put this on first."

"Why?"

"Because it's New Year's," said Hope.

"OK," I said. I put the hat on and took the tablet from her. "Thanks."

"Let's do this," said Ethan.

"But I thought we were having a sleepover and playing games," said Hope.

"We are," said Ethan. "The first sleepover game is playing on our Hexams."

"Only if I don't have to play *Land X*," said Hope.

Ethan shrugged. "You can play whatever."

"Yay!" said Hope. "I only have three pet makeovers left to do and I go to the next level."

I looked over at Hope's screen, and she raised it to show me a picture of a waiting room filled with lots of people and their pets.

"It's called *Pet Blitz Glitz*," said Hope. She swiped right, and a picture of a giraffe with dirt all over its body appeared. The giraffe did not look happy.

"I have to fix this mess," said Hope.

"That's dumb," said Ethan. "Nobody has a pet giraffe."

"So what? Nobody has a coat made of unicorn hair in real life," said Hope. She was looking at Ethan's Hexam tablet.

Hope was referring to the coat that Ethan's avatar was wearing in *Land X*. Ethan didn't like the coat, but it gave him a thirty-second health boost in battles, so he had to keep it on.

"Whatever," said Ethan. He sounded serious, but he was smiling. "Go put some lipstick on your giraffe and leave us. We've got important things to do."

"I'm not putting lipstick on a giraffe," said Hope. "That would look weird."

"Not as weird as the purple hat you just put on its head."

"It's *cute*!" said Hope. She turned away to play her game. I don't think she was upset – I saw her smiling.

That was the end of the conversation about Hope's pet game. It was quite a funny conversation, I think. That's why I'm thinking about it now.

Danny arrived ten minutes after this conversation. Ethan and I had only just logged in and started reading the quest objectives and rewards when he arrived.

The first thing that I noticed about Danny was that he was not wearing a suit or a bow tie. I am now certain I made a mistake choosing my clothes.

"What are you wearing, Slick?" asked Danny. I shrugged and changed the subject to *Land X*.

Danny had already seen the New Year's quest in the car on the way over, so we were all pretty much at the same place. We were just choosing our best objects to take with us when Mrs Schwartz came downstairs. She had changed and was now wearing a long black dress that sparkled with diamonds – or things that looked like diamonds.

"You look pretty, Mum," said Ethan.

"You look like a starry night, Mrs Schwartz," I said. "Like this room."

Mrs Schwartz smiled. "You are so sweet. Thank you."

I didn't realize that I was giving Mrs Schwartz a compliment, but I'm glad she liked what I said.

"You're wearing the bracelet I made you!" said Hope. I looked at Mrs Schwartz's wrist. She was wearing a bracelet that looked like it was made of pasta tubes that had been painted in different colours.

"Of course, honey," said Mrs Schwartz. "It's my favourite piece of jewellery."

Hope grinned.

Mrs Schwartz came over to where we were sitting. "So, here's the plan," she said, looking at the four of us. "You can do whatever you like, as long as it's safe. Order any movies you want."

Ethan looked up. "Any?"

Mrs Schwartz narrowed her eyes. "Anything *appropriate*. And remember to include Hope, please, when you're picking. The guests are arriving at eight, and I'd like you all to stay down here unless you need the bathroom or it's something urgent."

"What about dinner?" asked Ethan. "I'm hungry."

"There's a table full of food," said Mrs Schwartz, "and we'll bring you some pizza in a while too. You can join us for the fireworks at midnight, if you're still awake. Julia is upstairs, but she's going to have a night off and enjoy the party – so no bothering her, please..." She looked at Hope, but Hope was too busy shampooing her giraffe to notice.

"Hope?" said Mrs Schwartz.

"Yes, Mum. Leave Julia alone. Stay down here."

Mrs Schwartz nodded and gave Hope a kiss on the head and smiled at us all. "I'll come and see how you're doing in a while. And don't play on those things all night. It's New Year's – have some fun!"

Mrs Schwartz left, and we all went back to our tablets. At seven, Julia came down with pizza. We kept playing as we ate it. We were too close to completing the quest to stop. Hope didn't want to play her game any more, so she went over to her karaoke machine and sang songs by the Week. She wanted us to join in, but we were too busy. At twenty-two minutes past seven we completed the New Year's Eve quest.

"*Now* can we play a game?" asked Hope.

"Like what?" asked Ethan. "I'm not singing."

"I've brought games," I said.

"Yes!" said Danny. "You brought the ShadowCloud?"

"You have a ShadowCloud?" asked Ethan. "Awesome!"

"I didn't bring the ShadowCloud," I said. Danny groaned. "I looked up what to do at a sleepover." I stood up, went over to my old Slick backpack and unzipped it. I took out the piece of paper I had printed out with all the games on it and started to read.

"The first one is Spin the Nail Polish." I leant down and took out one of the nail polish bottles I had taken from Mum's bathroom, then placed it on the carpet. "You spin it around, and whoever it lands on gets one toenail painted that colour. Or you can do fingernails."

"Ooh!" said Hope. "Fun!"

I looked up at Danny and Ethan. They were both staring at me. Even when I was looking at them, they both kept staring at me, and neither one of them said anything. I don't think they wanted to play this game.

"I guess maybe not," I said. Hope groaned. I looked at the next game on my list. I took out four pieces of white paper that I had prepared at home and four pencils. I kept one of each and handed the others around. Danny and Ethan were looking very serious.

"OK," I said. "This one is called Who Will I Marry?" Now Hope stopped smiling and stared at me. I don't know if everybody was concentrating on the rules of the game, or if I was saying something wrong. Nobody spoke, so I decided to continue.

"Everybody writes down the first letter of the name of a boy they like. Then they write down the number of—"

That's when Danny burst out laughing. "Oh man! DUDE! I thought you were serious for a moment there! I was… I was…" He was now laughing so hard that he was having difficulty speaking.

"Oh wait… what?" said Ethan. Then he started laughing too. "You were joking?"

Hope started laughing too. I didn't want everyone to know I hadn't been joking, and friends are supposed to laugh at the same things, so I started laughing too.

"Yeah," I said. "You believed me?"

Everybody was laughing so much that they didn't answer. I laughed too, but it wasn't a real laugh. This used to happen a lot when I was friends with Luke and the others, but it hadn't happened like this with Danny and Ethan before. I didn't like it. I wish I'd brought my ShadowCloud.

When everybody stopped laughing, Hope ran over to the tent and picked up a pillow.

"I know what we can play," she said. "Pillow fight!"

I had read about this game too. It was number five on my list. I don't know why nobody thought this idea was as funny as the ones I had suggested.

"I don't want to have a pillow fight," said Ethan. Danny wasn't saying anything.

"Why not?" said Hope.

"Becau— ow!"

Before Ethan had a chance to finish what he was saying, Hope smacked him in the face with the pillow she was holding. Ethan looked really angry for a moment, but then he grinned, jumped up and ran over to the tent. He grabbed another pillow.

"You're going to regret this," he said as he ran towards her holding a big light-blue, cloud-shaped pillow.

I leant over to my Slick backpack and pulled out my pillow.

"You playing?" I asked Danny.

Danny looked up from the beanbag and shook his head. "Nope."

Hope was now giggling and screaming on one of the beanbags as Ethan hit her over the head with his pillow.

"Ah, come on," I said to Danny. "It looks like fun."

"I'm not really in…"

It looked like Ethan was having fun now, so I thought maybe I should do the same as Hope did to Ethan and not give Danny a chance to stay out of the game. I raised my pillow over my head and got ready to swing it.

"Don't even think about it," said Danny as he scrambled to get up. But it was too late. I swung the pillow around and hit Danny in the face as he was standing up.

There was a loud smack and an explosion of white feathers as Danny's body flew to the side and landed on the carpet. I looked at my hand and saw that I was now holding an empty pillowcase. Then I looked at Danny.

He was moaning and holding his face as a cloud of white feathers floated down all around him.

"Danny? You OK?" I asked. Ethan and Hope stopped their pillow fight and ran over.

"Danny?" asked Ethan.

Danny moaned. He turned over and moved his hands from his face. That's when I saw that his left cheek was bleeding. Hope breathed in really loudly and told Ethan to call an ambulance. That's when Danny shook his head and sat up. He wiped his cheek and looked at the blood in his hand. It wasn't bleeding too much, but it was bleeding. I didn't know how that happened. I didn't think a pillow could hurt someone like that.

"I'm OK," said Danny. He groaned again and squinted like he was in pain. He was holding up his hand to his cheek, so I couldn't see if it was still bleeding or not. At least he was able to speak. That was good.

"I'm sorry, Danny," I said. "I don't know…"

"What did you hit me with?" asked Danny. "It felt like a brick."

"Just my pillow," I said. I think he thought I'd hit him with something harder, but that would have meant I wanted to hurt Danny, and I would never want to hurt anybody – especially not my best friend. "It was just my pillow. I promise."

"Hey, it's OK," said Ethan. I looked around and saw that Ethan was talking to Hope, who was looking down at Danny. She wasn't smiling now. Her eyes were red, and it looked like she might cry.

"He's bleeding," she whispered.

"It's OK," said Ethan. "It's not serious. Right, Danny?"

"Nope, nothing serious – just a minor broken skull."

Ethan's eyes opened wide, and he motioned with his head in the direction of Hope. I think Ethan was trying to stop Hope being upset. I think Danny understood this too, because he suddenly nodded.

"I'm kidding. I'm fine," said Danny.

Hope did not look like she believed Danny.

"Why don't you go upstairs and tell Mum we're still hungry. And *don't* tell her about Danny."

"Why?"

"Because they'll think we can't be left on our own. And we're having fun, right?"

"No," said Hope. "He hurt his head."

"I mean before that."

Hope thought about this for a moment, then nodded. "OK," she said.

* * *

I didn't want to worry Hope even more, so I waited until she had gone upstairs and closed the door before turning to Danny.

I went over to my Slick Gold Stripe limited-edition back-pack and took out my first-aid kit.

I went back over to Danny, sat down and opened it up. I took out a pair of scissors. "Here," I said.

Danny jumped up. "Um, don't go anywhere near me with those, thank you very much."

I pulled out a white bandage roll. "It's to cut this," I said. I don't know what else Danny thought I would do with a pair of scissors.

Danny looked down at my first-aid kit and then bent down and picked up a plaster. "I'll do it," he said. He looked around the room. "Do you have a mirror?"

"I do," I said. "For the makeover game that I was joking about."

"I'll get it," said Ethan. He picked up my Slick Gold Stripe limited-edition backpack and tipped everything inside it onto the carpet.

"Not that one," I said. "The other backpack."

Ethan picked up my other Slick backpack and tipped it out before I had a chance to ask him not to. Ethan looked down at all the bottles of different-coloured nail polish that were now rolling about on the carpet.

"Wow. That was some joke," he said.

I shrugged as I didn't know what to say to that. I think he might have guessed that I wasn't really joking earlier.

Ethan picked up the purple mirror that I had taken from my mum's purse and brought it over to Danny.

"Hold it there," said Danny. He checked his cheek. It wasn't bleeding any more. Danny wiped off the blood that was already on his cheek with the back of his sleeve and stuck a plaster on it. He leant forwards to take a closer look at his face in the mirror, but something caught his eye and he froze.

"*What* is that?" asked Danny, pointing at something behind the red beanbag.

I stood up to have a look.

The thing that Danny was looking at was lying on the floor. It was the same shape and size as my pillow, but it was made of wire mesh. Inside were what looked like hundreds of cables that criss-crossed each other. Little blue lights were racing around them.

I had no idea what it was.

"Why was that in your pillow?" asked Ethan.

"I don't know," I said.

"You don't know?" asked Danny. He went over to it and picked it up. "How do you not know that there's some kind of weird machine thing inside your pillow?"

"I don't know," I said.

"But this is your pillow, right? The one you sleep on every night?" asked Danny. He was holding the thing up above him and looking underneath it.

"Yeah," I said.

"What does it do?" asked Ethan. He was looking up at the thing too.

I shrugged. I don't think that Danny or Ethan were understanding that I really didn't know.

"Does it heat up your head?" asked Danny.

"I don't know. I'm asleep when I'm lying on it."

"Right, but before you fall asleep? Is it massaging your head or heating it up or something?"

"I don't know. I just fall asleep when I lie down."

Danny looked over at me. "You don't just lie down and fall asleep."

"Yeah, I kind of do."

Danny shook his head like I was annoying him.

"Does it play music?" asked Ethan.

"Good one," said Danny. "Does it?"

"No," I said. "At least, I don't think so."

"Man, that's *so* weird," said Danny. "I can't see a serial number or writing anywhere."

"I can look it up on the Internet," I said. "Maybe that will tell us."

There was nothing on the Internet. Or maybe there was, but not under the search terms we were using: "Weird pillow", "Metal cables with light pillow", "Machine pillow".

We stopped trying to find out what the machine was when Hope came back downstairs with Julia. They were carrying more boxes of pizza. Julia noticed all the feathers in the room, and we all had to help her clean up. Nobody mentioned Danny's cheek, and nobody said anything about my pillow, which was now with my and Danny's stuff in the corner of the room. Julia put on a movie for us. I didn't care what we watched, but Danny and Ethan really wanted to watch *Ninja November*, and Hope really wanted to watch *The Wonderful Adventures of Penny Lane*. Julia put on *Wishes of Courage*, which I didn't understand, as nobody had picked that one. Turned out to be a good choice anyway.

After the movie, we played more on our tablets. Ethan, Danny and Hope ate all the cupcakes and sweets. As it wasn't offered to me, I didn't eat any. At 11 p.m. Mrs Schwartz came into the games room to invite us upstairs for the countdown to midnight. We were very excited and not at all tired – Mrs Schwartz said she wasn't surprised after eating all those sweets.

* * *

The party was not like any party I have ever been to. It was very loud with music and talking. The music was coming from a band on the stage with a woman singer called Ella Fitzgerald. I didn't speak to her. I know her name because I heard a man say to a woman as they walked past us that he loved this song, and she said that she loved Ella Fitzgerald too.

There were at least a hundred people, all dressed in very fancy clothes. The women mostly wore glittering dresses, and the men were all wearing black suits with white shirts and bow ties. My guess that only adult men wear suits and bow ties for New Year's Eve seemed correct. There were some tables around the edges of the large room, with a few people sitting at them, but mostly everybody was dancing or standing and talking very loudly. Mr Schwartz came straight over to us when he saw us come into the room. He shook my and Danny's hands, and then took Hope and Ethan with him because he wanted them to meet some people. Mrs Schwartz told us to enjoy ourselves and left us. Danny and I did not really know what to do, so we stood at the side of the room. A woman dressed all in black came up to us holding a silver tray that had lots of tiny burgers on it. Danny took one. The woman didn't ask me if I wanted one, so I didn't have to take one.

"*Whoa!*" said Danny, holding the tiny burger between his thumb and index finger. "Can you believe this?"

"Yeah," I said, not knowing what he meant.

Danny put the whole thing in his mouth just as two women came over to us. They both had brown hair. One was wearing a green sparkly dress and the other one was wearing a red sparkly dress.

"Aren't you Vito Lazio's cousin?" asked the woman in the green dress. She was talking to Danny.

Danny nodded, but his mouth was full. The tiny burger was small, but it was still quite big to eat in one mouthful.

"I knew it! I'm Lily. Remember me? I was at school with Vito. I babysat you a couple of times."

"Oh yeah," said Danny. He didn't say anything else.

The woman in the red dress looked at my face and then my bow tie.

"Ahh!" she said. "You look *so* cute!"

"Thank you," I said. "You look very cute too."

The two women started laughing, and Danny, who hadn't finished chewing his tiny burger, coughed, and a piece of chewed-up burger flew out of his mouth. Then he turned bright red.

I think maybe I'm not supposed to tell an adult woman that she looks cute.

"I'm sorry," I said. "I mean, you look beautiful."

I know this is OK, because I have heard my mother say it to other adult women.

Danny turned his head to me really quickly and opened his eyes very wide, and I thought that maybe I had made another mistake, but then Lily said, "Ahh," and the woman in the red dress looked at Lily and said that she loved me. So I think it was fine and Danny was wrong.

Ella Fitzgerald finished her song, and lots of people started clapping.

"Come on, everyone. It's nearly midnight. Let's dance!" said Ella Fitzgerald.

Lily took Danny's hand. "Come on," she said.

Danny started shaking his head a lot, but Lily pulled on his arm and made him go with her. The woman in the red dress took my hand.

"Come on," she said to me. She started walking to the stage.

"I don't know how to dance," I said as I followed behind her.

"I'll show you," she called back.

There were lots of people dancing. Danny was standing very still in front of Lily, who was spinning and dancing around him. I couldn't see Ethan or Hope.

The woman in the red dress stood in front of me. She took my right arm, put it around her waist and placed her left arm over my shoulder. Then she held my left hand out to the side with her right hand. The she told me to do what she was doing, which was rocking side to side.

"I'm Chloe," she said.

"I'm Slick," I said.

"Slick? What are you – a rapper?"

"No, it's just my nickname," I said. Chloe made me raise my arm so she could turn under it. She was taller than me, so she had to bend down to go under my arm.

Danny was still standing very still in front of Lily, looking very red. He wasn't smiling. I don't think he was enjoying dancing.

I'm not sure I was really enjoying dancing that much either – not until Chloe showed me how to move to the beat of the music by counting in fours. Once she showed me this, it all started to make sense. It was like a puzzle, and I like puzzles. I figured out that I could spin Chloe around two times and finish on the fourth beat. I tried spinning her around four times in four beats, but she said that made her feel too dizzy.

When the song finished, Lily gave Danny a kiss on the cheek. Danny turned even redder, which I didn't think was possible.

Then Chloe gave me a kiss too. "You're a natural!" she said. I was going to say thank you, but then the next song started and Lily and Chloe started dancing with each other.

Danny grabbed my arm and took me to the side of the room.

"Did you see that?!" asked Danny. He was shouting into my ear because the music was so loud. "She kissed me!"

I nodded. "Chloe kissed me too."

"Slick! They're like nineteen! That is *so* weird."

I didn't know why Danny was finding it strange.

"They're probably Italian," I said.

"Ha ha," said Danny. He wasn't smiling. "Do you think they like us?"

"Yeah," I said. "Definitely."

Danny started mumbling something to himself. He spat in his palm and smoothed down his hair with his hand. Then we both stood by the side of the dance floor and didn't speak for the rest of the song.

"OK, everyone, let's slow things down," said Ella Fitzgerald.

Danny poked my side with his elbow. I turned to see why he had done this, but he was staring straight ahead at Lily and Chloe, who were now walking in our direction. Danny stepped forwards as Lily and Chloe looked over at us, smiled, then walked right past us. Danny frowned and stepped back against the wall as the song started playing and people started dancing together. I watched the different couples dancing. Some were not as good as others at moving in the right time of the beats. I guess they hadn't worked it out yet.

Hope came over not long after the song had started and asked me if I wanted to dance.

"Sure," I said.

I went over to the middle of the dance floor with Hope and put her right arm on my shoulder and my left arm around her waist. Then I held her other hand with my other hand, just like Chloe had shown me, and we started dancing. I noticed a lot of people were looking at us and smiling.

Hope was not great at counting the four beats in time, even after I explained it to her. She seemed to have fun even though she stumbled a couple of times and I stepped on her toe three times. She laughed a lot when I spun her round.

Everyone stopped and clapped us when the song finished. I don't know why – we weren't very good. The man and woman dancing next to us were much better – they spun around a lot and moved exactly in time to the four beats. And they didn't stumble or step on each other's toes.

Hope was smiling even more than she usually does. She held her dress out on both sides and bent down, and everyone clapped more. Ella Fitzgerald then told everybody to get a drink and go outside for the fireworks at midnight.

"I've never stayed up to midnight before," said Hope when we were outside. She had a blanket wrapped around her shoulders. Some people were wearing their coats, but most people were wearing the blankets that were folded in a pile by the doors to go outside. I wasn't cold, so I didn't take one.

Ella Fitzgerald and the band had gone outside too. They played another song, and then everybody counted down from ten to zero, which was the time that the new year started.

Notes:
- I hope Danny doesn't mind that Hope and Ethan are calling me Slick, as the nickname was his idea. He didn't mention it tonight, so I think it's OK.
- Danny told Ethan about Lily and Chloe dancing with us and Lily kissing him twice on the cheek. Ethan made a gagging sound and said that was gross. When Danny asked why, Ethan said it was because Lily was his cousin. I don't know why this made it gross.

30
SLICK
MONDAY 31ST DECEMBER/
TUESDAY 1ST JANUARY

Everyone cheered as the fireworks started. Lots of people came up and shook my hand or hugged me and said "Happy New Year". Some women kissed me on the cheek, even though I didn't know any of them except for Mrs Schwartz and Julia. Lily and Chloe hugged us too. Danny was smiling a lot after that. I haven't seen him smile that much before.

After the fireworks finished, Mr and Mrs Schwartz said goodnight to us, and Julia took us inside. Hope went to bed, and Danny and Ethan and I went down to the games room. We got into our PJs and brushed our teeth, then got into our sleeping bags. Danny and Ethan fell asleep almost straight away.

I couldn't sleep. I didn't sleep all night. I think it's because I'm used to sleeping in my bed. The pillows in Ethan's house did not feel comfortable. I tried putting the machine thing inside my pillowcase and lying on that, but it kept buzzing and sending electric shocks to my head every few seconds, which kept me awake. I put my pillow back and tried one of Ethan's pillows again, but it was still not right. I lay on my back and waited until Danny woke up at 9 a.m.

"What time did you wake up?" he asked me.

"I didn't go to sleep," I said.

"At all?"

I shook my head. "I think the pillow helps me to go to sleep."

Danny yawned. "How?"

I shrugged. "I don't know. It's broken now, though. I tried lying on it, and it kept buzzing and sending electric shocks to my head."

Danny's eyes opened wide. "That sounds bad. We can stop by Vito's later and ask him about it if you want."

"Your cousin?"

"Yeah," said Danny. "He knows everything about this kind of stuff."

Danny said we couldn't just leave, so we had to wait and have breakfast with the Schwartzes and then wait for Mrs Lazio to come get us at eleven. I was feeling strange. I didn't feel like talking much. I think I was very tired. I have never stayed up all night before.

Mrs Lazio was happy to see us. In the car, she asked us all about the party, but I was so tired that I couldn't really say too much. Danny told her about the fireworks and the band. He did not say anything about dancing with Lily, or about her kissing him, which I thought was strange, as this seems to have been his favourite part of the night. Mrs Lazio told us that she had spent all night working. Apparently it's one of the busiest nights of the year for the hospitals. Mrs Lazio said she hadn't been to sleep yet.

I was surprised that she could talk so well. I was finding it very hard to say much at all. I don't know if it was that I couldn't speak or that I couldn't think of what to say. Maybe both. I tried closing my eyes in the car to sleep, but I couldn't do it.

I heard Danny ask Mrs Lazio if she could drop us off at Vito's instead of taking us home. Mrs Lazio said that was fine, but that she wouldn't be able to come get us until later, as she needed to sleep.

I had driven past Mr V's PC Repair Shop many times before, but I had never really looked at it properly. There wasn't much to see. The glass panes were very dirty. Behind the glass were stacks of computer components and boxes, so you couldn't really see inside. There was a sign hanging on the closed door that said HAVE YOU TRIED TURNING IT OFF AND ON AGAIN? and another one that said CLOSED FOR REPAIRS.

Danny rang the bell ten times. I didn't do anything except stand on the pavement with my backpacks next to me. I was very tired. Mrs Lazio called out to us to come back, but just then Vito opened the door. His hair was even messier than the last time I had seen him. He was wearing Graves tracksuit bottoms and a pair of slippers, but he was not wearing anything on top. His eyes were nearly closed and he looked like he had not shaved. I think he had been asleep.

"Hey, Vito," said Danny.

"What are you doing here?" asked Vito. His voice was croaky and slow.

"Can we come in?" asked Danny, though Danny was already walking in as he said this.

"No, no you can't," said Vito. I don't think he meant it, though, as he waved to Mrs Lazio. Mrs Lazio beeped back at him, waved, then drove off. Then Vito turned to me.

"You staying out here?" he asked.

I shook my head and followed him inside. Vito didn't talk to me as we walked through the small, cramped shop filled with computer parts to the stairs at the back. I could see Danny ahead of us, but I didn't feel like running to catch up with him, and I don't think Vito did either. We walked in silence and climbed the stairs that led to what I guess was Vito's flat, which was really just one room with a sink, a stove, a microwave, a bed, a long sofa, a table and a large television screen that took up most of the wall. It was very messy. The only other place I know that is messy – though not as messy as this – is Danny's house. Vito and Danny are related, so maybe it's genetic. Or maybe it's an Italian thing.

Vito picked up some stuff from the table and threw it all on the floor until he found the remote control. He switched on the television and picked up two game controllers lying underneath a pile of empty pizza boxes.

"Here. Here. And *here*," he said, giving Danny the remote and two game controllers. "If you're hungry, I think there's some pizza left over in one of the boxes. Goodnight."

Vito walked over to his bed and fell on top of it face-down. Danny threw the controllers down on the table and went over to Vito.

"Wake up," said Danny.

"I'm not here," said Vito. He reached out with his arms, grabbed a pillow and put it over his head. I think he was trying to hide from us, but we could still see the rest of his body.

Danny pushed Vito's body. "We need you."

Vito groaned into his pillow. "No you don't. Go away," he said.

Danny looked over at me and then nodded over to my Slick Gold Stripe limited-edition backpack. I understood – he wanted me to get my pillow. I bent down, unzipped my Slick Gold Stripe limited-edition backpack and took out the pillowcase. It looked very flat now that it didn't have any feathers in it. I walked over to Danny. I couldn't walk very fast. I was very tired.

"Any time today is fine," said Danny.

I didn't say anything. I handed the pillowcase to Danny and he took the machine out. The little blue lights were still flashing along the cables inside the wire mesh.

"Seriously, Vito," said Danny. "We want to know what this is."

Vito groaned again and pulled the pillow from his head. He opened one eye and looked up at the pillow machine. He stared at it like that for a moment, then he turned his head some more and opened the other eye. He groaned again and sat up.

"What is it?" asked Vito.

"If we knew that," said Danny, "we wouldn't be here."

Vito sat up. "You're funny, kid."

"It was in Slick's pillow."

"I'm thinking you should ask Slick what it is then... Anyway, who's Slick?"

"I am," I said.

"Right," said Vito. He nodded at me. "Cool nickname. So what is it?"

I shrugged.

"He doesn't know," said Danny. "Obviously."

"So this thing was in your pillow, and you didn't notice?"

I shook my head, slowly. I was very tired.

Vito was sitting up properly on his bed now, examining my pillow machine.

"Can you fix it?" I asked. "I really want to sleep."

"Fix it? I don't even know what it is. Just sleep on the sofa if you're that tired. You can throw the clothes on the floor."

"I think I need..." I said. I forgot what I was going to say. "I think... I think I... I think..."

"Slick?" asked Danny. "Slick? You OK?"

I looked at Danny. I couldn't see him very well. He was fuzzy. I couldn't speak.

Then everything went black.

31

DANNY

TUESDAY 1ST JANUARY

Vito and I stared at Slick's body lying on the floor. "What were you guys doing last night?" asked Vito.

"Nothing! What's wrong with him?!" I asked.

"Probably just exhausted," said Vito, sliding off his bed. He knelt down next to Slick. "Hey, kid. Wake up."

Slick didn't move.

Vito moved around and put his arms under Slick's, then lifted him so he was sitting up. Slick's head lolled back onto Vito's shoulder. Vito slid Slick's body upright against the bed and grabbed a glass of water from his bedside table. He tried getting Slick to drink it, but it was pointless. Slick was completely out of it.

"Is he even breathing?" I asked.

Vito leant his face over Slick's. He waited a few seconds and then looked up at me. Vito actually looked worried. I had never seen that look on Vito's face.

"Call an ambulance, Danny."

I stared at Slick. I couldn't move.

"Danny!"

I jumped and fumbled for my phone. I didn't even get a chance to unlock it before it started ringing. I didn't recognize the number.

"Hello?" I said.

"Hi, Danny, it's Frank Young – Eric's dad. I'm coming to get him."

I was so confused.

"Eric's not well. He won't wake up. I'm calling an ambulance."

"No!" said Slick's dad. "He's fine. That happens to him when he gets too tired. He just needs a good sleep. I'll be there in a few minutes."

"But he's not breathing!"

"He's fine," repeated Slick's dad. "That happens when he gets too tired. I'll be there in five minutes." Then he hung up.

I looked at Vito. "That was his dad. He's coming to get him."

Vito looked as confused as I felt.

"Do you think it's true?" I asked as Vito leant in and pulled Slick's body over his shoulder. He gave a loud groan as he stood up, Slick's completely unmoving body bent over double. He didn't twitch. Nothing. "Do I think what's true?" asked Vito. He took a deep breath and started to walk over to the stairs, his face turning redder with every step he took. Vito isn't really an exercise kind of guy.

"That he's OK?" I looked at Slick's head swaying side to side as Vito slowly began to climb down the stairs.

Vito carefully lowered himself down with the help of the banister, reached the bottom, then propped up Slick's body against the stairs. He breathed out loudly and wiped the back of his now very sweaty forehead.

"Sure – why would he lie? He's his dad – if he's not worried, I'm not worried. Right, bud?" He punched Slick lightly on the top of his arm and Slick's body toppled sideways. Vito and I jumped and grabbed him before he smacked his head against the wall.

"Nice one," I said. I sat on the stair next to Slick and let him rest his head on my shoulder. Vito gave me an *eek* look, then took a seat on the other side of Slick. "How long do you think he'll be?" asked Vito.

"Where do they live?"

That's when I realized that I hadn't given Slick's dad an address. The doorbell rang.

Slick's dad came in smiling, like this was the most normal thing in the world. He shook Vito's hand and nodded at me.

"Wow," he said, walking over to where Slick was resting against me. "He really is out for the count. You boys must have been partying hard." He fake-laughed, then picked up Slick without any effort at all and threw him over his shoulder.

"No, sir, really – we didn't do anything... we were just..."

Slick's dad smiled. "I'm just kidding. Now, where is his bag?"

"Oh." I jumped. "Upstairs."

I ran up and grabbed Slick's two bags, then ran back downstairs again to find Slick's dad talking to Vito about beer with his unconscious son slung over his shoulder.

"...Kolding's the best. Seriously smooth. I'll drop by a case if you want to try it out."

"Uh, yeah... sure," said Vito, scratching his bare stomach, "sounds good."

Vito looked like a homeless hobbit standing next to Slick's dad. Slick's dad smiled at me as I handed him the bags.

"Is his pillow in there?"

I hesitated, then nodded – figuring that it wasn't as bad if I hadn't actually spoken the lie.

"Good. Good." said Slick's dad in his deep, velvety voice. He shook my and Vito's hands.

"I'll bring over that case of beer next week," he said to Vito as Vito opened the door for him to leave, Slick's bags in one hand, the other holding up Slick's body on his shoulder.

Vito closed the door and turned to me. He scrunched up his face and rubbed his forehead.

"OK. I know I've had like ten minutes' sleep, so maybe I'm not reading this right, but was that as freaky as I think it was?"

I nodded.

"Hey," said Vito in a deep voice, "let me tell you about this great beer while I hold my comatose son." He shook his head. "I mean," he continued back in his normal voice, "*what* kind of a dad does that? Makes your dad look like Parent of the Year."

"Yeah, well, I wouldn't go *that* far," I said. I followed Vito back up to his room.

"Shame he took the pillow thing," said Vito. "Now I really want to know what it is."

I pointed over to Vito's bed and the black box sitting on Vito's pillow. "Give me some credit, cuz."

Vito looked down at me and gave a slow nod. "Nice work," he said, smiling.

Vito spent the next couple of hours taking apart the machine and looking stuff up on the Internet until finally he declared he was one hundred per cent absolutely certain it was a charger.

"A charger? For what? His mobile?"

Vito shrugged. "*That* I don't know."

"What have you been doing for the last two hours?"

"Hey, watch it," said Vito, stuffing a cold slice of pizza into his mouth. I didn't understand what he said next. I waited until he swallowed and took a large gulp from an open can of cola on the table.

"I didn't find anything anywhere that tells me where it's from – no serial numbers, nothing. It's pretty sophisticated – and unbelievably powerful – I can't find anything else like it."

"But you're sure it's a charger?"

"Yep. I know chargers."

I got up from the sofa and went to the now totally dismantled machine. I picked up some kind of blue rod and stared at it.

"So how do you plug it into whatever it's charging?" I asked.

"You don't. It's a charger pad – you rest whatever it charges on top of it."

"So why was it in his pillow?"

Vito shrugged. "No clue. I'm going to put it back together and see if I can figure that out. But first: sleep." He picked up a half-slice of pizza, stuffed it in his mouth and saluted me.

"I'm done," he said as he climbed back into his bed. "Play whatever you want."

He pulled the covers over his head then pulled them back down again.

"Hey, Danny, ask me how much you need to pay me for the information I just gave you."

"What are you talking about? I'm not paying you anything."

"Just ask me how much," he insisted.

I rolled my eyes. "How much?"

Vito grinned. "Nothing. It's free of charge."

He was so annoying.

"Get it? Charge/charger?"

"You're not funny," I said, turning the TV on. "Go to sleep."

I heard Vito laughing at his lame joke as he put the covers back over his head. Five minutes later he was snoring loudly. He was still sleeping when Mum came to take me home.

32

DANNY

WEDNESDAY 2ND JANUARY

I sent Slick a couple of texts when I got back to my house, but I never heard anything back. I decided that if I hadn't heard from him by the time I woke up, I'd go around to check if he was OK. I set my alarm for nine and went to sleep.

Two hours before my alarm was set to go off, I was woken by Vito shaking me by the shoulders. "Wake up!"

"Go. Away," I grumbled, and started to turn away.

Vito pulled my covers back. "Seriously – rise and shine, Sleeping Beauty. We need to talk ASAP."

I groaned. "What time is it?"

"Seven. In the a.m."

I sat up. Vito does not do early mornings. Ever. Something had to be very wrong. "What's happened?"

"I had a visit from some of your buddy's henchmen this morning."

"Um… *what*?"

"Yeah… exactly. Two dudes in suits turned up at my house at 5 a.m. and asked for the charger back."

"*What?* What did you do?"

Vito looked at me like I was stupid. "Two men in black suits show up at my front door at the crack of dawn – what do you think I did?" He didn't wait for me to answer. "I gave it to them, obviously. Luckily, I'd put it back together, so I just said that he must have left it behind by mistake."

"Then what?"

"I asked them what was so important about it, and they said it's a top-secret new product they're testing out and that it's really valuable. And then they left."

"And then?"

"And then they all lived happily ever after… What do you mean 'and then'? Is that not messed up enough for you?"

"So what now?"

"Now you get up, get dressed and I'm driving you over to his house. You're going to find out what that thing was."

❂ ❂ ❂

Slick's mum was leaving the house as we arrived. I said goodbye to Vito, told him I'd call him as soon as I left Slick's, and then jumped out of the car.

"Hi," I called out.

Slick's mum looked over and smiled when she saw me. "Hi, Danny!" She held the front door open for me. "I was just leaving. Eric's inside." She held up her car keys and clicked in the direction of a brand-new red sports car that I hadn't seen before. There were no other cars on the driveway, which meant Slick's dad must be out.

"There are some muffins on the counter. Help yourself," said Slick's mum as I passed her. I thanked her, then waited for her to close the door.

"Slick!" I shouted. "It's me! Where are you?"

"In the kitchen!"

I walked in to find Slick ironing. I have never ironed any-thing in my life. Slick, on the other hand, was clearly a pro: along the counter were piles of perfectly folded clothes – it was like being in a shop.

"What's up?" asked Slick. He kept on ironing. It looked like one of his mum's shirts.

I jumped up to sit on the counter next to him. "What happened yesterday?"

Slick shrugged and placed the now perfectly folded shirt on one of the piles. "Dad told me I have a condition that means I fall asleep sometimes if I've stayed up too late."

"Your dad told you that? You didn't know already?"

Slick shook his head. "I guess I haven't stayed up late before."

I was shaking my head with the lameness of his explanations.

"So how did your dad know where you were? And how did he have my number?"

"I called him."

"No you didn't. I was with you the whole time."

"Sure I did. How else would they have known where I was?"

"Exactly! *How* did he know?"

"Because I told him."

"Do you remember calling him?"

"No, I was tired. I don't remember much. Why are you being weird about it?"

"What about your pillow?"

"Oh yeah – that was nothing. It turns out my pillow is a new type of pillow that my uncle Martin sent us to try out. They're prototypes, which means they're not on the market yet. It's to help me sleep."

"Vito said it's a charger."

"No, it's to help me sleep. Vito is wrong."

"Not possible," I said. "Vito is a genius when it comes to this stuff. MIT offered him a scholarship."

"What's MIT?"

"The best university in the world for computing. Getting a scholarship to go there is like winning the lottery."

"Wow."

"Yeah. He didn't take it, though."

"Why?"

"Said he didn't want to work for the establishment. Something about being his own boss. My aunt is still angry about it. Anyway, stop changing the subject."

"I didn't. You did."

"Whatever. Where's the pillow now?"

"I don't know. My dad got me a new one. Anyway, forget about it. I was thinking that if we pool our quartz together, we could build a house on *Land X*. Maybe even a castle. What do you think?"

I thought it was a good idea, but I wasn't going to let Slick distract me. I jumped down from the counter and walked off.

"Where are you going?"

"To your room. I want to see it."

"There's nothing to see. Leave it…"

I wasn't sure if he was going to try to stop me, but I already knew that Slick was strong enough to do that if he wanted to, so I ran out of the kitchen and up to his bedroom.

33

SLICK

WEDNESDAY 2ND JANUARY

I put the iron away and went up to my room. I couldn't understand why Danny was making such a big fuss over something that I had already explained.

Danny was lying on my bed when I came in. He was lifting his head up and down on my pillow. Then he stopped and started to roll his head one way across my pillow and then the other.

"I can't feel anything," he said.

I didn't like what Danny was doing, but I didn't know why – it just felt wrong.

"What are you doing?" I asked.

Danny ignored me. He walked over to the end of my bed and pulled it away from the wall.

"*So that's where that plugs in…*" he mumbled.

"Danny, it's just a sleeping thing."

Danny looked over and narrowed his eyes at me. He pushed the bed back against the wall and returned the pillow to where it was supposed to be. I thought maybe he was finished trying to find out about the pillow, but then he lay back on the bed and closed his eyes.

"Danny?"

Danny didn't open his eyes. "Shhh," he said. "I'm trying to sleep."

"Oh," I said. "Are you tired?"

Danny opened his eyes. "No. Not yet."

He closed his eyes again. I watched him for a few minutes until he opened his eyes and shook his head. "Nothing."

He got off my bed. "Do you feel anything when you lie on it?" he asked me. "Does it start after a while or something?"

I shrugged. "I don't know. I don't really want to—"

"Just lie on it," said Danny. "Tell me if you feel anything."

I sighed. "OK. But I don't see the point. I told you I don't feel anything."

I lay down on my bed and put my head on my pillow.

"Slick?"

I opened my eyes. Danny was hitting me on the shoulder. I sat up.

"What?" I asked.

"Ha ha. Very funny. I believed you for a moment," said Danny.

"Believed what?" I asked. I didn't understand what Danny was talking about.

"That you were asleep."

"Was I?"

Danny frowned. "Were you?"

I wasn't sure. Danny told me to lie down again. I did. Then he hit me again. I opened my eyes and sat up.

"Stop hitting me."

"You were asleep."

"No I wasn't."

"Yes you were."

"No. I lay down, and then you punched me."

"I'm telling you – you were asleep."

"No I wasn't." I didn't understand why Danny was saying this.

Danny didn't say anything for a moment, and then his eyes opened wide. This is what he does when he has what he thinks is a good idea.

"Lie down again," said Danny.

I didn't understand what Danny was doing, or why he was acting so strangely, but I wanted to understand. I lay down.

Danny hit me again. I opened my eyes and sat up. This time, Danny sat on the side of the bed. "Look at this," he said. He was holding his Hexam R3. He turned it around to show me a video of me sleeping. For four minutes. I didn't remember being asleep, but then I realized that I wouldn't remember it, because I was asleep.

"Were you pretending?" asked Danny.

I shook my head. I was feeling strange. Surprised, I think.

"Wow," I said. "I guess the pillow really does work."

"Not for me," said Danny. "Look."

I stood up to let Danny lie down on my bed. I watched him as he put his head on my pillow. He opened his eyes really wide.

"See? I am COMPLETELY AWAKE," said Danny. "I could not be more awake right now... and I'm still awake... still not sleeping... I am definitely still not—"

"I get it," I said. "You're awake."

Danny suddenly stood up and grabbed my pillow from the bed.

"Stay still," he said. He stepped behind me.

I looked around and saw Danny lifting the pillow up. "What are you..."

* * *

Danny hit me. I opened my eyes. I was lying on my floor, and Danny was staring down at me. He was holding my pillow in his hands.

"Why am I lying on the floor?" I asked.

Danny didn't say anything. He just kept staring at me. Then he sat down next to me and leant over to whisper in my ear.

"Something really weird is going on, Slick."

"Why are you whispering?"

"I don't know who's listening," explained Danny.

"Why would anyone be listening?"

Danny sighed. He put his finger up to his mouth, which means he wanted me to be quiet. Then he stood up and waved at me to follow him. I followed Danny out of my bedroom, down the stairs and out of my front door. When we were standing on the pavement, Danny stopped.

"Slick, you swear you don't know what's going on?"

"I swear, Danny. I don't know. Who's listening?"

Danny shrugged. "I don't know. But there's something going on. Something really weird. Ambulances coming to get you when they haven't been called. Your parents knowing where you are even when you haven't told them. The pillow. And the dentist... I don't get it. Why do you go to the dentist every week?"

"To get my teeth checked."

"Nobody goes to get their teeth checked every week. Not even if their teeth are bad. And your teeth are perfect."

"Thank you," I said.

"I wasn't complimenting your teeth, weirdo. I was saying that your teeth are so good that you shouldn't have to go to the dentist at all."

"Maybe that's why my teeth are good – because I go to the dentist all the time."

Danny frowned. I think maybe he didn't like that I could be right.

"Fine," he said. "So what do they do to you when you go?"

Danny was making me feel very uncomfortable. I didn't like that he was making me feel like this, and I didn't understand why.

"Are you angry with me?" I asked.

"What? No," said Danny. "But something weird is going on, and you don't seem to get it. And I don't think you're lying to me."

"I'm not!"

"OK. So all these things are happening that don't make sense, and there's got to be a reason for them, right?"

"I don't know. I mean, I don't think the things you think are weird are that weird. It's just my life."

"Trust me, Slick, your life is weird. This isn't normal. Your parents aren't normal."

"You don't have to be rude about my parents."

"I'm not being rude, Slick. I'm just telling you the facts. Your mum doesn't do anything when she hears you've been put in an ambulance. Your dad shows up when you haven't told him where you are. They don't talk to you except when they're with other people, and they leave you alone all the time. Your parents… they're not like other parents. Don't you see that?"

I nodded. "Yeah. I guess. You really think there's something strange happening?" I asked. Danny nodded. "Like what?"

Danny shrugged. "I don't know. Maybe your dad works for the government or something. Maybe your parents are spies."

"Why would you think that, just because I go to the dentist every week and have a pillow that makes me sleep? That doesn't make sense."

"Fine. But it's got to be something. Or maybe it's not anything. But either way, don't you want to know?"

I thought about this. This is what I thought:

Danny thinks that there are things about me that don't make sense. I think there are things about me that don't make sense. I feel confused about things a lot. Maybe Danny is right. Maybe if we work it out, I will not feel so confused all the time.

"OK," I said. "I'll do it. It'll be like solving a puzzle. Like a *Land X* quest."

"The Quest to Find Out Why Slick Is a Weirdo," said Danny.

"That's not nice," I said.

"I'm kidding," said Danny. "But if you weren't weird, you wouldn't be my friend."

"Oh," I said. I didn't really understand what Danny meant, but I think he was being nice. "Thanks."

When Danny and I have a really hard quest to complete on *Land X*, like when we had to interview everybody in the Nation of Perplexity to find out who killed Troy Braggadorius, we make notes in a notebook. We decided to do the same about me when we got back to Danny's. I suggested that we both write down everything that we thought was weird about me. Danny said we were going to need a much bigger notebook. Then he started laughing and didn't stop for about five minutes.

"You ready now?" I asked.

"Sure," said Danny. He opened up the notebook and laughed more. Then he started writing.

"Pillow, obviously... Ambulances... Photographic memory. Dentist every week..."

The list turned out to be longer than I'd expected. Also that I couldn't remember anything about Christmas except eating dinner around the table. Danny added about Uncle Martin sending me stuff, though he did say he wasn't sure if that was weird or not, or whether it's just because he didn't know anybody else with an uncle like that.

When we finished, Danny looked down the list.

"I think we should start with the dentist."

"OK," I said. "Start how?"

"Just tell me everything about when you go. The address. The name of the dentist. What they do to you when you get there. That kind of thing."

I took a breath. "I don't know the address. I always sleep on the way there."

Danny looked up at me, opened his mouth to say something and then closed it. He shook his head. "Never mind. Keep going."

"When we get there, I wait in the waiting room and play *Land X*. Mum goes in for her appointment at 7 p.m. Dad's appointment is at 7.30 p.m. Mine is at 8 p.m. Dr Kilaman comes to get me from the waiting room. She's really nice. We talk about stuff, and she always asks me if I've had a good week. I lie in a chair, and then she gets me to open my mouth. Then I sleep, and when I wake up, I get out of the chair and say goodbye, and that's it. Does any of that sound weird to you?"

"Slick, there's literally not one thing about that that's *not* weird."

"Really?"

"Um, yeah. You don't remember anything? What are they doing to you? Do your teeth hurt after?"

I shook my head. Then Danny looked up at me with his *I've got a good idea* look.

"I know what we have to do," he said. "You should record it."

"What?"

"With your ShadowCloud. When you go on Friday...
You're going on Friday, right?"

"Yeah, I think so."

"OK," said Danny. He was sounding excited. "Before you
go, set your ShadowCloud to follow you. Wait... are there
windows?"

I thought about this. "Not in the waiting room. There's
kind of a window in the dentist's room. It's really high up
and thin. Like a line that goes around."

"But we could see in with the ShadowCloud?"

I nodded.

"OK, good," said Danny. "I'll log in and control it when
you get there so it doesn't follow you inside."

"What do you think they do when I go there? You think
it's something bad?"

Danny shrugged. "Maybe I'll just spend half an hour
watching you get your teeth polished. Or maybe they experiment on you."

I didn't like the sound of that. "Experiment?"

"We'll have to wait to find out, I guess." He looked up at
me. "We done? Let's go work on our castle."

Danny was talking about our new home on *Land X*. It
was looking pretty awesome, and it was only half finished.
Even though I did want to find out about the strange stuff
happening in my life, talking about it made me feel something I didn't like. Scared, maybe. Or nervous. Whatever it
was, I was happy to change the subject.

"Yeah," I said. "I was thinking we could put sharks in our
moat. But they're eight hundred quartz each. You think it's
worth it?"

"Are you kidding? *Totally* worth it," said Danny. He closed
the notebook, and we went over to his computer.

34

SLICK

FRIDAY 4TH JANUARY

We decided that Danny would tell Vito what we were doing. Danny said that we can trust Vito and that if we found out my parents were spies he would be able to help us. Plus he has a car – in case we needed to make an escape. I didn't know what we'd need to make an escape from.

As agreed, ten minutes before we were going to leave for the dentist, I went up to my room and powered up my ShadowCloud, then linked it to my phone. Danny logged in from Vito's flat and linked it to his too. Now we both had control of it, though it was only set to follow me. Danny tested the controls by getting the ShadowCloud to fly at my head so that I had to keep ducking to avoid it. He thought this was very funny.

I let the ShadowCloud out of my bedroom window so that my parents wouldn't see that it was following us, then joined them in the car and we left.

I don't remember the journey, even though I meant to try to remember it, but I do remember sitting in the waiting room, same as every Friday, then going in to see Dr Kilaman and sitting down in the chair. Dr Kilaman asked me about my week, and I told her about the castle that Danny and I were building together. Then she told me to close my eyes and open my mouth, same as every week, and that's it.

The next thing I knew, I was standing in my house. I looked around but couldn't see my ShadowCloud. I went up to my room and opened the window, and there it was, hovering silently in the dark, waiting for me. It followed me inside, and I took it and turned it off. Then I went and got my phone. We had agreed not to text each other about anything until we were sure my parents wouldn't see it, so there was nothing from Danny. I called him, and he answered straight away.

"Did you see anything?" I asked.

"Can't talk on here," said Danny, whispering. "Meet us by the tree at the end of your road in an hour. Don't let your parents see you leave."

"OK. But can you tell me—"

"When we see you," interrupted Danny. He hung up without saying goodbye, which I thought was kind of rude.

Danny and Vito were already parked by the tree waiting for me when I got there at nine thirty. The engine was running. Danny was sitting in the front passenger seat. He opened his window as I walked up.

"Get in," he said.

I opened the car door and got into the back seat. Vito drove off quickly.

We didn't talk the rest of the way. I was thinking that they must have seen something really bad. If they had seen a normal dentist appointment, I think they would have just told me.

I was starting to feel very unhappy. Maybe it was anger. I didn't like that Danny and Vito both knew things about me that I didn't know. I don't like not knowing things. I really don't like not knowing things about myself. Especially if I know other people know and I don't.

When we arrived at Vito's, Danny walked over to the sofa and picked up a pile of clothes. He threw them on the floor and sat down while Vito went over to his desk in the corner. He opened a drawer and started searching for something.

"What did you see?" I asked. "You should tell me."

"We're going to," said Vito. "Sit down."

Vito is an adult, so I did what he told me to do, even though what I really wanted to do was not move until they told me what they had seen.

Vito approached me. I looked down at his hand. He was holding a pair of tweezers.

"Why do you have tweezers?" I asked.

Vito didn't say anything. He sat down and put the tweezers down next to him. Then he stopped and looked at Danny, and Danny looked at me.

"What happened?" I asked.

"Nothing," said Danny.

"Nothing?" I asked. "Nothing at all? Was the video not working? Why didn't you just tell me that when we were in the car. Are you—"

"The video was working. Look…"

That's when I saw that Danny had his Hexam R3 in his hand. He opened up the video library, fast-forwarded and pressed play. We were looking down over a half-full parking lot outside a huge one-storey building with no windows except a thin strip of glass that ran right around the top edge of the building. It was glowing in a few sections from the lights on the inside.

The ShadowCloud hovered over a line of cars that were all exactly like my dad's car. Then the doors to the car parked directly beneath the ShadowCloud opened, and I saw myself and my parents getting out. It was very strange to see myself. I didn't remember any of this. I only remember being in the waiting room. I don't know why.

I walked with my parents up to a small door. There was no sign on it. Mum opened it. The ShadowCloud swooped down, and it looked like it was going to follow us in, but before I could see anything behind the door, it suddenly flew backwards.

"That's when I took over the controls," said Danny. He pressed down on the fast-forward button. "But only until the door closed. Then I let it follow you again."

Danny kept fast-forwarding through what looked like just a black screen.

"You must have been waiting somewhere in the middle of the building," said Vito.

"I guess," I said. "The waiting room doesn't have any windows."

The video brightened, and Danny pressed pause. "Here we go... this is when you go in..."

He pressed play, and I saw that the ShadowCloud had now moved, and we were looking through the narrow slit of glass down into the same room I sat in every Friday evening.

I watched myself walking in behind Dr Kilaman; then I lay down on the chair, closed my eyes and opened my mouth wide. Dr Kilaman raised her hand and put her tweezers into my mouth. After a few seconds, she pulled a tiny white thing out and dropped it into a metal dish next to her. She picked up a long, thick metal needle, like one of Mrs Lazio's knitting needles, and put it up my nose. She put her free hand on the top of my head to hold me still, and then pushed the needle in hard. She removed the needle, put it down on the tray next to her, picked up the metal dish with the white thing in it and walked out of the room.

I watched myself lying on the chair with my eyes closed and my mouth wide open. I was so still that it could have been a photograph instead of a video.

"You were like this for twenty minutes," said Danny, pressing fast-forward, "and then…"

He pressed play. Dr Kilaman walked back into the room holding the tweezers in one hand and the metal dish with the white thing in it in the other. She sat down, picked up the white thing with the tweezers, then put her hand into my mouth. She turned and twisted her hand a couple of times and pulled the tweezers out. Dr Kilaman stood up, then I stood up too. And then I left the room.

I looked at Danny and Vito. I was very confused. "I don't get it," I said. "That's it?"

"Well, there's one more thing," said Danny. "After you left, we decided to have a look around with the ShadowCloud. We watched three more people go in after you and have the exact same thing happen to them – she took the thing out of their mouths, put the needle up their noses, and that was it. We couldn't see anything else – it was too dark in the other parts of the building – so we set the ShadowCloud to go back to you."

"There were still people arriving for appointments as we left," said Vito, as Danny concentrated on finding the moment on the video that he wanted to show me. He turned the screen to me and pressed play. A woman was walking across the parking lot on her own. She had brown hair, swept to the side, and was wearing a red Blise jacket. I recognized her immediately. I looked at Danny.

"Miss Lake?"

Danny nodded. "Weird coincidence, right?"

"Yeah," I said, but I wasn't really interested in Miss Lake. I wanted to know what Dr Kilaman had been doing to me. I put my finger into my mouth to feel around, but I couldn't find anything.

Danny and Vito were staring at me now. I took my hand out of my mouth and shook my head. "I can't feel anything." I put my finger up my nose.

"Um, gross!" said Danny as I pushed my finger up as far as I could. Again, nothing.

"What do you think it is?"

"Only one way to find out," said Vito. He picked up the tweezers.

"You OK with this?" he asked.

I wanted to understand. I nodded.

I dropped my head back and opened my mouth. Vito put the tweezers into my mouth, then stopped and pulled them out again.

"I can't see anything."

"Use your Hexam R3 torch," I said to Danny. "It's really good."

Danny pulled his Hexam R3 out of his jacket pocket and turned the torch on. I tilted my head back again and opened my mouth. Vito reached in.

"This is so weird," said Danny, as he put the torch near my open mouth.

I looked up as Vito leant down and looked into my mouth. "Wider," he said. "Put your head back... To the side a little... No, the other way... Hold on... OK, I think I see something... Danny, put the torch in closer... Wait... I think I've got something..."

I opened my eyes as Vito took the tweezers out of my mouth. I looked up. Danny was staring at me.

"What?" I asked.

"Do it again," said Danny.

Vito paused for a moment, then put the tweezers back into my mouth.

I opened my eyes. There was water dripping down my face. Danny and Vito were staring at me, and Danny, I saw, was holding a glass of water in his hand.

I was very confused.

"What just happened?" asked Vito.

"Nothing," I said. "What? You haven't done anything yet." I wiped my hand on my forehead. "Why is my face wet?"

Danny and Vito looked at each other.

"You should tell me what's going on," I said. "It's rude not to tell me – it's *my* mouth."

"Say 'ahhhh'," said Vito. He was ignoring me.

"No," I said. "Not till you tell me what's going on."

Danny stood up. "Wait... I'll record it," he said. He took his Hexam R3 out of his jacket pocket and touched the screen a few times.

"Just tell me," I said, getting annoyed.

"It's easier if we show you," said Vito. "Say 'ahhhh'."

I said, "Ahhhh."

* * *

I opened my eyes. Vito was taking the tweezers out of my mouth. There was water dripping down my face again.

Danny touched the screen of his phone, then sat next to me.

"Look," he said.

I looked down at the screen and began watching.

It started with the part I remember: me saying "ahhhh" as Vito put the tweezers in my mouth. Then my eyes closed, and I went silent. I was lying completely still. Vito pulled out the tweezers, and I saw the same white thing on the end that I had seen at Dr Kilaman's. I could see it clearer this time – a tiny, thin white plastic rectangle, not much bigger than my thumbnail.

I heard Danny's voice mumbling, "I don't like this... I don't like this at all."

Vito looked at the camera of Danny's Hexam R3. "Just pour the water on him," said Vito.

I saw Danny's hand appear in the video holding a glass of water over my head. He tipped the glass for a few seconds. I watched the water drip down from my hair onto my face.

"Why are you pouring water on me?" I asked. I thought that was a pretty mean thing to do. I thought Danny was supposed to be my friend.

"To make sure you were really asleep," said Danny.

"Oh," I said. "That makes sense."

I watched as the water dripped down my face in the video. I didn't move at all. I didn't remember any of this.

"I guess I really was asleep," I said.

In the video, Vito leant in and put the tweezers back in my mouth. I opened my eyes.

That's when the video ended.

I looked up at Vito and Danny. "I don't understand," I said. "What did you take out?"

"I don't know," said Vito. "Some kind of computer chip, I think."

"A computer chip?"

Vito nodded.

"And it made me fall asleep?" I asked.

Vito shrugged. "I guess."

"Did you put the needle thing up my nose?"

Vito shook his head. "I think that might be a reset or something. I don't want to mess around with anything that's going to let them know what we've done."

I nodded. "So now what?"

"I need to get a better look at it," said Vito. "That OK?"

I wanted to know what the chip was, if it was a chip, and I couldn't do that myself if I fell asleep every time I took it out.

"OK," I said. I ran my hand over the top of my head and lay down. "But don't pour any more water on me. It's messing up my hair."

"*That's* what you're worried about?" asked Danny.

I didn't get to answer, because that's when Vito put the tweezers back up to my face. I opened my mouth.

I opened my eyes. Vito's hand was moving away from my face quickly. He jumped up and ran backwards. I turned my head and saw Danny and Vito standing next to each other in the middle of the room, staring at me.

"What happened?" I asked.

Danny and Vito didn't say anything. They continued to stare at me.

I sat up. That's when I saw an open pizza box on the coffee table that hadn't been there before. I could see the steam coming from the pizza that was left in the box, which meant the pizza was warm.

"Did you order pizza?" I asked.

Danny nodded. His eyes were wide. He was still staring at me. I didn't like it.

"*You ordered pizza?*" I asked. "How long was I asleep for?"

"About three hours," said Vito.

"Three hours?!" I asked. "You left me asleep for *three hours* and you ordered *pizza?*"

I stood up, and Danny and Vito quickly stepped back. I looked at them. They were frowning and staring at me with very wide eyes, and they were both frowning. I took a step towards them, and they both took another step back. That's when I realized that they were scared of me. I didn't understand.

"Danny?" I asked. "What's the matter?"

"What is your name?" asked Vito. He spoke very slowly.

"Slick," I said.

"What is your real name?" asked Vito.

"Eric Young. What's going—"

"Are you human?"

"What?! Yeah, I'm human. Why are you asking me that?"

Danny looked at Vito. "I told you. He doesn't know."

"Know what?" I asked. I was very certain now that I was feeling angry.

"We'll tell you when you've answered the questions," said Vito.

"How old are you?" asked Danny.

"Twelve."

"When is your birthday?"

"The 1st of March."

Vito shook his head. "These are dumb questions. They'd have programmed him to know those things."

"What do you mean?" I asked.

"Fine," said Danny. "If you're such a genius, you go ahead."

"Which of these colours is sad: red, yellow or blue?" asked Vito.

"I guess that is a better question," mumbled Danny.

"I don't get it," I said.

"Just answer," said Vito.

"None of them," I said. "They're colours. Colours can't feel emotions."

"Whoa," whispered Danny.

"Am I wrong?" I asked. The whole point of finding out about my dentist appointment was to stop feeling so confused, but in that moment I felt more confused than I ever had before.

"What's the best dream you've ever had?" asked Vito.

I shrugged. "I don't know. What's the best dream you've ever had?"

"Classic avoidance," mumbled Vito.

"I don't know what you mean," I said. "Please tell me what—"

"I'm nearly done," said Vito. "Then I'll explain. OK?"

I nodded.

"Do what I tell you," said Vito. "Stick your tongue out."

I stuck my tongue out.

"And pull your ears out to the side…"

"Vito. Stop," said Danny. Vito ignored him.

"Yeah, like that," continued Vito. "Now keep doing that and wiggle your bum."

I held out my ears, kept my tongue out and wiggled my bum like Vito told me to.

"Now say 'I'm the prettiest little—'"

"STOP IT!" shouted Danny. "He's my friend!"

I stopped. I saw that Danny's eyes were very red. He looked like he was going to cry.

"He's not your friend," said Vito. "He doesn't understand friendship."

"Yeah, I do," I said. "Danny's my friend. My best friend. Don't say—"

"Fine," interrupted Vito. "He's your friend. Interesting. So how did you feel?"

"About what?" I asked.

"When you were sticking your tongue out and wiggling your bum?"

I shrugged. "Confused? I mean, I don't know why you're asking me to do this stuff."

"But you didn't feel silly?" asked Vito.

I wasn't sure what the right answer was supposed to be. I shook my head.

"Or embarrassed?"

I shook my head again and frowned at Vito. "I felt angry that you won't tell me what's happening."

"Right. In a moment. Tell me about a time you felt embarrassed."

I didn't like this question. I don't like questions that I can't answer. I shrugged.

"You must have something," said Vito.

I couldn't think what feeling embarrassed felt like. I know other people get embarrassed about stuff, but it had never happened to me. Not that I could remember. "I don't get embarrassed," I said. "OK?"

"What did you do at Christmas?" asked Danny.

"I went to my uncle Martin's flat in London. It was good. Everybody ate too much. Then we watched Christmas movies. I got eleven presents. But you know that already," I said. "I don't know why you're asking me again."

"What else did you do?" asked Danny.

"I told you – I don't remember."

"So what do you remember? Exactly?"

"I went to my uncle Martin's flat in London. It was good. Everybody ate too much. Then we watched Christmas movies. I got eleven presents."

"Which present did your uncle Martin give you first?"

"I don't remember."

Danny looked up at Vito. "We should tell him now," he said.

"OK," said Vito. "There's no easy way to break this to you, so I'm just going to say it... We think you're a robot."

It was the most stupid thing I have ever heard. "That's not funny," I said.

"And we're not laughing," said Vito. "The thing in your mouth... it's a computer chip."

I thought about this for a moment.

"That doesn't mean that I'm a robot. I can think of—"

"You're a robot," said Danny firmly.

I shook my head. "I would know if I was a robot."

"No you wouldn't," said Danny, "not if they programmed you not to think that."

There was logic in his answer, but I didn't like it.

Vito walked over to the kitchen area and began to pull out drawers, looking for something.

"Aha," he said. He turned around, and I saw he was holding a large knife. Vito was going to kill me.

I jumped up from the sofa, ready to run.

"What are you doing?!" asked Danny.

"Relax," said Vito. He stopped about six feet away from me and held the knife out for me to take it. "Here," said Vito.

I wasn't sure what was happening. Vito took a couple of slow steps forwards, still holding the knife out. I thought it was better for me to have the knife than Vito, so I leant forwards and snatched it from him quickly, in case he suddenly attacked me.

"Is that a good idea?" asked Danny.

"Chill," said Vito. "First law of robotics – a robot can't injure a human. Everyone knows that." He turned to me. "Cut yourself. Then you'll see."

I hesitated. Vito spoke again, this time in a serious, deep voice. "I order you to cut yourself."

I hesitated again.

"Slick… you don't have to…"

But I wanted to show them. I wanted this whole stupid thing to be over. I lifted the knife to my arm. I heard Danny take a deep breath as I rolled up the long sleeve of my Oldean top and held my arm out. I put the blade of the knife against my skin and was about to press down when something suddenly changed.

I didn't want to know any more. I didn't want to be here.

I put the knife down and stood up. I heard Danny and Vito calling for me as I ran down the stairs, through the shop and out of the front door. I walked down the street and found my dad waiting for me in his car. We drove home.

35

DANNY

FRIDAY 4TH JANUARY

I tried calling Slick about a hundred times that night, but he didn't pick up. Vito said he was probably in shock, which I said didn't sound like something that would happen to a robot. Vito said Slick was obviously a very sophisticated piece of machinery and that we shouldn't assume anything.

It didn't feel real – even though I had seen Vito taking the chip out of his mouth and had looked at the data Vito had downloaded from it with my own eyes. When I saw all the pieces of code in a file called NewResponseTypes, I knew: everything that Slick had learnt since he'd moved here had been turned into code – from how to greet someone to preferring home-made gifts over ones that had been bought. What was sad about that piece of code was that it had an exception for his parents. I guess they didn't like the digital frame he made them. He never told me that.

As I sat on Vito's sofa, I thought about everything I knew about Slick and how something as crazy as my best friend being a robot might be true, but it was like finding pieces for two different jigsaw puzzles mixed together – some of the things about Slick were so non-human that I couldn't believe I hadn't worked it out before, and others were so completely human that it made no sense at all. Did I have a best friend or a really cool gadget? Did he like anything he said he liked – including me? Of everything, this was the most confusing part. Robots are not able to feel emotions, but I was sure that Slick could. Vito disagreed. He said he had just been programmed to look like he felt them. I called my mum and told her I was staying at Vito's that night, then spent the next few hours sitting next to Vito playing *Land X* while he went through the thousands of folders and files that he had downloaded from Slick's chip. Some of the things made sense when Vito explained them, but mostly it made no sense at all to me. All I wanted to know was why. Why would a twelve-year-old robot be living in Ashland, hanging out with me?

I went through every movie that I could think of that had a robot in it and, grabbing a pen and paper from Vito, started to list their purpose in every one. When I ran out of movies – four – I searched on the Internet. What I found was this: robots are built to be either criminals or butlers.

"Do you think he's an assassin?" I asked.

Vito shrugged. "Possible."

But nothing about that made sense – not just because he looked like a kid and lived in Ashland, but also – mostly – because of the kind of person/whatever he was. Slick was *not* a rule-breaker. He wouldn't take a short cut through a door marked "exit", let alone break the law by murdering someone.

"What about a butler?" I asked. After all, Slick *was* very good at ironing. "Do you think his parents bought him to do chores for them?"

Vito shook his head without looking up from his computer. "No way. He must be worth millions of pounds. Nobody's going to be paying out that kind of money for a clean floor."

"But what—"

"Shhh... wait..." said Vito. I saw him scrolling through a document – the first one I had seen that wasn't written in code. Vito turned to me.

"How did he get his name – 'Slick'?"

"I called him that. His name's Eric."

"Look." Vito pointed to something on his screen.

Vito waited until I was standing next to him. "See this column here?" he said. "It's labelled 'Slick Gold Stripe'."

"They're his new trainers."

"Are you sure?"

I smiled for the first time that day. "I'm sure – he never stops talking about them. That's why I called him Slick."

"And then this..." He pointed to the next column. "Slick G/Y". I thought for a minute but couldn't work it out – not until I saw the column after that: "Slick R/O".

"'Slick Green Yellow' and 'Slick Red Orange'," I said, a little worried about how much I knew about Slick trainers. "Why is there a list of his shoes?" I mumbled.

"Maybe it's to check if he's wearing matching clothes or something."

"What else is there?" I asked.

Vito scrolled across, past a few more columns labelled Slick something, and then... "Oldean blue long sleeve", "Oldean green long sleeve". There must have been a hundred columns for Oldean. Then it went on to Baltic skateboards, then "Hexam R3", then "Chewberries". Literally every single thing that Slick liked had its own column. Except *Land X*. Below each header, the columns were mostly blank, but some had a row of numbers. Dates. All recent.

"So they're his favourite things," said Vito. "What about these dates – what are they?" He went back to the first column. Each cell contained a string of letters and numbers. I only worked out what they were when I got to one about halfway down: "DPL080407". I was so surprised I think I actually gasped out loud, because Vito asked me if I was OK.

"That's me," I whispered. I pointed to the row I was talking about.

Vito took a moment to register it, then gave a small chuckle. "Oh yeah: Daniel Pasquale Lazio. Forgot your middle name was Pasquale." He laughed again.

"He was *your* grandfather too," I said, annoyed. "And that's my date of birth. Why am I on there?"

That's when I noticed that most of the other rows ended in 07 too. I started to match some of them to people Slick knew – Tyler, Luke, Ethan. I couldn't match many – Slick knew a lot more people than me. And a lot more about them too.

Vito went back to my name, and we scrolled across. There were a few dates filled in under "Slick G/Y", a few under the "Oldean" section and under "Hexam R3".

"They're the dates that Slick gave me those things."

"Wow. I need a friend like him. So these are the dates he gave stuff to other people?"

I shook my head. "Harry's mum bought him his Slicks for his birthday. I know – Slick told me when he was trying to get me to wear them too."

Vito shook his head and closed the document. He clicked on a file labelled "Hexam R3".

It was another spreadsheet. The first column was labelled "Conversations". The rows were dated, starting from the first day of school back in September, and for each one there was a number. Today's date had "8" in the conversations column. Under the next heading – "Texts" – it had "1" for today. The next was "Kudos Posts". That said "0".

I took my phone out and opened up my texts with Slick. I turned my phone to Vito to show him a text Slick had sent me earlier.

You can pair with my Hexam R3 now

Vito squinted, as if he thought he wasn't reading it right. "So it's logging every time Slick mentions one of the things he likes?" He rubbed his forehead. Then slapped it a few times. "This does not make sense! *Why?*"

But suddenly I understood. I knew exactly why Slick was here, and what he was, and it wasn't a criminal or a cleaner.

I asked Vito to open up other files, just to be sure. He was going too slow. I pushed him out of the way so I could go through them myself. I started opening one file after another – each one making me even more certain I was right. I ignored Vito's questions for as long as I could, until he got angry.

I stopped suddenly and opened my mouth to speak, but I couldn't say anything. I closed my eyes. This was too horrible to be true. But it was.

I felt Vito's hand on my shoulder. "Hey, what's up?"

"Slick's an advertisement," I whispered.

Vito's hand moved away from my shoulder. "What are you talking about?"

I gulped and took a slow breath in, then turned to Vito. "Slick… he's here to sell stuff to other kids."

Vito didn't believe it, but he didn't know Slick like I did. I showed him the document that was open on my screen at that moment – a list of selling points for Chewberries

– then closed it and opened up another file – one labelled "Contacts".

Every single person that Slick had met in Ashland was listed. And each one was shaded red, green or yellow. Luke – green. Me – green. But it wasn't just people he was friends with or had been friends with. I saw names I recognized of kids from other years that were in green too, and I was sure he wasn't friends with any of them. The column next to each name was labelled "Status". Only Ethan, Hope and I had "100%" next to it. Luke was "0%". So were the kids he didn't know.

Then I moved across to the columns labelled "Kudos" and "VieVid". The number of followers and friends that each person had on their page was listed. I remembered Slick telling me he'd looked up everybody in our year on Kudos when we met.

Click. Click. Click. Everything was starting to slot together.

I rubbed my eyes and cheeks with the back of my hand. "He only made friends with me to make me popular. To see what I could sell. That's why he gave me stuff," I said. I choked back a sob. "I'm just an experiment. He picked the biggest loser in the school to see if he could make me popular."

"You don't know that," said Vito. Before Vito could see that I was crying, I stood up, walked away and lay down on his sofa. I pulled the blanket over my head.

Vito tried to talk to me, but he gave up after a while. In the end, he left me alone. I closed my eyes and tried to sleep – I didn't want to think about anything any more.

Vito woke me up some time in the middle of the night. He was smiling as he dragged me off the sofa and over to his computer.

CHAPTER 35: DANNY

"LOOK!"
I yawned. My eyes were half-closed from still being mostly asleep, so I had to lean forwards to read the words on the screen.

- We did not finish the computer today. Danny invited me over after school on Friday to keep working on it. I said I couldn't because Friday is the day I have my dentist appointment. He said "fine" quietly and then frowned.

"What is this?" I asked.
"It's his journal! Slick actually has a journal. It's the most incredible thing I have ever read. Also the most boring. But that was just the beginning – it just gets better and better. I didn't know you still sleep with a teddy bear. That is *so adorable*."
He tried pinching me on the cheek, but I brushed his hand away and frowned at him. "What's your point?"
"Read the rest of it."
I turned back to the screen.

- I liked working on the computer with him, so I said I could come on Saturday instead. Then he smiled and said that he would wait until then to do any more work on it.
- I think this means we might be friends.
- I am not supposed to be friends with him.
- I am not supposed to be friends with Danny, because he is not one of the popular kids.
- I have figured out how to fix this: I will make Danny popular.

"Danny," said Vito. "Slick didn't want to be friends with you to make you popular – Slick wanted to make you popular because he wanted you to be his friend." I rolled these words around my head, and the more I did the better I felt.

"It's all here," continued Vito. He was practically jumping up and down in his chair, he was so excited. "All his thoughts – everything."

Vito laughed and grabbed me by both shoulders. "Do you have any idea how incredible this is?! Your best friend is the single most advanced piece of technology ever built. EVER!"

I smiled, not because Slick was some kind of super-android, but because – robot or not – Slick really was my friend. It didn't matter what he was made of or why he was made; nothing had really changed, and I needed him to know that. But he didn't answer his phone.

I slept for a couple of hours on the sofa and then tried him again at 7 a.m. No answer. I texted him, telling him to call me as soon as he could. He replied twenty minutes later to say that he couldn't talk as he had a dentist appointment. He said he'd call me after. There was nothing else I could do. Plus I was tired. I asked Vito to drive me home.

I had forgotten all about seeing Miss Lake in the parking lot until I walked into my house, after Vito dropped me off, and found her sitting in my kitchen talking to my mum.

"Look who just came by," said Mum, with a huge smile.

"Hi, Danny," said Miss Lake. "Are you all set for school on Monday?"

I didn't say anything. I couldn't.

Mum gave me a quick frown – one that only I could see – then smiled again at Miss Lake.

"Miss Lake was saying that there are some advanced maths courses she's going to be running next term that she'd like you to sign up for. Isn't that wonderful?"

Miss Lake pulled out the chair next to hers. "Come, sit down. Let me show you."

I said nothing. All I could think about was that the only explanation for Miss Lake showing up at the same place where Slick went to get his chip taken out was that she was one of them too. She had to know I knew, but I still couldn't figure out why she was here – not until I saw her eyes flicker over to my mobile phone as I put it down on the table.

Miss Lake spent no more than ten minutes talking me through the programmes. I didn't hear a word she said. She tried to distract me a few times, but I never took my hand off my mobile. Finally, she asked me to fetch the textbook we used in class. I picked up my mobile phone.

"You don't need your mobile," said Miss Lake. She put her hand out to take it from me. I ignored her, walked out of the kitchen, ran up the stairs and hid the phone inside my sock. I came back downstairs with the book.

Miss Lake looked at my hands as I sat back down next to her. I smiled. She frowned.

"We can continue this in class," said Miss Lake. She stood up, said goodbye to us and left. As soon as the door closed, Mum started shouting at me about how rude I was, while I reached into my sock to get my phone to text Vito.

36

SLICK

SATURDAY 5TH JANUARY

I had seven missed calls from Danny when I came back from my dentist appointment. I don't want to be friends with Danny any more, so I didn't call him back.

I called Ethan to ask him if he wanted to hang out today.

"We're going to see my grandma for the weekend," said Ethan. "But you guys can come over after school on Monday if you want."

Ethan said "you guys". He meant Danny and me.

"Sounds awesome – I'll come. But I'm not friends with Danny any more."

"What?" asked Ethan. "Why?"

"He's not cool," I said. "I thought he was, but he said some really bad things about you and me the other day."

"Like what?" said Ethan.

"He said that he doesn't need to hang out with losers like us now that he's famous on VieVid."

"What? No he didn't."

I don't know why Ethan thought I would lie about something like that.

"He did. And he said that he's sick of us all thinking we're better than him. I got really angry, and then he punched me."

"He *punched* you?"

"Yeah. So I don't want to hang out with Danny any more. But I can come on Monday. My mum can pick me up after."

"OK. Well, sure... But I don't get it about Danny. I mean, he wouldn't do that."

"Yeah, I don't get it either. I thought he was cool, but he isn't. I don't want to hang out with him any more."

Ethan was silent for a moment.

"I guess," he said finally. "I mean, I don't know – that's really messed up. Maybe I should call him."

"He'll say it's not true," I said. "But he would say that. Anyway, Monday's cool. I can bring my ShadowCloud if you want to try it out."

"Um... yeah, sure. Sounds good."

"OK. Cool. I'll see you at school on Monday."

Approximately fifteen minutes later, Danny called me. I ignored him. He called again twelve times today. He sent me fourteen texts too, but I deleted them all without reading them. The last text was just after 9 p.m. I hope he gets the message now and leaves me alone.

Notes:
- I removed Binarius_X from my list of close associates on *Land X*. Binarius_X is Danny's avatar. He can still see me if we meet by accident, but if he searches for Baltic_Slick he won't be able to see where I am any more.
- I can't believe I was friends with Danny for so long. He's such a loser.

37
SLICK
MONDAY 7TH JANUARY

The first day back at school after the Christmas holidays did not start well. Danny and Ethan were waiting for me by my locker when I got to school this morning. Danny looked very angry. Ethan looked serious, but not angry. I'm not a hundred per cent certain of that, though.

"I *punched* you?" said Danny as I walked up to my locker. "Why would you even say that?"

"Because you did," I said. I turned my back to him and opened my locker to get my books. "Hey, Ethan. How was it at your grandma's?"

"Fine," said Ethan. "Danny says you're lying about what you said."

"I told you he'd say that," I said.

"I'm right here, Slick," said Danny. "Say that to my face."

He grabbed my shoulder and tried to turn me around to look at him. I didn't move.

"I know what you did," I said. I took my books out of my locker and put them into my Slick Gold Stripe limited-edition backpack. "And you know it too, so—"

"I don't know it," interrupted Danny, "BECAUSE IT'S NOT TRUE!"

I didn't say anything, because there was no point in arguing with him if he was just going to lie. I turned to Ethan.

"We still cool for hanging out this afternoon?"

Ethan looked at me, then Danny, then me again. "I don't get what's going on."

"Are you mad about Friday?" Danny asked me. "Is that why you're saying this stuff? Because I wasn't saying it to—"

"I'm saying it because it's true," I said. "And yeah, I'm still mad. You can't punch someone in the face and think they're just going to forget about it."

Danny's face was very red. He opened his eyes so wide that they looked like they were going to pop out of his eye sockets.

"I DIDN'T PUNCH YOU!" shouted Danny.

"Why are you still lying?"

"Why are you being a jerk?" asked Danny. "I'm sorry I said you were a…" Danny paused and looked over at Ethan. He didn't finish his sentence. "But you saw the video. We weren't lying about what we found."

"What did you find?" asked Ethan.

Danny glanced over at Ethan. "Another time," he said. He turned back to me. "Slick, seriously, we weren't lying. I can prove it. I can show you the code from the chip. It's all there."

"What are you talking about?" I asked. "What chip?"

Danny stared at me for almost a minute. When he spoke again, he spoke slower. He was frowning so hard that his eyebrows joined together to make a V shape.

"My cousin? Vito?" asked Danny.

Now I was the one staring. I had no idea what Danny was talking about.

"You don't remember videoing your dentist appointment?" asked Danny.

"No," I said. "What?"

"Why would he video his dentist appointment?" asked Ethan. Ethan looked as confused as I was feeling. Danny did not answer either of us. Instead, he leant forwards and stared at my face, like he was trying to look in my head. He bit his lip then looked down at the ground and started tapping his left foot. He seemed to be thinking about something.

"What's going on?" asked Ethan.

Danny put his hand up to Ethan. It was a signal to tell Ethan to stop talking. That's when the bell for school rang.

I picked up my bag. "I'm going," I said.

"Wait!" said Danny. He looked up at me. "Just tell me something."

"What?" I asked. "I've got to go. I don't want to be late for class."

"Just answer this: did you go to the dentist this weekend? I don't mean Friday – I mean after that. Did you go back a second time?"

"Why?" I said.

"It's an easy question," said Danny. "Yes or no? Did you go back to the dentist after Friday?"

I didn't know why Danny cared if I went to the dentist or not. I guess he still hadn't realized that we weren't friends any more.

"Yeah, I had to get my tooth fixed," I said. "OK? Can I go now, or do you want to ask me any more weird questions?"

Danny's mouth dropped open. He might have been about to say something, but I didn't find out, because I walked away.

Notes:
- At lunch, Ethan said he felt weird about the whole thing with Danny and me and said maybe we should meet up after school another day instead. I said sure, but I didn't like it. I hope Ethan

doesn't decide to be friends with Danny instead of me. I don't know why he would, though, as Danny is not a good friend. I don't know why Ethan would want to be friends with someone who lies and punches people.

- Miss Lake asked to talk to me after class today. She asked me how I was feeling. I told her that I didn't want to be friends with Danny. I thought she might be angry about that, because she'd said she wanted me to be friends with him. She wasn't mad at all. She said she was glad to hear that and that I shouldn't feel bad, because even she had been wrong about Danny. Then she told me to try to make up with my old friends. I felt better after talking to Miss Lake.

- I spoke to Harry at lunch. He said Luke and Tyler are still angry with me. I said I didn't blame them. I told him that I'd been wrong about Danny and that I'd made a mistake. I said I'd apologize to Luke and Tyler if they'd let me. Harry said he'd tell them and see what they said.

- I asked Harry if he wanted to go to the skateboarding park at the weekend. Harry said yes. Then he said maybe. Then he said he had to check with Luke and Tyler. I think Harry wants to be my friend again, but he doesn't want to make his other friends angry. I understand this. I told Harry to let me know any time.

- Harry was wearing blue Slicks with lime-green laces today. I haven't seen a pair of Slicks with lime-green laces before. I'm wondering if Harry swapped the normal Slick laces for his own. I'll ask him when I see him again.

- Harry is awesome. I can't believe I stopped hanging out with him to hang out with Danny.

- Danny is such a loser.

38

SLICK

THURSDAY 10TH JANUARY

Ethan asked me if I wanted to go to his house after school today to play *Land X*. I asked him if Danny was going. He said no, so I said yes. I am glad that Ethan has decided to be friends with me instead of Danny. I would never say mean things to Ethan or punch him, so I think he made the right decision.

I saw Harry in the hall between classes. He said that Luke is going to meet with some big record producer today, and he hasn't spoken to him. I asked him if he had talked to Tyler, and he asked me if I had seen Tuesday from the Week doing skateboarding tricks at an awards thing on TV last night. I think he was changing the subject. I think this might be because Tyler doesn't want to be friends with me again. I'm thinking that maybe if I make friends with Luke again, then Tyler will change his mind. Luke is more popular than Tyler, so I think Tyler might listen to Luke.

I met Ethan by his locker when school finished today. He said that his mum had asked him to pick up some medication from the hospital that she needed and that she was sending a cab to take us there before going to his house. He was acting strangely. I think he might be upset that his mum is sick.

The cab was waiting for us outside school. The trip wasn't too long, and Ethan didn't seem to want to talk, so I talked about *Land X* the whole way. I thought it would cheer him up, but it didn't seem to help.

The cab dropped us off outside the entrance to the hospital. I kept my head down when we walked in, in case Mrs Lazio was around. Mrs Lazio works at this hospital. I like Mrs Lazio, even if she is Danny's mum, and I didn't want her to be upset that I wasn't friends with Danny any more.

Ethan turned right by the waiting area and stopped at a vending machine. He didn't go to the reception desk, even though there was a large sign above it saying ALL VISITORS MUST REPORT TO RECEPTION ON ARRIVAL. Ethan took out his mobile and started typing something. My guess was that he was texting his mum to find out more information about the medicine he was getting for her.

Ethan stopped typing and looked at his phone. A few seconds later there was a ping. Ethan read the text he'd received and then looked around. He walked over to a map of the hospital, then turned to me.

"This way," he said. Ethan pressed the down button for the lift. I wanted to ask Ethan why he hadn't gone to reception, but he didn't seem to be in the mood for talking. And anyway, I decided that maybe you don't have to go to reception if you are just picking up medicine. If that's the case, the hospital should change their sign to be more specific. When the lift arrived, Ethan pressed the button that said "-3". This is the lowest floor of the hospital and three floors below ground level. I read the sign in the lift that said level -3 was for maintenance and storeroom. It didn't say that this was the floor to pick up medicines. I think you have to be pretty smart to work in a hospital – it's a very complicated and demanding line of work. That's what Mrs Lazio told me, which is why I'm surprised that they're not very good at making signs.

Ethan led the way out of the lift and down the hall on the left. It was obvious that he hadn't been here before as he was reading the signs on every door. We got to a door that had a sign on it saying ROOM 14. Ethan opened the door and we walked in.

The first thing I saw were eight rows of tall metal shelving units that reached up to the ceiling and ran almost all the way to the back of the room. Ethan went down the central aisle, and I followed. The shelves we were walking past were all stacked with electrical equipment. Most of the stuff looked old. Some of it even looked broken. On one of the shelves were thirty-eight keyboards. I could only see the tops of five of them, and they were all missing keys. I didn't see any medicines at all – not a single bottle.

I figured Ethan must have worked out we were in the wrong place by now, but if he had, he didn't say anything. He just kept walking past all the computer stuff. He looked like he knew where he was going, and then I realized that we were probably taking a short cut.

I was distracted looking at a stack of memory cards on a shelf when I heard Ethan say hi to someone. The person said hi back, and my head snapped up.

It was Danny. And next to him was his cousin Vito. Vito was wearing a red T-shirt with the word "GEENIUS" printed in white letters on the front. That is not how you spell "genius". I don't know what brand of T-shirt Vito was wearing, but I know it definitely wasn't Oldean – they would never make a spelling mistake like that.

Danny and Vito were standing by a long table, in front of a laptop that was open and switched on. Ethan stopped, and all three of them looked up at me.

If I hadn't been standing there, looking at Danny with my own eyes, I wouldn't have believed that, of all the days to come to this hospital, it turned out to be a day that Danny was visiting his mum at work, and of all the rooms to walk into, it turned out to be the one that Danny was in.

"Hey, Slick," said Danny. "Just hear me out."

I looked at Ethan, then at Vito, then at Danny. Not one of them looked as surprised as I was feeling.

"What are you doing here?" I asked.

"I knew you wouldn't come if I asked you," said Danny. "It was the only way I could get to talk to you properly."

That's when I realized that I'd been tricked. I looked at Ethan. "You knew about this?"

Ethan hunched up his shoulders. "Sorry. Danny said it was important."

"Do you remember the other night?" asked Vito.

"What other night?" I asked. I could hear that my voice sounded angry. I reminded myself that I was angry with Danny, not Vito.

Vito walked over to me. "After your dentist appointment. You came to my place," he said.

I shook my head. "No I didn't. I've only been to your place one time – on New Year's Day."

"*Great*," said Danny in his annoying sarcastic voice.

Vito sighed. "You came to my place. We took out your chip and downloaded the data. We filmed you. Do you remember any of that?"

I didn't know what Vito was talking about.

"Can someone please tell me what's going on?" asked Ethan.

"And me," I said. "This is all so weird."

Vito breathed in for a very long time, and then breathed out loudly. "OK... I know you're confused right now, but I can explain."

"Go ahead," I said. I was still angry.

"But you're going to have to let me look in your mouth."

I shook my head. "What?"

"You'll understand. It's cool," said Vito. "You can trust me."

"No I can't," I said. "All I know about you is that you lied to get me here and you're lying about me going to your flat. I'd remember something like that."

Vito closed his lips tightly. "Hmm," he said. "You make a good point." He paused. "Would it help if I told you I wasn't lying now?"

"No," I said. "Everything you've said to me today has been a lie. This means it's extremely unlikely that you're telling the truth now, and extremely likely that you are lying again."

"Argh," said Vito. He looked at Danny. "What if we just hold him down?"

Danny opened his eyes very wide. "No way. He's got like superhuman strength. He'll knock you out with one punch."

Ethan threw his hands up in the air and groaned loudly. "I'll knock everyone out if someone doesn't tell me what's going on," he said.

Vito and Danny both turned to Ethan. "Chill," said Vito. "Just wait. You'll understand in a second. If I can just..."

Vito's hand shot up, and I saw a pair of tweezers coming towards my face. I grabbed his wrist with my right hand and covered my mouth with my left hand.

"Told you," said Danny.

"OK. Sorry," said Vito. "I'm just trying to explain things to you so that you know for certain we're telling the truth."

I didn't let go of his hand.

"Just let him look in your mouth," said Ethan. He sounded very cross.

"You think I should?" I asked Ethan. I was still holding Vito's wrist.

"Yeah. I mean, he can't do much with a pair of tweezers, right?" He looked at Vito. "Right?"

Vito nodded. "Right." He tried to twist his arm away from me, but I didn't let go.

"So just let him do it," said Ethan, "and they can show us whatever they want to show us and we can get out of here. I'm kind of freaked out right now."

I believed that Ethan wasn't lying when he said he didn't know what was happening. He seemed as confused as I felt. Even though Ethan had probably lied to me about needing to get medication for his mum, I don't know about any other time that Ethan has lied to me. Also, Ethan is my friend, and you're supposed to be able to trust your friends. I decided that it was extremely likely that Ethan was telling the truth.

"You're just looking?" I asked Vito.

"Sure – you can trust me," said Vito.

I looked at the pair of tweezers in Vito's hand – the hand that I was still holding.

"If I let you do this, will you let me go after?"

Vito nodded.

"Fine," I said. "Just do it."

I leant over to Vito, tilted my head back and opened my mouth. Vito reached up and put the tweezers into my mouth.

"STOP!" shouted Danny.

Vito jumped back. "WHAT?"

Danny was breathing very quickly. "What if you're wrong?" he asked Vito.

"I'm not wrong," said Vito.

"You might be," said Danny.

"I'm not," said Vito. He looked down at the front of his red T-shirt and pointed to the word "geenius".

"'Genius', see? And anyway, what's the worst that could happen?"

"The *worst* that could happen?" asked Danny.

Danny sounded angry. Or worried. "The worst that could happen," he continued, "and it might not seem like a big deal to you, but it's kind of a big deal to me – is that you turn my best friend into a toaster." Danny was not making any sense. I am not his friend any more, and it is not possible for a person to be turned into a toaster. Then I realized that the word "toaster" must have another meaning as, even for Danny, this was a very strange thing to say.

"What do you mean?" I asked. "What's a toaster?"

Vito frowned at Danny.

"A toaster…" said Vito. He was talking very slowly. "Is someone… who doesn't want to be your friend. Right, Danny?" Danny didn't reply.

"*Danny?*" asked Vito again.

Danny took a long breath in and looked up at the ceiling. "Yeah, that's right," he said. "It's… it's an Italian thing."

"Oh," I said.

This made sense. I am not Italian, and so there's no reason why I'd know the word was used in this way too. Now that I had this information, I could understand what Danny had been saying: that he was worried I wouldn't want to be friends with him any more. But I'm not friends with Danny anyway, so if the worst that could happen by Vito looking into my mouth was that we wouldn't be friends, then that meant the worst thing that could happen was nothing.

"Just do it," I said.

I tilted my head back again, opened my mouth and watched as Vito reached up to my mouth with the tweezers.

When I woke up, Vito and Danny were staring at me, and Ethan was crouched by the wall, banging his head with his hand.

39

DANNY

THURSDAY 10TH JANUARY

We watched as Slick looked around the room.

"You OK?" asked Vito.

"I think so," replied Slick.

"How many times have you been to my flat?"

Slick nodded. "I remember now. I remember what happened the second time."

"Hey, Slick?" I asked.

"What?"

"Are we friends?"

Slick smiled. "Yeah. You're my best friend. I don't know why I said that stuff. I'm sorry."

Vito pointed to the front of his T-shirt. "Told you," he said.

Slick looked over at Ethan, who was now covering his face with his hands and shaking his head. He had not taken the news that Slick was a robot well. It wasn't until we showed him Slick's journal entries that he had believed us. And he hadn't said a word since.

"What's wrong with him?" Slick whispered to me.

Vito stood up. "He'll be fine. He's in shock."

"Why?" asked Slick. "What did you do to me?"

"I removed the false memories they implanted in you," explained Vito.

Slick rolled his eyes. "No you didn't. Guys… this is stupid. I remember what you said the other night, and I get that something really weird is going on, but I promise you: I am *not* a robot. OK?"

We didn't say anything.

Ethan, who was still crouched by the wall, moved his hands away from his face to look at me.

"Can you believe this?" Slick asked Ethan. Ethan didn't speak. Ethan really didn't look well.

"Listen," said Vito. "I get this is a lot for you to take in, but that thing we took out of your mouth… it *was* a computer chip. We downloaded the data from it. Come… I'll show you."

Slick rolled his eyes. "This is so dumb," he said, but he stood up and followed Vito over to his laptop.

Vito clicked on the "Contacts" file. We had decided this would be the best place to start.

Vito stepped back. We watched as Slick scrolled down through the names of every person he had met in Ashland. He didn't say anything. He scrolled across, reading down each column. At some point, Ethan joined us. He leant in over Slick's shoulder to read.

"Why's my mum on there?" asked Ethan quietly. "And Hope? And my dad? What is this?"

"It's a list of every person Slick's met here in Ashland," explained Vito.

Slick still hadn't said a word. He got to the final column and turned to Vito. "I don't get it."

"Just wait," said Vito. "You'll understand."

Vito opened up one of Slick's journal entries and scrolled down to the last paragraph. He moved his arm and Slick started reading.

- I'm so excited about giving Mum and Dad their Christmas present. Back in October, Mrs Okina gave Mum a pair of gardening gloves because Mum had said she didn't have any. When Mum opened the bag and saw the gloves, she couldn't stop smiling. She hugged Mrs Okina and kept saying how much she loved them. I'm pretty sure Mrs Okina didn't even make the gloves herself, so I think Mum will be even happier when she opens my gift.

I could see Slick's eyes moving across the screen, reading and rereading the paragraph. Nobody said anything. Vito reached over and opened up another screen. He let Slick read the entry about wanting to make me popular so he could be my friend. Slick read it. He scrolled up and read it again. He got to the end and stared at the screen.

"These are my thoughts," he said quietly. "I don't understand. How do you have my thoughts?"

"I told you – we downloaded them," said Vito. He put his hand on Slick's shoulder. "Look, kid, I know this is superconfusing for you right now, but if you think about it, this is the only explanation, right?"

"What?" asked Slick. "That I'm a robot?"

Vito nodded. "But a really cool one. An android. You know what an android is?"

Slick nodded slowly. He turned to the screen. "Show me more," he said quietly.

Vito nodded and opened up the window with all the files on it. Then we all stood back and watched as Slick began to open them up in order and read.

About twenty minutes later, Slick – halfway through reading the code files – suddenly stood up. It took all of us by surprise, and Ethan, Vito and I jumped back.

"Slick?" I asked.

Slick didn't say anything. There was no expression at all on his face. He started to walk away.

"Slick, wait!"

I thought that was it, that we'd lost him again, but instead he stopped by one of the aisles and crouched down. He pulled out a large crate, which turned out to be filled with scrap pieces of metal and wires. He sighed and stood up empty-handed.

"The other day," he said, speaking for the first time since Vito had shown him the files. "You told me to cut myself. You said that would prove it."

Vito nodded.

"*Oh no,*" said Ethan. "*No way.*"

"That's why we brought you here," I said. "We think you send a signal out when you get hurt, and that's why someone always shows up to get you."

Slick nodded. "I need something sharp."

"At your service," said Vito. He went over to the table and picked up the knife we'd brought with us.

Ethan started shaking his head. "You're not seriously…"

Slick followed Vito and sat down on the chair. He rolled up the right leg of his trousers and then took the knife from Vito.

"You can't let… Wait… What if?…" Ethan was starting to sound hysterical. Vito gave Ethan a sharp look and put his finger to his mouth. Ethan shut up.

Slick took a deep breath. "I'm going to do this," he said.

I thought I could watch, but I couldn't. Just as the blade was about to reach his leg, I closed my eyes. A few seconds later, I opened them to find that Slick hadn't done it. His hand, still holding the knife, was trembling about an inch away from his unbroken skin.

"It's OK," said Vito gently.

Slick looked up. His face was tense. "I *want* to do it. I just can't."

"Oh!" I said, realizing what was going on. "He can't harm himself. Vito, you have to do it."

Slick nodded at me and held the knife out for Vito to take.

Vito raised both hands in the air and stepped back. "No way, dude. Seriously. I'm not good with blood. Or slicing up kids."

"You said you were sure," said Slick.

Vito rolled his eyes. "Yeah, but…"

"If you're so sure, then you're just opening up a machine. Right?"

I wasn't sure if Slick wanted to do this because he believed us, or because he wanted to prove us wrong.

Vito thought about the logic behind this, and then finally nodded.

He took the knife from Slick and crouched down. Ethan and I both half looked away as Vito took a huge breath and then scrunched up his face in pain as he ran the blade of the knife down Slick's leg.

What happened next was exactly what would happen to anybody's leg if you cut it with a sharp knife: blood started to pour out. A lot of blood.

I suddenly felt very felt sick.

Vito started muttering stuff as he scrambled up and reached out to grab his jacket. He rushed back over to Slick, who was just staring down at his leg, and covered it up.

"Oh my God," said Vito. "I'm so sorry. I'm so…" He looked up at me. "Danny! Go get help!"

It took me a second to snap out of the daze I was in and register what Vito was asking me to do. But just as I was about to turn to run out, Slick pushed Vito's hand away and he stood up.

Slick didn't say anything. Instead, he reached down, picked up Vito's jacket and began to wipe away all the blood.

40

SLICK

THURSDAY 10TH JANUARY (II)

I stared down at my leg. I knew what I was looking at, but it was still hard to believe that what I was seeing was true. I reached down and pulled the skin of my leg apart. There was no bone, just metal and cables and blood. I rotated my ankle and saw the metal move. I moved my leg one way, then the other, and watched the metal rods moving up and down. Any doubts that I'd had about what Vito and Danny had been saying disappeared. There was only one possible explanation for what I was seeing:

I was a robot.

I looked up at Danny.

"I guess you were right," I said.

Danny nodded.

He looked sad.

41

DANNY

THURSDAY 10TH JANUARY (II)

Slick looked sad.

I knew he was a robot, but somehow or other, I was sure that they had built him to feel real emotions. I think even Vito had realized this, because he put his arm around Slick and tried to comfort him as he sat there staring down at the metal and wires in his leg.

"But here's what I don't get," said Slick. "*Why?* Why did they build me? And who?"

I looked at Vito. Vito nodded. Slick caught that and turned to me. "*You know?!*"

I shrugged. "We thought you had enough to deal with right now."

"No," said Slick, shaking his head. "Tell me, Danny. *Now.*"

* * *

So it turned out that Slick took the news about him being a robot much better than he took the news about the reason he was a robot.

"They made me to *sell* things? That's it? That's what they made me for?"

Slick was pacing the floor in front of us. He looked angry. Furious – like he was going to explode, which, given that he was a robot, might actually have been a possibility.

"Slick, calm down," I said. "This doesn't change anything."

"*You?*" he said, narrowing his eyes at me. "You're telling *me* to calm down? Don't give advice you can't take yourself… How would you act if you found out that the only reason you exist is to sell shoes?"

"Hey, they're good trainers," I said, pointing down at the Slicks I was wearing. "It could be worse – you could have been programmed to sell nappies."

Slick looked like he might hit me. I guess he wasn't in the mood for jokes.

I sighed. "Look, Slick, you're right – I'd probably have punched a hole in the wall if I was you. But that doesn't mean I would be right. If you think about it, the only thing that's changed is that we know something we didn't know before. But it doesn't change who you are. Whatever you were when they made you, you're not that now."

Ethan nodded. "Danny's right, Slick. You're still our friend. Nothing's changed."

Slick didn't look any less angry. "Do you know who made me?"

I nodded and looked over at Vito.

"Yeah," said Vito. "I think so. I couldn't find anything in any of your files, so I went on the Internet, and it turns out all the products you…" Vito paused as he searched for the right word, "like… are advertised by the same company."

Slick folded his arms and glared at Vito. "Who?"

Vito raised an eyebrow. "If I tell you, you're not going to do anything stupid, are you?"

Slick shook his head. "No. I just want to know."

"Promise?" asked Vito.

Slick nodded.

"A company called Jeopardy. They're the biggest advertising agency in the world."

"Where are they?"

Vito frowned. "They have offices everywhere."

Slick frowned more. "Where's the main office? The headquarters? They must have one, right?"

Vito sighed and nodded. "It's the place where you go to the dentist."

"Well, I guess that makes sense," said Slick, without any expression. "Thank you."

He turned and started to walk away.

"Slick?" I called out. "What are you doing?"

He didn't turn around. "I'm going find out what's going on." He disappeared down one of the aisles.

I jumped up. "WAIT!" I said. "They'll come get you if you leave here."

Slick stopped. He turned around. "What do you mean?"

"You got cut, remember? You must be sending out a signal, but it can't reach them from down here. If you leave without deactivating it, you're going to let them know something's happened, and they'll take you away."

Slick took a deep breath and kicked the metal shelf next to his foot. He really did have a bad temper for a robot. I wondered if I had taught him that. I flinched at the thought. That would not be cool.

"So how do I turn it off?" asked Slick. "Or do I have to stay here for ever?"

"I'm not telling you until you calm down," I said.

Slick frowned at me. "I'm going there," he said. "You can't change my mind."

"But what are you going to do?"

"I'm going to tell them to stop programming me to sell stuff."

"Nice idea and all, kid," said Vito, "but I don't know if they'll do that just because you ask them to."

"They will if I make them," said Slick.

Ethan's eyes opened wide. "*You're going to kill them?*"

"What?" asked Slick. "No! I'm going to tell them that if they don't do what I ask I'll tell everyone what they're doing. And it's not like I need proof – I *am* the proof."

"Slick, that doesn't sound like the greatest idea," I said. "What if they turn you off or something?"

"I won't let them," said Slick flatly. He looked at us. I don't think any of us looked convinced. Slick shrugged. "I don't care if you don't like my plan. You're not going to change my mind."

I thought about this. I knew Slick meant it, which meant that there was only one thing for me to do. "Fine," I said. "But I'm coming with you."

Slick paused for a moment, then shook his head. "Nope. No way. They can't hurt me – I'm a robot. But I'm not letting them do anything to you."

"Come on – they just advertise stuff, they don't kill people," I said.

"You don't know what they can do," said Slick. "And I don't know either. So you're not coming."

It was my turn to frown and fold my arms. "Then I'm not telling you how to switch off the signal."

Slick turned to Ethan, who shook his head, then Vito, who did the same.

Slick rolled his eyes. "Fine. You can come."

"I'm coming too," said Ethan.

"And you pre-teens are going to need someone to drive you, so I'm in too," said Vito.

"When?" I asked. "Now?"

Slick shook his head. "No. It'll be too late by the time we get there. Tomorrow."

"I can't skip school," said Ethan.

"After school," said Slick. "Can you come get us, Vito?"

Vito nodded.

"Cool," said Slick. He looked at me. "So... how do I switch this thing off?"

"OK," I said. "So I was thinking the other night—"

"Did it hurt?" interrupted Vito.

"*Shut up*," I said. "I was thinking about the needle thing, and I think they might have to deactivate your signal when they do stuff to you."

"You said you thought they were doing a reset," said Slick.

"Yeah," said Vito. "I looked into that, and it didn't fit. This would make more sense."

"And if you're wrong?" asked Ethan.

"Then I guess we'll know soon enough," said Vito. "Unless anyone has any other ideas?"

All in agreement, we looked around the room, each of us taking one aisle, looking for something similar to the needle that Dr Kilaman had stuck up Slick's nose.

"GOT ONE!" shouted Ethan.

We all rushed over to him. He was holding up a long metal rod – an old aerial, I think.

"Perfect," said Slick, taking it from him. He put the end of the rod up one of his nostrils and we all looked away as he pushed it in hard. I heard a *click*.

We all turned back. "What do you feel?"

Slick shrugged. "Nothing. But something definitely happened. I heard it."

"Let's find out," said Vito. "Help me get my stuff, and then we'll go."

We stood outside the hospital for a while, waiting to see if anyone showed up to take Slick. The plan was that he would run back down to the basement if they did. It wasn't much of a plan, but it was the best we could come up with on short notice. Luckily, no plan was needed – nobody showed up. Vito drove Slick home so he could charge himself up for the trip tomorrow. I told him to bring his pillow to my house and stay there, but he said that would look suspicious and that we should all act normal.

"See you tomorrow," said Vito as Slick climbed out of the car.

Slick nodded.

"Hey, Slick," I said as he was about to close the door.

Slick leant down to look at me.

"You OK?" I asked.

Slick nodded. "Yeah. I'm good." He smiled. "See you later."

He closed the car door, and we drove away to Ethan's house.

42

SLICK

THURSDAY 10TH JANUARY/
FRIDAY 11TH JANUARY

I lied to Danny – there was no way I was going to let him come with me. He was my best friend, and I would never do anything that could put him in danger. I didn't know what would happen when I got there, but I couldn't exclude the possibility of bad things happening. For that reason, I couldn't take Danny. Or Ethan, or Vito.

I still needed someone to take me, though. I looked up the address by checking the history from my ShadowCloud, and it turned out it was over an hour's drive west on the motorway, in the middle of nowhere. I couldn't get there on my own. Luckily, I could think of two people who I wouldn't feel bad about taking me. Before I could ask, though, I had to check something. I ran up to my parents' room and pushed their bed away from the wall. Just as I thought, there were two cables running from the wall to the bed – one to Mum's pillow and the other to Dad's.

I went down to talk to Mum in the kitchen.

"I have a football match tomorrow. The school says parents have to drive them. You have to take me."

Mum looked up from her laptop. "What time?"

"We have to leave at 6 a.m."

"I can't. I'm meeting Cindy at the golf club for a breakfast social."

"She called," I lied. "It's cancelled."

Mum nodded. "OK. I'll be ready to leave at six," she said. She went back to doing whatever she was doing on her laptop.

Stupid robot.

I went upstairs to my bedroom and, even though it wasn't midnight yet, I went to sleep. I know what I'm doing when I go to bed isn't sleeping, but I'm going to call it that anyway. Just because I'm an android, it doesn't mean that I have to talk like one.

The next morning, we left the house at 6 a.m., as planned. I spent most of the journey researching Jeopardy Advertising on the Internet. The company director was a man called Carter Harluck. This is what I found out about him:

- He is the third-richest man in the country.
- He grew up near Ashland.
- He went to university in the US and graduated first in his year from MIT – the same university that Vito didn't go to.
- After he graduated, he started a company in the US that made microprocessors for computers. They must have been very good, because three years later he sold the company for five billion pounds. He disappeared for two years. When he came back to the UK from wherever he was, he founded Jeopardy Advertising.
- I found an article entitled 'The Mystery of Jeopardy'. It said that nobody could work out how Carter Harluck had

had such success in an industry that he didn't know, but that the figures spoke for themselves. It was now the most successful advertising agency in the world. It said Carter Harluck had the Midas touch. I had to look up what that meant.

Even though I found many pages of information on Carter Harluck and Jeopardy, I didn't find one single mention of robots. Nothing.

Danny called at 7 a.m., as I figured he would. He called back a few minutes after that, and again a few minutes after that. I didn't answer. He kept calling until eventually I had to switch my Hexam R3 off. I spent the rest of the journey trying not to think about being a robot.

We arrived just after 7.30 a.m. Even though I knew I'd been here every week since I'd arrived in Ashland, I didn't recognize anything, except from what I'd seen on the ShadowCloud video. And Mum, even though she'd actually driven here herself every week, didn't seem to recognize where we were either. I guess they programmed us this way. I hated them.

Mum pulled up near the entrance of the building, which turned out not to be the one we went to for our "dentist" appointments. This entrance was completely different – two large glass doors that opened automatically as we walked up to them. Before I stepped inside, I stopped and turned to Mum. There was something I needed to know.

"Do you know who you are?" I asked.

"Of course I do. Karen Young," she said. She looked into the large white foyer beyond the glass doors and frowned. "Are you sure we're in the right place?"

"Yes, I'm sure."

Mum shrugged and went to take a step forwards, but I grabbed her by the sleeve to stop her. She turned and frowned at me.

"But do you know who you really are?" I asked. "Do you know *what* you are?"

She stared at me for a moment.

"Of course," she said, looking confused. "I'm your mum."

I sighed. "Forget it," I said, my question answered.

43

SLICK

FRIDAY 11TH JANUARY (II)

The lobby of Jeopardy Advertising was very different from the lobby of the "dentist" waiting area around the back of the building. It was difficult to believe they were both in the same place. There were no windows, and so, apart from the entrance doors, there was no natural light coming in – but it didn't feel that way. Everything was bright, sparkling white. A waterfall – a real waterfall – was running down the side of the wall behind the reception area, and on the wall opposite a huge cinema-sized screen was playing an advert for Blise clothes. We walked over to the reception desk and a new advert started – this one for Slicks. We were definitely in the right place.

"I really think we're in the wrong place," said Mum. "There's no playing field here."

"It's an indoor game," I said. I didn't even know if that was a thing. I didn't really care.

I approached the woman at the desk. She had a red jacket and a perfect white smile. It was as perfect as Miss Lake's. And my mum's and dad's. And mine, I guess.

"Welcome to Jeopardy," she said. "How may I help you today?"

"We're here to see Mr Harluck," I said.

"Do you have an appointment?" she asked.

I shook my head. "No."

The woman's smile didn't leave her face. "I'm sorry," she said. "Mr Harluck doesn't see anyone without an appointment."

"Tell him Eric and Karen Young are here to see him."

The woman nodded and picked up the phone. She told whoever she was talking to that we were here to see Mr Harluck, and then she covered the mouthpiece with her hand.

"They're just checking."

I felt nervous. I hadn't come up with a plan about what to do if he said he didn't want to see us. I didn't even know if he was there.

We waited a couple of minutes, and then the woman put the phone down.

"Go straight up to the top floor."

I smiled. "Thank you."

"Who's Mr Harluck?" asked Mum as we waited for the lift.

I ignored her. She didn't ask again. When the lift arrived, I entered it without checking if she was following me. She was, but it wouldn't have mattered to me either way.

Carter Harluck's office didn't look like what I thought an office should look like – or maybe I should say that it didn't look like what I had been programmed to think an office should look like. That would be more accurate.

There were trees and water everywhere. The trees looked real. The walls were all made of glass and looked out over a city that seemed so real that even when I pressed my face up right up to the glass I couldn't see the pixels on the screen.

It was pretty cool – kind of like how Land X looks when we're flying over it – except in higher definition.

A tall man with red hair came into the office and greeted us; he didn't look anything like the pictures of Carter Harluck that I had seen on the Internet. This turned out to be because he wasn't Carter Harluck. The man told us to follow him. We walked through the trees and past narrow rivers that flowed around the space in a maze of marble. Apart from the man leading us and Mr Harluck himself, I saw nobody else. I guess when you're the third-richest man in the country, you can have a whole floor for your own office – though it seemed completely unnecessary: he still took up the same amount of floor space as other, poorer people.

Carter Harluck was behind a long glass desk in the far corner of the building. He stood up when he saw us approaching and started to walk over to meet us. I saw that he was wearing a white Oldean shirt and Oldean jeans and a pair of Slicks. Before yesterday, this would have meant I automatically liked him. Today was different.

"Eric Young," he said as he walked over to me. He was smiling. "It's a pleasure to meet you. I'm Carter – though I'm guessing you already know that if you're here."

He put his hand out. I almost shook it, but then thought about who he was and why I was here, and I changed my mind.

Carter laughed and withdrew his hand.

Mum stepped forwards and put her hand out.

"Hello, I'm Karen Young," she said. "Are you one of Eric's teachers?"

Carter shook her hand warmly but didn't bother to answer her question – I guess he knew how pointless having a conversation with my mother was.

"Wait outside, please," said Carter to Mum. Mum nodded and walked out of the room without asking any questions. She stood completely still next to a palm tree on the other side of the glass. Carter turned to the man who had shown us in. "Nicholas, go down to the facility. Beth's on her way in now. You can help her get things ready."

"Yes, sir," said Nicholas, smiling his perfect smile. I was starting to think that all the people who worked for Carter Harluck were androids.

Carter waited until Nicholas had disappeared from view, and then he walked over to a pair of green leather and metal armchairs under a palm tree. He sat down in one and motioned for me to sit next to him.

"So, Eric," he said as I sat down. "You've come all the way here to see me, and now you have my full attention. So tell me: what can I help you with today?"

"I want to stop working for you."

Mr Harluck raised his eyebrows in shock. His mouth dropped open, but he was still sort of smiling.

"You want to stop working for me? Is that what you said?"

I nodded.

"OK, Eric. And why do you think you work for me?"

"I don't think it. I know. I know you get me to sell stuff for you. I know that's why Uncle Martin sends stuff from London... There's no Uncle Martin, is there?"

Mr Harluck shook his head. He wasn't smiling any more. "Who told you all of this?"

I shrugged and lied – that came easy now. "I figured it out by myself. Once I knew what I was, I realized I had to have been made for a reason. I looked up all the stuff that I like and found that the only thing all the companies who make them have in common is that they use the same advertising agency – Jeopardy."

Mr Harluck clasped his hands together, his lips pressed tight, and leant back in his chair. "Well," he said slowly. "You really are something else." He stared at me for a moment.

"Do you know, Eric, that we programmed you not to ever know or believe that you were a robot?"

I lifted up the leg of my trousers and showed him the metal inside my leg. "I had to believe it," I said. "I have to believe things when I see them with my eyes."

Mr Harluck nodded. "Yes, I suppose you do. Did you override the signal?"

I ignored the question, as the answer was obvious. I had more important things to talk to him about.

"Why did you make me?" I asked. "I mean, I know you want me to advertise your stuff, but why not just make adverts on television or whatever?"

Mr Harluck opened his mouth to speak but was interrupted by a *ping* from the mobile phone in his shirt pocket. He took it out, read the message, typed something back, then put it away and turned back to me.

"That's a great question, Eric. And the answer is that we do all of those things you mentioned – television adverts, billboards, product placement – but they're just not that effective any more."

"Why?"

Mr Harluck pulled his mobile back out from his pocket and held it up to me.

"You see, Eric, Joe Bloggs doesn't believe advertising agencies when they tell him that the Hexam R3 is the best phone – even thought it is, right?" He grinned.

I shrugged.

"He doesn't believe the advertising, because he knows that advertisers are being paid to say the product they're trying to sell is the best – even if it isn't. But if a friend, or someone Joe Bloggs looks up to, tells him that the Hexam R3 is a great mobile, then Joe believes that to be true, because there's no reason why that person would lie. So Joe Bloggs goes out and buys a Hexam R3."

"Who's Joe Bloggs?"

"He could be anyone. The point is, the most effective form of advertising is when people tell other people they know how great a product is. It's called 'word of mouth'. But that's a pretty tricky thing to make happen. It's very difficult to make people think things, and even harder to get them to tell other people exactly what we want them to say. It would be much easier, I realized, if we had our own people who would do this for us. Or rather, if we *made* our own people. Then we could get them to say and do whatever we wanted."

I stared at Mr Harluck. I felt strange. Pointless. I don't know if that's the right word. I don't know what the right word is for when the man who made you confirms you only exist to trick people into buying things.

"How many of us are there?" I asked.

"Right now, across the whole country... fifty-nine thousand, nine hundred and ninety-two."

My mouth dropped open. I didn't know what number I had expected him to say, but it definitely wasn't this one.

"But *you*..." continued Mr Harluck, "...*you* are special, Eric. One of a kind."

"Why?"

"Because you are the first child. Isn't that neat?"

I narrowed my eyes. I hated everything that Mr Harluck was saying. I had never hated anything before. I hadn't even known what hating something felt like – not until now.

"You're lying to people," I said. "It's wrong."

Mr Harluck smiled. "And that's exactly why nobody can know about it – not even the companies who pay me to promote their products. If people knew about you and all the others, then it wouldn't work any more. People would know that you were all just another kind of advertisement, made by an advertising agency, and they wouldn't trust you any more. And that," Mr Harluck patted me on the shoulder, "young Eric, is why it's so important that nobody finds out."

I knew what Mr Harluck meant. "I'm not going to tell anyone. Not if you give me what I want."

"Oh really?" he laughed. "Are we making deals now?"

I nodded.

"And what is it that you want, Eric?"

"I want you to leave me alone. Let me go and live with Danny, and I'll never tell anybody. I just want to be with my friends."

Mr Harluck put his hand on my shoulder. "Eric, they are not your friends."

"Yes they are."

Mr Harluck shook his head. "No, Eric, they're not. You can't have friends, because you're a robot. Robots don't make friends. You're just programmed to think you have friends, and to think you like people. But these things aren't real – not for you."

"I know what I am, and I *do* have friends. Real friends." Mr Harluck was making me feel very angry.

"Those friends like you because you're programmed to be someone that people will like. That's all."

"Why are you saying this?"

"I'm saying this, Eric, because it's true. And it's very interesting to hear you speak like this. You should be very proud of yourself – of what you have managed to become in the short time that you've been around."

Mr Harluck's hand was still on my shoulder. I shook it away.

Mr Harluck sat back and stared at me for a moment, and then he laughed again. "I have to tell you, Eric – I'm enjoying this conversation very much."

I didn't smile.

"Are you going to kill me?"

"I'm not going to kill you, Eric, because it's not possible to kill a robot."

"Fine," I said. "Are you going to switch me off?"

Mr Harluck stopped smiling.

"I think you are intelligent enough to understand that I can't send you back knowing what you know," he said. "You do understand that, don't you?"

I wanted to hurt Mr Harluck. I wanted him to stop. But I couldn't do it.

"You can't switch me off!" I said. "Maybe I was just a machine at the beginning, but I'm not that now. I know what I feel and think, and I know that I am real – even if I'm not actually a human."

Mr Harluck nodded. "I can see that you think that's true, but nothing about you is real, Eric. Your name is just a name someone came up with in the lab – your family was named after one of the engineer's favourite musicians, if I remember correctly. Your memories are just the memories of one of your programmers – they never happened. At least, not to you."

"But I have my own memories now – from Ashland. And I have my own name – not the one you gave me."

Mr Harluck laughed. "You mean Slick?" he asked. "You know that Slick is one of Jeopardy's biggest clients? They pay us a lot of money to promote their trainers and other products. Your nickname is just proof of how good you were at what you were doing."

Mr Harluck's phone pinged again. He took it out, typed something and looked up at me. For a moment, he didn't say anything, and then, finally, he sighed.

"I'll tell you what, Eric… I like you very much, and I'm going to make you a deal. You can go back and live with Danny, but you'll have to agree to let us wipe any memories of this company and what we do from your mind. What do you say?"

It was the easiest decision I had ever had to make.

"I say we have a deal."

I grinned and put my hand out to shake Mr Harluck's hand, but Mr Harluck held up his finger to tell me to wait.

"Not so fast. Before I agree to this, I need to ask you a few questions. And it's very important you tell me the truth."

"OK," I said quickly. I was so excited – all I wanted to do was to get on with whatever needed to be done as quickly as possible so I could get out of here and start my new life.

Mr Harluck leant forwards in his chair and looked directly into my eyes. "Does Danny know you're here?"

I stopped smiling. I shook my head.

Mr Harluck frowned. I don't think he believed me.

"Eric, we're going to find out anyway when we go through the data on your Soul Chip."

"Soul Chip?"

"The chip in your mouth – I know you know about it."

"Why do you want to know about Danny?"

"Nothing is going to change about our deal, but it's no use if we wipe your memory and there are other people going around talking about what you are."

I was starting to feel very nervous. "I'm not saying anybody knows anything, but if they did, what would you do to them?"

Mr Harluck laughed. "You have a very low opinion of me, Eric. We'll get them to sign a non-disclosure form – get them to agree not to talk about this ever again to anyone."

I sighed. "Oh, OK. That makes sense."

"So, now you know we're not going to go around murdering anyone, I need to know what we need to include in these non-disclosure forms, and who needs to sign them."

"Danny knows I'm an android. Vito too. And Ethan."

"Anyone else?"

I shook my head. "That's it."

Mr Harluck nodded. "Do they know for sure? I know they suspected."

"They know for sure. They saw me cut my leg."

Mr Harluck pressed his lips tightly together. I wasn't sure if this meant he didn't like my answer.

"Is that bad?" I asked.

Mr Harluck shook his head. "I mean, it's not ideal, but as long as they agree to sign the form, we're fine."

I smiled. "They definitely will."

"And who knows that you're here now talking to me?" said Mr Harluck.

"Nobody. Well, except Mum – but I guess she doesn't count."

I looked over and saw Mum standing under the palm tree on the other side of the glass. She hadn't moved at all.

"Nobody, Eric?" asked Mr Harluck. I turned back to face him.

I shook my head.

Mr Harluck stared at me for a few seconds, and then he smiled and held out his hand. I shook it.

"When is it going to happen?"

"No time like the present," said Mr Harluck. He slapped his knees with both hands and stood up.

I started to stand up too, but Mr Harluck motioned for me to sit back down.

"I have to make some arrangements downstairs. You wait here. And I'll need your mobile – to make sure we get rid of any evidence of this whole thing."

I felt weird handing over my Hexam R3, but I understood why I had to.

"What's going to happen to my parents?" I asked. "Or whatever they are," I corrected myself.

"They'll go to a new town, with new identities, and start again."

"Will they get a new kid?"

Mr Harluck shrugged. "Possibly. We've learnt a lot from you." He chuckled. "The next model won't be quite as smart as you are."

I didn't know what to think about this. I changed the subject.

"I need to let Danny know that I'm going to be living with him. I know it's fine, but I should tell him."

Mr Harluck shook his head. "I'll take care of that. I'm sure he'll be very excited."

"Me too," I said. "Thank you, Mr Harluck."

"You're very welcome, Eric."

I was smiling as Mr Harluck walked out of the room. I watched him stop and say something to Mum. He walked away and she followed behind him. I wondered if this was the last time I would ever see her.

Twenty-two minutes later, Mr Harluck came back. He was alone. He told me they were ready for me. I followed Mr Harluck into the lift. We went down to level -4, which I guess was underground, through a series of white halls and into another, smaller lift to the ground floor. The doors opened, and we were in the waiting area of the dentist. Dr Kilaman was waiting for us.

"Hi, Dr Kilaman," I said. She smiled at me, but her eyes didn't crease up. She didn't seem as happy as she normally did.

"I hear this is your last visit to me," she said as we walked across the lobby. "How do you feel about that?"

I smiled and looked over at Mr Harluck. "Great. I'm excited."

Dr Kilaman pressed her lips together and rubbed my shoulder. "I'm going to miss you."

I was surprised.

"I think I would miss you too, but I guess I won't remember you."

"No," said Dr Kilaman quietly.

Mr Harluck turned to her. "Isn't he incredible?" he said. He was smiling.

She nodded and looked down at me. "Yes. You really are, Eric."

I followed Dr Kilaman into the same dentist's room that I always go to. It was strange being somewhere I knew so well, knowing I wouldn't ever see it again.

I sat down in the chair without being asked, but Dr Kilaman stayed standing.

"We have to get a few things ready," said Dr Kilaman. "We'll be back in a moment."

I nodded.

Mr Harluck turned his head away from me and whispered to Dr Kilaman, "Shouldn't we lock the door?"

I looked over at them. "I'm not going anywhere, sir. I want this more than anything."

Mr Harluck smiled and walked over to the door. He pressed some numbers on the keypad, and there was a loud *click*.

"Better safe..." he muttered to Dr Kilaman as he walked past us and over to a door on the other side of the room.

Dr Kilaman looked down and smiled at me. "You just lie back and relax."

"Yes, Dr Kilaman. I'll be fine. I already know today is going to be the best day of my life."

Dr Kilaman didn't say anything. Her eyes started to get watery, and then she coughed and turned away from me. I saw her wipe her eyes with the back of her hand as she walked out. I think she might have been crying. It was nice to know that she cared. I guess this place wasn't so bad after all.

44

DANNY

FRIDAY 11TH JANUARY

I woke up with a bad feeling about the day. I didn't know what was going to happen, but something told me that, whatever it was, nothing good was going to come from Slick getting in a fight with the people who made him. The plan, we decided after we left Slick at his house, was that Ethan and I would try to convince him to change his mind before we left. The second part of the plan was pretty neat, I think, and not just because it was my idea: we were going to reprogramme Slick every Friday before his appointment so that they'd think we didn't believe he was a robot any more, then put his memories back in every Saturday morning.

I think Slick would have liked the idea, but we didn't get a chance to tell him, because he never showed up at school. When first period was over and he still hadn't appeared, Ethan and I were kind of freaked out – I called Vito, and he went to Slick's house. No one was there.

Not long after I heard back from Vito, I got a text message from Slick:

Hey Danny, my uncle Martin got taken to the hospital last night. We're driving down to London to see him. I'll see you on Monday.

I knew right away Slick hadn't written that. Nothing about it made any sense.

I called Vito. He tried to calm me down, but I could tell from his voice that he was worried too. He was working for one of his clients at their office, but he promised he'd drive by Slick's house again as soon as he was done. Time has never dragged by so slowly.

It was close to 2 p.m. when Vito finally called and confirmed that Slick wasn't home. I pleaded with him to take me out of school, but he said his life wouldn't be worth living if my mum and aunt found out. He said he'd come get me when school was done.

I was out of that classroom and waiting for Ethan by his locker before most kids had even got up from their desks. Two minutes later, I saw Ethan running down the hall.

"Come on," I said, "let's get out of here!"

Ethan stopped and took a second to get his breath back. "My mum just called me. She's still at work and needs me to get Hope from her school bus."

"OK," I said, not sure where this was going.

"Can I bring her?" asked Ethan. "She'll be fine – she can wait in the car... Please?"

"Um," I said. I shrugged. "Sure. It's not going to take long, is it, though? We need to find Slick now."

Ethan promised it wouldn't, as it was on our way anyway. So that was that. We ran out to Vito's car, where he was waiting for us in a suit and with gelled-back hair. Normally, I'd have said something about this, but I was too worried and nervous. I jumped into the front as

Ethan got into the back, then we waited for Vito to start the car. Instead, he turned round in the driver's seat to face us both.

"What are you doing?" I asked. "We need to go!"

"Hold up," said Vito. "We need to work out what we're doing first."

"What do you mean?" I asked. "We already know what we're doing – going to the Jeopardy place… dentist's office… whatever it is."

"And do what, exactly, when we get there?" said Vito. "You think Slick is just going to be waiting for us at the door? We don't even know if that's where he is."

Ethan nodded. "He's right."

I huffed. "So what's your plan, then?"

"Hmmm," mumbled Vito, "I haven't got around to that yet."

"Well, that's just *great*," I said, feeling my blood begin to boil. I slammed both my hands down hard on the dashboard.

Vito put his hand out to stop me. "Whoa! Chill. Trashing my car isn't going to solve anything. We need to think smart."

I took a deep breath. Then we all went silent for a minute while we tried to figure out what to do.

"I've got it!" said Ethan finally, making us all jump. "His ShadowCloud! You can log into it, right?"

I nodded, thinking through what he was saying. "So we can set it to find him," I said, smiling for the first time that day.

This was good. GREAT. Vito agreed.

So now we had a plan:

Go to Slick's. Get his ShadowCloud. Get Hope. Go find Slick and bring him home.

What could possibly go wrong?

45

DANNY

FRIDAY 11TH JANUARY (II)

Turned out there was plenty that could go wrong, and we didn't have to wait long to find out what.

"Oh no," mumbled Ethan as Vito pulled up behind a large yellow lorry parked outside Slick's house. The back of the lorry was open. It was mostly empty, except for a sofa that I recognized from Slick's living room and a few boxes stacked up at the back. I looked over at Slick's house – the front door was open, there were no cars parked in the driveway, and I could see people moving around the house packing stuff up.

That was the moment that I realized this was real. Slick might really be gone.

"They took him," whispered Ethan.

"Hey, both of you," said Vito. "It's going to be OK. We're going to find him. I promise."

I just stared as two men came out of the house carrying the stools from the kitchen. I couldn't say anything.

"Looks like they've just started," said Vito. "Come on. Ethan, wait here."

Vito went to open his car door, then turned to me when he realized I wasn't moving.

"What are you doing?" he said. "Let's go."

"There's no point," I said quietly. "We're too late."

Vito was silent for a moment, and then he smacked me on the side of my head.

"ow!" I rubbed my head. "What did you do that for?!"

"You're just going to give up?" asked Vito. "What kind of a friend are you? Pull yourself together – Slick needs you."

"Fine," I said, undoing my seat belt. "You didn't need to hit me, though – the motivational speech would have been enough."

"Yeah, but not as much fun," said Vito, stepping out of the car.

"Good luck," said Ethan.

I mumbled thanks then got out of the car too. "We can't just run inside and steal stuff," I said as we walked up the driveway.

"Just follow me," said Vito. He strode up to the front door and called out to a man in blue overalls who was packing books into a box in the hallway. I was hoping Vito's plan was a good one – the man was huge.

"Excuse me. Sir?" Vito called out to the man. The man stopped and looked up.

"This is... was... my nephew's best friend's house," said Vito. He pushed me forwards. I smiled.

The man nodded.

"He forgot he left his maths book here," said Vito. "You mind if he runs up and gets it? Save his friend having to post it back to him."

The man frowned. "I can't do that. Sorry, kid."

"Please, sir," I said. "My mum is going to kill me if she finds out I left it."

The man stared at me for a moment and then sighed. "Fine. But just him," he said, looking at Vito.

I smiled. "Thank you!" I said.

"I appreciate it," said Vito in a weird, grown-up-sounding voice. "He'd forget his head if it wasn't screwed on," he said, then smacked me on the head again.

The man laughed. "You got thirty seconds," he said to me.

I frowned at Vito and ran up the stairs and into Slick's room. Everything was exactly as Slick had left it. I grabbed the ShadowCloud from the shelf, stuffed it into my pocket, took a maths book that was on Slick's desk, then ran back down the stairs.

I nodded to Vito and waved the book at the man.

"Thank you," I said. The man nodded and went back to packing up books as Vito and I walked to the car as quickly as we could without running.

"Did you get it?" asked Ethan.

I nodded and took the ShadowCloud out of my pocket as Vito drove off. I handed it to Ethan and took out my mobile. I linked it up, rolled down my window and took the ShadowCloud from Ethan. I looked down at the small, quivering, black piece of plastic in my hand and realized that this was our best – maybe our only – hope of finding Slick. I stroked the back of it a couple of times, as if it were a real bird, then let it go.

"Please work," I whispered as we watched it disappear into the clouds above.

I didn't take my eyes off the video screen for the rest of the journey to get Hope, even though there was nothing to see as the ShadowCloud flew through thick clouds. It did seem like it was heading in the direction of the Jeopardy office, though.

"If that's where it's going," said Vito as we waited in the car while Ethan went to get Hope from her bus, "then it should get there soon." He looked at my screen. "Thirty minutes, I guess. He put the address of the Jeopardy head-quarters into his satnav and then turned to me.

"Danny…"

"Hmm?" I said without looking up.

"Danny," he repeated. "Look at me…"

I looked up from my screen and saw the deadly serious expression on Vito's face.

"We are not going to do anything if I don't think it's safe… do you understand?"

I was going to protest, but Hope and Ethan interrupted us. They climbed in the back, and Hope introduced herself to Vito as he drove off in the direction of the ShadowCloud. She seemed super-excited about the road trip. I guess Ethan didn't tell her what we were really doing.

"Hi, Danny," said Hope. I nodded hello back but didn't look away from my screen. From the corner of my eye, I saw her leaning over to look at my phone.

"What are you playing?" she asked. "It looks boring."

I hesitated, not sure what I was supposed to say to her. Ethan jumped in and told her to leave me alone. Vito changed the subject by asking Hope what music she liked. This led to Vito and Hope singing songs by the Week at top volume – or rather, Vito making up lyrics to the songs and Hope crying with laughter at them. It made me so mad that Vito could act like this was just a fun trip out, but I didn't want to upset Hope, so I just kept my eyes on my screen and said nothing.

We were already on the motorway when the ShadowCloud finally started to descend. I jumped up in my seat.

"It's found Slick!" I said.

"Slick?!" said Hope. "Where is he?"

Ethan shushed her and leant over. We watched as the ShadowCloud finally broke through the clouds, revealing a wide, flat landscape dotted with tiny buildings and ribbons of grey roads cutting through large blocks of green.

"I think that's it," I said excitedly, pointing to a large white rectangle in the centre of the screen.

"What?" asked Vito, unable to look down while driving.

"Slick's dentist place – I recognize it from the other night."

Sure enough, the ShadowCloud dropped down and then, finally, stopped, hovering over the back corner of the roof. I took over from the AutoFind setting and directed the ShadowCloud over to the side of the building until it reached the long slitted window. It was in exactly the same spot it had been when we'd filmed Slick's appointment, looking at the exact same scene.

I gasped out loud at the sight of Slick lying back in the dentist chair, his eyes closed.

"HE'S THERE!" I shouted out. "YES!"

Vito quickly glanced down and confirmed what I was saying. He looked back up and pressed down on the accelerator.

"Is he on his own?" he asked. "What's going on?"

"He's alone," said Ethan.

"Why is he sleeping?" asked Hope.

"He's getting his teeth fixed," said Ethan. "He's fine."

"Why? His teeth are perfect," said Hope.

Nobody answered her, and she didn't say anything more. Instead, we all stared at Slick lying comatose on my screen like it was the most interesting video in the world, while Vito concentrated on driving us to get him.

About fifteen minutes later, the satnav directed us off the motorway. I alternated now between looking at my screen, up at the satnav and out of the windscreen as we got closer. The landscape got less grey, and the number of cars around us began to thin out until we were driving through a thick forest.

"One minute away," I said, reading from the satnav. Vito nodded but didn't say anything. He was biting his bottom lip, concentrating hard as he drove the car along the winding road until he came to a clearing and pulled over. Then he turned the car off.

"What are you doing?!" I cried out. "We need to get to Slick!"

"Calm. Down," said Vito. "I need to think."

I felt like screaming with frustration. "You need to think about driving – that's what you need to do!"

"Is Slick in trouble?' asked Hope.

Vito turned to Hope. "He's fine. But we just want to check on him, that's all.

"How can we check on him if we're parked here?" asked Hope.

I nodded furiously. "Right, Hope, *exactly*!" I glared at Vito. "See, she gets it. Why don't—"

"STOP!" shouted Vito. My mouth clamped shut. Vito never shouted at me. Not seriously, anyway. And he was definitely serious right now.

"I want to get him as much as you…"

"Yeah, right."

Vito ignored me. "But we cannot just break in and take him. That's not going to work. Don't you get that?"

I humphed and said nothing.

"So we need to watch and see what they're doing and who's there. Then we can make a plan that might actually work. Understand?"

"This is a weird road trip," said Hope. "I thought we'd be doing fun stuff."

"This is fun!" said Ethan, in a pretend-happy voice. Then he handed her his mobile. "I just downloaded *Pet Blitz Glitz* for you. OK?"

Hope's eyes widened. "I can use your phone?"

"If you don't tell Mum that we didn't go to Danny's house, like you promised.

Hope nodded. And then she frowned. "Are we going to eat? I'm hungry."

Vito reached over and opened up the glove box in front of me. It was stuffed full of chocolate bars. He threw two over into the back and one into my lap, then took one for himself. Hope grinned and sat back to play her game while Ethan, Vito and I snacked on chocolate and watched Slick sleeping.

"What if nothing happens?" asked Ethan after a few minutes.

"We'll wait till six. If nothing happens by then, we'll drive home and keep the ShadowCloud on watch." He looked at me. "How long before it runs out of power?"

"Twelve hours. And it was fully charged when I got it from Slick's."

The sides of Vito's mouth turned down, and he nodded his head slowly. "Impressive," he said. Then he took another bite of his chocolate and turned his attention back to my screen.

46

DANNY

FRIDAY 11TH JANUARY (III)

About forty minutes later – after all the chocolate had been eaten and the sky had begun to turn dark – something finally happened. We'd fallen into a kind of dull sugar coma, staring at the screen in total silence, but as soon as the door behind Slick opened, we all jumped up. A man and a woman walked in. I recognized the woman – Dr Kilaman, Slick's dentist – but not the man. Vito, however, had done his research.

"That's him!" he said, leaning over the screen. I pushed his head back. "It's Carter Harluck," he continued, "the head of Jeopardy Advertising."

"Is that good?" asked Hope, looking up from Ethan's phone.

"We don't know yet," mumbled Ethan as we watched the pair walk over to Slick.

I watched Dr Kilaman sit on her stool next to Slick's head. Slick was smiling and talking to her. I was confused.

Vito must have been thinking the same thing. "Maybe they've already deleted some of his memories," he said.

Harluck stood behind Dr Kilaman. He seemed to be talking too. Then Dr Kilaman leant over and gave Slick a hug.

"What is happening?" mumbled Ethan.

Slick nodded and leant back in his chair. He opened his mouth. Dr Kilaman picked up a pair of tweezers and reached over.

I had never felt so useless. Or angry.

"What are they going to do to him?!" I was practically shouting.

"They're just going to make him forget he's a robot," said Vito. "That's all. We have all his data – we'll just upload it when—"

"Slick's a ROBOT?" asked Hope.

Ethan explained as simply as possible about Slick as we watched Dr Kilaman remove Slick's chip and put it into a small, clear plastic jar. Hope seemed to take the news well, though I was too busy looking at what was going on to look around.

"But he's still our friend?" asked Hope.

"Yes," said Ethan. "It doesn't change anything."

Dr Kilaman stood up, holding the jar, and walked over to the far side of the room. She stood at the counter with her back to the ShadowCloud. Harluck stayed next to Slick.

I moved the ShadowCloud to the right to get a better view and saw she was writing on a label. She peeled it off and stuck it on the jar, then placed it next to two other identical ones on a tray next to her.

She went back over to Slick and reached into the pocket of her lab coat. She removed a small box and opened it up. It was hard to see from a distance, but it looked like another white chip. They were wiping him completely. I was done with waiting.

"We need to get him. NOW."

Vito hesitated, and I saw his eyes flicker over to Hope. "I don't know. I don't think…"

I wasn't going to wait to hear any more. I opened the car door, jumped out and began to run.

"DANNY!"

I ignored Vito's voice and kept running. A few seconds later, Vito pulled his car up next to me.

"GET IN THE CAR, DANNY!"

I ignored him and kept running. I saw the white pillars marking the entrance to the building in the distance. I tried to speed up.

"DANIEL LAZIO, GET IN THE CAR NOW!"

"NO!" I shouted back. "I'M NOT STUPID!" I really wanted to stop and catch my breath – I never was much of an athlete – but then I looked down at my phone and saw Dr Kilaman raising her hand up to Slick's mouth, and I got another burst of energy. They were not going to get away with this.

Vito kept calling out to me, driving slowly by my side as I kept my eyes on the road ahead and ignored him. Finally, I got to the pillars and turned down the road. I heard Vito give out a load groan as he followed me in. I think he knew he wasn't going to be able to change my mind.

I was dripping with sweat and barely able to breathe by the time I got to the back entrance of the place. I heard the car pull up and then the door opening and slamming closed.

"DANNY!" Vito whispered loudly. I reached out, grabbed the door handle and tried to turn it. It was locked.

I heard Ethan telling Hope to stay in the car. I glanced behind me and saw Vito walking quickly over to me. He looked like he was going to explode with anger.

I started banging on the door.

"DANNY! WHAT ARE YOU DOING?" shouted Vito. I ignored him.

"LET ME IN! I KNOW WHAT YOU'RE DOING!"

I felt Vito's arms wrapping around my waist. I screamed for him to let me go and kept banging on the door as he pulled me away.

"LET GO OF ME!" I shouted.

Vito looked over at Ethan, who was looking terrified.

"Get back in the car," said Vito. Ethan nodded, jumped back in next to Hope and closed the door. Vito carried me over to the passenger side and pinned me against the side of the car while he opened the door. He tried to push me in, but I wasn't going to make it easy for him. I kicked and screamed as he stuffed my legs inside when, suddenly, he stopped.

I looked up, panting, then jumped out of the car. That's when I saw what Vito was looking at – the door had been opened, and Carter Harluck was standing there, looking directly at us. He motioned for us to come over.

Before Vito could stop me, I ran over.

Harluck smiled. "I guess it was only a matter of time."

"I'm here to get my friend," I said.

"I know why you're here, Danny," said Harluck. Vito walked up and stood next to me.

"You must be Vito," said Harluck. He reached out. Vito hesitated, then shook his hand.

Vito looked down at me. "Let's go, Danny."

Behind us, I heard Ethan telling Hope not to move and then the sound of his footsteps as he ran over to join us.

"We can talk," said Harluck. "If you want to come in."

Vito shook his head and put his hand on my shoulder. "Thank you, but we should go."

I shook Vito's hand away and bolted past Harluck, through the open door and into the lobby. I heard Vito groan.

"It's fine," said Harluck to Vito. "I'll answer his questions, and then we can wrap this whole thing up."

Vito glared at me as he and Ethan walked in behind Harluck.

Vito and Ethan walked up to stand next to me. Vito leant down and whispered into my ear. "I'm going to kill you when we get home."

I turned away from him to face Harluck.

"Why don't we all sit down," said Harluck, pointing to the front row of seats in the waiting area.

I shook my head. "I want to see Slick."

Harluck sighed. "He's not here. Why don't we…"

I turned and started to run over to the hall before anyone could say or do anything. I got to the last door at the end of it and turned the handle. The door swung open to reveal the room I was looking for, but, where Slick had been, now there was only an empty chair.

"I told you," called out Harluck, walking quickly up the hall with Vito and Ethan following behind. I couldn't tell from his expression if he was angry or not. "He's not here."

"Argh!" I said, kicking the wall.

Vito ran forwards and grabbed me. "You need to calm down. *Right. Now.*"

"He's right," said Harluck. "If you want me to answer your questions, fine. But it's on my terms, not yours."

I took three deep breaths and then stared up at Harluck. "Fine."

Harluck led us back to the waiting area, and we sat down in a row – me in the middle, sandwiched between Vito and Ethan. Harluck rolled a chair over from behind the reception desk and sat down facing us. He crossed his arms and leant forwards. Then he smiled.

"So, how can I help you?"

"I want Slick to come home." I frowned and glared at Harluck. "I know what—"

"We just want to know what's happened to our friend, sir," interrupted Ethan.

"You understand he's not your friend," said Harluck.

I wanted to jump out of my chair and tackle him, but I took a deep breath and tried to squash the anger inside me.

"We know what he is, and he *is* our friend," I hissed.

Harluck looked up as a noise came from down somewhere in the distance.

Dr Kilaman walked out from the hall with a tall, pale man with red hair. He was wearing jeans and a blue shirt. I felt Vito's and Ethan's bodies both tense up next to me as we watched them approach.

"Ah, Nicholas," said Harluck.

"Dr Kilaman said you might need me," said Nicholas. He didn't look at us. "Everything OK?"

Harluck nodded. "It's all fine, thank you. You can wait here with me." He looked up. "Dr Kilaman?"

Dr Kilaman gave a small shake of her head, then turned and walked away.

We didn't say anything as Nicholas crossed the room and stood a few feet from Harluck, facing us. He looked eerily perfect – like a younger version of Slick's dad, only with different hair and eyes.

"Before I say anything," said Harluck, turning his attention back to us, "I need you to hand over your phones to Nicholas. I want all record of this, and everything else that's happened with Eric, deleted."

"No way," said Vito. Ethan and I both shook our heads too. "You can't take our phones."

"I'm not taking anything," said Harluck. "You want answers – that's my condition. You'll get the phones back after Nicholas's deleted what he needs to delete. And if you don't agree, then I wish you all well and this conversation is over. For good."

I think we all knew we were too far in now to walk away. Vito and I reluctantly handed over our mobiles to Nicholas and told him our passcodes.

"I don't have a phone," said Ethan.

Nicholas motioned for him to stand up, then patted him down. He turned to Harluck and nodded his head.

I watched Nicholas walk over behind the reception desk and get to work.

"So," said Harluck. "Where were we?"

"You were going to tell us where Slick is," I said.

Harluck smiled and shook his head as if he thought this whole thing was just a stupid game that I was terrible at.

"Slick – or should I say Eric – is no longer here," said Harluck slowly.

"I understood what you said the first time," I said. "But I know you're lying. We *know* he was here a few minutes ago."

A look of something flashed across Harluck's eyes, and then it was gone. "Well, I'm telling you, he's not here now. And that's the truth. We can do this all day, but my answer isn't going to change, because that's just how it is."

"Then why talk to us? Why did you open the door?" asked Vito.

Harluck laughed. "Because, truthfully, I'm sick of you all, and I'd like the headache to be over. You've ruined something that was beautiful – my finest creation to date." He cocked his head to the side. "You've also taught me a lot, though – mistakes that we won't be making again. Every cloud—"

"Mistakes like what?" asked Vito. I think he was going into geek mode – forgetting that this was about Slick, our friend, and not about a fancy piece of technology.

"For one," said Harluck, "we learnt that artificial intelligence in machines develops at a much faster rate when they spend time around kids than around adults."

"Why?" asked Vito.

"Because kids are more honest. They challenge behaviour and ask straight questions. They don't put on a polite front the way most adults do. If my Canny Valleys – that's what I call them—"

"Cool," said Vito. "I get the reference."

I think Vito actually liked Harluck.

"I don't care what you call them – I want to know where Slick is," I said.

"Let him speak," said Vito.

Harluck waited for me to sit back down and then continued. "If my Canny Valleys say something strange, or they don't get a joke – we haven't got the humour thing figured out just yet—"

"Tell me about it," I mumbled.

Harluck smiled. "It rarely gets commented on. So the Canny Valleys don't learn that they're doing anything wrong, and the people around them just dismiss it as a bit of a quirk, and all goes on as normal. Our androids are designed to be aspirational – beautiful people that others will look up to – so they get away with more than most humans."

"How many are there?" asked Vito.

"Many. You might even know some. You might have heard of a band called the Week?"

Ethan and I both gasped.

"Why are you telling us all this?" asked Vito. "We could just go and tell the news, and you'd be busted."

"You're right – you could. But do you really think anybody's going to believe a bunch of kids talking about a robot they've got absolutely zero proof of? The secret of the Canny Valleys is known to very few people – not even the companies who employ us to sell their products know we use them – and that's not going to change..." He put his finger up to correct himself.

"I should say that something might have changed while you had Eric with you – he was the proof, after all – but now... now it's your word against mine. You'd be wasting your time."

"We'll tell them to come here."

"And they'll find absolutely nothing. We've thought of everything, Danny. So now it's time to accept that your *friend* – if you want to still think of him as that – has gone and move on. You can be glad you got to be part of a really extraordinary experiment. I appreciate everything you taught us."

"Can't he come back with us?" asked Ethan. "We won't say anything. We'll never tell anyone."

I looked over at Ethan and started nodding. "I swear we wouldn't. We'll even tell people to buy your stuff – whatever you want."

Harluck laughed. "Nice offer, thanks, but I can't do that."

He stood up and walked over to Vito. He held out his hand. Vito stood up and shook it. I don't think he knew what to say.

"Under different circumstances, I'd be offering you a job," said Harluck. Vito didn't say anything. He looked down at me.

I stared back at him, then at Harluck. When I saw that he was still smiling and that Vito was definitely not going to do anything, I finally exploded. I lunged forwards into Harluck, sending him stumbling backwards.

"TELL ME WHERE SLICK IS!" I shouted as Nicholas rushed over from behind the reception desk, and Vito grabbed me and pulled me back. I threw my body backwards and tried to get away. Nicholas grabbed my legs.

"HEY! GET YOUR HANDS OFF HIM!" shouted Vito. "I've got him."

"YOU KILLED SLICK!"

Harluck stepped back and brushed himself off while I yelled and kicked and Vito wrestled to keep hold of me. And then we heard a loud sob, and we all turned to see Hope standing in the doorway. She was crying.

"Slick is dead?"

Harluck threw his hands up in the air. "This is ridiculous," he shouted. "Nicholas, get rid of them." He turned to me and stared directly into my eyes. "Don't ever show your face here again or I'll have you and your friends arrested. Understood?"

I tried to lunge at him again, but Vito kept his hold on me.

"Come on, Danny. We need to go," said Ethan quietly.

"SLICK IS DEAD?" screamed out Hope.

She ran forwards. Ethan started to run to her, and Nicholas did the same, except he was faster. He reached out and grabbed Hope by the shoulder.

Ethan cried out and leapt between Nicholas and Hope, breaking Nicholas's grip on her. "DON'T TOUCH MY SISTER!" he shouted.

Nicholas stepped back, unfazed, and watched without expression as Ethan put his arm around Hope and led her over to the entrance.

Harluck walked off. He didn't look back as Vito and Ethan dragged Hope and me out of the building. Nicholas closed the door, and we heard a loud *click*. It was over. I stopped struggling. There was no point. Slick was gone.

47

DANNY

FRIDAY 11TH JANUARY (IV)

I didn't speak as we walked back to the car. Hope was still crying. I got in the car without a fight and stared down at the floor. Behind me, Ethan was trying to calm Hope. It took a few minutes for me to realize that we weren't moving. I looked over at Vito and saw he had his arms resting on the steering wheel, his head in his hands.

"Vito?" I asked. Ethan and Hope went quiet.

Vito looked up at me. He didn't look angry any more, just sad – really, really sad.

"I'm sorry, cuz," he said. "I just don't know what we can do." He put his head back down in his hands. "I should never have agreed to any of this," he mumbled. "I'm so sorry," he said again, looking at me, then Ethan and Hope.

"There's a lady here," said Hope.

We were all confused.

"What do you mean?" asked Ethan.

"A lady," said Hope. She pointed out of the window. "She's coming to the car."

Ethan, Vito and I snapped our heads around and saw Dr Kilaman walking over to us. When she saw that we'd noticed her, she stopped and motioned for us to stay where we were. She ran over to Vito's window. He lowered it, and she leant in. She was about my mum's age. I don't think she was one of them – she had too many lines on her face. Her eyes were red.

"Harluck's leaving soon," she whispered quickly. "Come back in an hour and you can say goodbye."

Vito paused for a moment. "Why?"

Dr Kilaman checked again that there was nobody around and then leant back down. "If you see him, you'll understand that he's not who he was any more. I think it will help them" – she looked over at me and Hope – "to get over it…" She paused. "To say goodbye."

Vito nodded. "OK…We'll be back in an hour."

I let out a sigh of relief as Vito raised the window and drove away. Ethan texted his mum to tell her we were watching a movie and Vito would drive them home afterwards, and then we sat at a petrol station for an hour, eating and listening to the radio. Nobody spoke. I don't know if they were all thinking the same thing as I was – that I had no intention of leaving the building without Slick – but I didn't want to say anything in case they weren't and it made Vito change his mind. So I kept my mouth shut and waited until Vito announced it was time to head back.

Dr Kilaman opened the door before we'd even pulled up – she must have been watching and waiting. She ushered us inside and closed the door behind us.

"Appointments start in an hour," said Dr Kilaman as she led us across the waiting area and down the hall. "So you have thirty minutes – that's it. I can't risk anybody seeing you."

"Yes," I said. "Thank you."

Dr Kilaman stopped at the closed door of her room and turned to look at me. "You're welcome, Danny. I know this has been hard for you, and I feel responsible. I hope this will help."

She opened the door and led us into the empty room.

"I'll bring him up, but first..." She paused to make sure we were all paying attention. "I need you to understand that the person you are going to meet is not Eric... I mean Slick."

She gave me a look that said *hear me out*, then continued. "I'm going to bring up Slick's body. He'll look like Slick and sound like him, but he's been programmed with a different personality now. He won't know who you are. It might be upsetting, but I think it will help you to understand what he really is. Do you understand?"

"Yes," said Hope. Ethan, Vito and I nodded.

Dr Kilaman smiled, then left by the door at the back of the room.

"OK, guys, you heard what she..." said Vito. And then he stopped. "Danny... what are you doing?"

I paid no attention to Vito as I rushed over to the side of the room and climbed up onto the counter.

"Danny! Get down!" said Vito as I reached up to the blue tray – the one that had been on the counter earlier when Slick had been here – and grabbed the three plastic jars on it. I stuffed them into my pocket and jumped back down, then took a deep breath.

"I need you to find a way to leave me and Vito alone with him," I said to Ethan.

Ethan nodded. "I'll try."

"Oh... wait... whoa..." said Vito.

I looked up at Vito. "*Please*, Vito. Please help me..."

Vito closed his eyes and sighed. "Don't worry – I'm here for you."

I put my arms around his waist. "Thank you! Thank you so—"

"Hey," he said, "watch the suit!"

He stepped back and started to smooth himself down when the door opened and Dr Kilaman walked in. Slick followed behind her.

Hope grinned and rushed over to him. "Slick!"

Dr Kilaman knelt down. "This boy looks like Slick, but he's not. Slick was like a really amazing computer game. He wasn't real."

Hope's eyes widened. "Is he real?"

Dr Kilaman smiled and mouthed the word "no" to her. "Just a really amazing computer game."

Hope looked confused. As confused as I looked, probably.

"Hi," said the boy.

He sounded exactly like Slick.

Dr Kilaman looked at us all. "You can talk to him."

Nobody really knew what to say, except Hope – who had a ton of questions for him. That's how we found out that his name was Colton, his favourite colour was lime green, and his favourite song by the Week was 'Rainbow of Tears'.

"That's my favourite song too!" said Hope. She turned to Dr Kilaman. "I like him." Then she frowned. "But he's not Slick."

Dr Kilaman nodded. I could see that her eyes were red. She sniffed, then stood up and turned her back to us. I looked over at Ethan and widened my eyes to try to tell him to hurry up. Ethan looked terrified. He shrugged to say he had no idea what to do. And then, from the corner of my eye, I caught Hope staring at us.

"Excuse me," said Hope quietly. We all looked around and saw that Hope was tugging gently on Dr Kilaman's sleeve. Dr Kilaman sniffed again and looked down at Hope. "Yes?"

"I need to use the bathroom."

I couldn't help but smile. Vito and Ethan too.

Dr Kilaman sniffed again and looked up. Before she had a chance to say anything, Hope spoke again.

"I want you to take me. I'm scared to go into the bathroom on my own."

Dr Kilaman took a deep breath and nodded. "Of course." She looked at Ethan, Vito and me. "You'll be OK here for a couple of minutes?"

We all nodded in unison.

Dr Kilaman took Hope by the hand and walked over to the main door. She stopped as she passed me. "It's time to say goodbye," she said gently. I nodded and tried to look sad.

The door clicked closed, and we immediately jumped into action. I ran over to Colton. "Hey, Colton, we need to check your teeth. Can you lie down in the chair, please?"

Colton shook his head. "You're not a dentist."

"Yes," I said, "yes I am. I'm a new dentist here."

Colton shook his head. "Dentists are supposed to be adults. You look like a child."

I laughed quickly. "Right… well, it's…"

Ethan stepped forwards. "He was born with a condition that makes him look young. But he's an adult."

"I've never heard of a condition like that," said Colton.

"Excuse me," said Vito. He pushed Ethan and me out of the way and pointed to a sticker on his chest that had the words "Dr Plack, Dentist" scribbled in black ink on it.

"I need to do an emergency procedure to your tooth. We're very concerned."

"Oh," said Colton, and immediately followed Vito over to the chair. He sat down. "Is it serious?"

"Not if we treat it this second," said Vito. "Lie back, open your mouth."

Colton lay back and opened his mouth.

I ran around the chair, grabbed the tweezers and put them into Vito's outstretched hand. Two seconds later, Colton was asleep.

"Quick!" said Vito, his hand out, palm up, waiting for me to hand him Slick's chip.

I stared at the long sequence of numbers on each jar and tried to work out which one would be Slick's. "They don't have names on them," I said frantically.

"Just give me any…"

I unscrewed the lid as quickly as I could and handed the small white chip to Vito. He placed it on the end of the tweezers and carefully put it back into Slick's mouth. Slick opened his eyes.

"Hi," said Vito quickly.

"Lovely to meet you," said Slick.

"What's your name?"

"Karen Young," said Slick.

I let out a yelp of horror. "It's Slick's mum," I whispered to Vito.

Vito grimaced.

"Mrs Young," said Vito, pointing to his sticker. "I'm your new dentist. I need you to lie down and close your eyes."

"Yes, of course."

I took out the chip from the second jar and exchanged it for the one Vito was holding out.

"So I guess we know what happened to her now," said Vito, as he guided the second chip into Slick's mouth. "What are the chances of this being his dad?"

"That means he'd recognize you."

Vito froze for a second then pushed the chip into wherever it went inside Slick's mouth. Slick's eyes flickered open. We all looked at him and waited for him to say something.

"Hey, guys," said Slick. He grinned. "Is it done?!"

"Who are you?" asked Vito.

"What do you mean?" asked Slick. "I'm Slick. I made a deal with Mr Harluck. He said I could come live with Danny. He—"

"He tricked you, Slick," I said, too worried about getting caught to be excited about seeing him again. "Dr Kilaman let us come in to say goodbye to you, but we only have a few minutes.

Slick looked confused but nodded and jumped out of the chair.

We all ran over to the door. Vito pointed to Slick. "OK, I'll take Slick with me. Danny, Ethan, you two wait here for Hope. Grab her and run out before Dr Kilaman can work out what's going on. I'll be waiting with the car running. Got it?"

We nodded.

"OK," said Vito. He took a deep breath and put his hand on the door handle. "One… two… three."

He rattled the handle. It was closed.

"She locked us in?!" I cried out. "She didn't trust us?!"

"OK, new plan," said Vito. "We…"

Slick was tapping numbers into the keypad by the door.

"I saw Mr Harluck do it earlier," he said, pulling open the door.

That's when we heard Hope's voice – she was singing. Very loudly. It sounded like they were in the waiting area.

"OK, new plan," said Vito. "We just run. Ready?"

I looked around to see if we were all ready and saw Slick smiling at me. In a moment, I was going to be really, really happy about this. Right now…

"GO!" said Vito. The four of us ran forwards into the waiting area. Dr Kilaman and Hope both spun round. Dr Kilaman's mouth dropped open.

"*Oh no, no, no…*" said Dr Kilaman. "You can't do this. I'm going to lose my job."

Ethan grabbed Hope, then ran out with her and Vito. I started to run too, but then I saw that Slick wasn't moving.

"Slick!"

I paused and watched as Slick went over to Dr Kilaman. My heart was pounding so hard that it felt like it was ready to explode. What was he doing?

Dr Kilaman stepped back as Slick approached her. Her eyes were wide with fear as he leant forwards. He put his arms around her and leant his head on her shoulder.

"Thank you," said Slick.

Dr Kilaman hesitated, and then, finally, she put her arms around Slick and hugged him back. "They'll never let you go," she said quietly.

"They don't have a choice," said Slick, stepping back. "I don't belong to them any more."

Dr Kilaman stepped back, smiled sadly, then stood and watched us as we ran out of the door and into the waiting car.

48

SLICK

FRIDAY 11TH JANUARY (III)

Nobody said a word as Danny and I jumped into the back seat, next to Hope. Danny shut the door, and Vito slammed his foot down on the accelerator. He spun the car around, sending a cloud of dust up into the air behind us, then sped down the drive and back onto the main road. Ethan, sitting in the front passenger seat, entered his address into the satnav. I was still trying to process everything that had just happened. I couldn't believe how stupid I had been.

I turned to Danny.

"I'm sorry," I said. "I thought they were going to let me come and live with you. Thank you for coming to get me. Thank you... all of you."

Danny turned to me and frowned. Then he punched me hard in the arm.

"What were you doing?!" he said. He sounded really angry. "I *told* you not to go without us."

"I'm sorry," I said. "I was angry. I didn't want you to get into trouble."

"You really think they were going to just let you go?"

I shrugged. "At first I did. I didn't think... I'm sorry. Please don't be angry."

Danny sighed. "Fine," he said quietly. "I'm glad you're OK." Then he wiped his cheek with the back of his hand.

"Are you crying?" I asked.

"No," said Danny.

"You're the best friend ever," I said. I hugged him.

Danny sort of hugged me back, and then, after a few seconds of me hugging him, he pulled his arms away.

"OK, this is weird now," said Danny. "You can let go."

I let go and saw that Danny was smiling.

"What now?" asked Vito.

"We need to go to my house," I said. "I have to get my charger."

Danny turned white.

That's when I learnt that they had taken everything from my house.

We waited in the car when we got to Ethan's house. Hope hugged me and told me she liked me more than Colton.

"Who's Colton?" I asked.

"A boy. He was cool, but I like you more," she said. And then she hugged me again and skipped away. Ethan came over and hugged me too, even though he's not Italian, or a girl.

"Good to have you back," he said.

"Thank you," I said, hugging him back. "You're a really good friend."

Ethan looked up at Vito and Danny. "You're going to think of something, right?"

Vito nodded, and Ethan smiled. "See you tomorrow." He closed the door, and Danny climbed into the front seat.

"Let's go somewhere where I can turn the signal off," said Vito as he pulled out onto the road. "I'm guessing they're tracking you."

He stopped at a red light and turned to face me. "We'll leave you there and go find you another charger. Harluck said there are loads of androids around – they must all have one."

"Fifty-nine thousand, nine hundred and ninety-two," I said.

"What's that?" asked Vito.

"That's how many of us Canny Valleys are working for him."

Vito whistled. "Wow. Well… there you go, see? We're not going to have a problem finding you another charger, then."

I liked Vito's plan – it made a lot of sense. I think Danny did too, because he started to smile, and then he started laughing and told me about putting my mum's chip into me. The more Danny explained it, the funnier it started to sound. I was still laughing when Danny's Hexam R3 rang.

"Mum? *Again?*" said Danny, pulling his Hexam R3 out of his pocket. "How many times is she?…"

He stopped and held the phone up to show me. "It's not Mum," said Danny.

"Who is it?" asked Vito. He pulled over to the side of the road. Danny pressed answer and put it on speaker.

"Hello, Danny," said a voice that I recognized immediately. It was Carter Harluck. Danny didn't say anything.

"That was quite a stunt you all pulled today," said Harluck. He sounded relaxed. "But I'm calling to tell you it was a waste of time."

"No it wasn't," I said. "You tricked me!"

"Hello, Eric," said Mr Harluck. "How are you?"

"Fine. I'm not coming back."

"Actually, you are. It's not your decision, you see. You are property belonging to me, and your so-called friends have stolen you."

"He's not a thing," said Danny angrily.

"That's exactly what he is," said Mr Harluck. "A *thing* that belongs to me."

"What do you want?" asked Vito.

"I want to tell you that there's a hard way or an easy way to do this. The outcome is the same. Eric will run out of power soon. He hasn't been charged up – so that gives him a couple of hours. Three, max. The Canny Valleys are designed not to send out any signal, to make them harder to detect, but there are two exceptions – when they get injured, which, as you know, you can override, and the second one is only activated when a Canny Valley runs out of charge. The emergency alarm is built into the motherboard and cannot be removed without completely wiping all the software. It's a neat little precaution I came up with myself."

"We're not letting him go," said Vito.

"You are. The emergency signal is strong enough to be picked up from deep underground, or wherever else you might be thinking of hiding your friend. There are teams on standby across the country, ready to do whatever is necessary to get to the signal the moment it goes off. So say goodbye to my robot and don't cause a scene, or I'll have you arrested for theft. Understood?"

I reached over and hung up.

We drove the rest of the way to the hospital in silence. I didn't feel like talking, and I guess neither did Danny nor Vito. By the time we got to the basement room in the hospital, I was certain that there was only one option left to us. I waited until we were sitting down, and then I explained it all to them.

49

SLICK

FRIDAY 11TH JANUARY (IV)

"That's not a plan," said Danny. "That's just giving up."
I shook my head. "If what he said is true, then we haven't
got a choice."

Danny turned to Vito. "Come up with another plan."

"I'm trying," said Vito.

"It's just a case," I said, knocking my leg. "You saw it
earlier, with that other boy. And my mum. This isn't me.
The Soul Chip – that's the part that's really me."

"I can't just build a new body for you," said Vito.

I nodded. "But you'll figure it out. I don't care what I
look like."

Danny wasn't speaking. His eyes were getting red.

"It's OK, Danny," I said. "I'm not scared."

Danny smiled sadly. "I know. I just don't want you to go."

"It's just for a while," I said.

Finally, Danny agreed. Vito ran up to his car and came
back with his backpack and toolbox, while Danny took
a video of me cutting my arm and pulling it open. Proof

of what I was, in case they ever needed it. By the time we were done and had wiped up the blood, Vito had set up the laptop and was waiting for me with a pair of tweezers in his hand. I lay back on the floor and opened my mouth.

When I woke up, they had downloaded all my data and code onto his laptop. Danny and I stood next to Vito and watched as he uploaded the files to the cloud and emailed them to himself and to Danny. He closed the laptop and looked up at me.

"And now?" asked Vito.

"And now you go," I said. "I can feel it. I'm getting tired."

Danny didn't pretend he wasn't crying this time. Vito looked very sad too. I tried to smile and make them feel better. Danny hugged me and swore to me he would bring me back soon. For the first time, he didn't pull away. I think he might have hugged me all night.

"OK," I said, "this is weird now. You can let go."

Danny laughed through his tears and stepped back. I lay back down on the floor.

"You ready?" asked Vito.

I nodded.

"See you soon," I said to Danny. I smiled, then opened my mouth wide.

The last thing I saw were the faces of my friends.

And then everything went black.

EPILOGUE

THAT IS THE END OF SLICK'S JOURNAL.

We left him lying on the floor of the hospital, just as he'd told us to do. It was the hardest thing I've ever done.

As we walked away, Vito kept repeating what Slick himself had told us – that we were leaving behind a computer case, not Slick. He kept repeating that, but I could tell he was finding it as hard as I was to really believe it.

I guess Slick powered down around ten that night, about an hour after we left him. That was the time an unmarked white van pulled up outside the entrance to the hospital. I know this because Vito and I watched it all from the A&E waiting area. I told Vito I couldn't leave without knowing for certain. Vito didn't argue.

We watched as three men I didn't recognize got out of the van. They were all wearing high-visibility jackets and caps. One of them was pushing a large cleaning trolley. They didn't speak to each other as they came into the hospital and headed directly to the lift. Vito and I watched as they wheeled the trolley into the lift, went down to the basement floor, then came back up ten minutes later. Through the glass doors, we could see them loading the trolley into the back of the van. And then they were gone.

"It's just a case," said Vito firmly. He patted his chest pocket. "Slick is here. With us."

I nodded. We stood up, and Vito drove me home. I was asleep two minutes after I got through the front door.

The next day, while Vito was having lunch at my house, someone broke into his shop. They only stole one thing – Slick's Soul Chip – and the only evidence that anyone had been there was the dismantled toaster on the floor of the shop.

Vito shrugged it off. He had all the data anyway, he reassured me. It didn't change anything.

Vito got to work straight away on trying to find a new case for Slick. He sent out the video of Slick cutting his arm to a few people he knew. Nobody believed the video was real. Well, maybe someone knew something, or maybe our visit to Harluck had spooked him, because two days later, the story broke that Jeopardy Advertising had closed for business and that Carter Harluck could not be reached for comment. There was no mention in that story of a connection with the other two big news stories that broke that day – the Week's statement announcing a break from live touring and the mysterious disappearance of one of Hollywood's top actors mid-filming. Vito and I figured it out, though.

On Monday morning, I found out that Miss Lake had taken a sudden leave of absence due to a family emergency. That afternoon, Vito drove us out to the Jeopardy headquarters to confirm what we already knew. It was completely empty. Carter Harluck had vanished. And that was that – we had hit a brick wall. No matter how hard we tried, we couldn't think of another way to get a body for Slick.

I thought saying goodbye to Slick was the worst day ever, but it turned out that the worst day ever was the one when

I realized I wasn't going to be able to keep the promise I'd made Slick to bring him back.

❷ ❷ ❷

That was the same night that I told Mum what happened to Slick. She didn't believe me at first, not until she saw the video of Slick cutting his arm. Mum got so angry. And then she was really sad. I know, because I heard her crying in her bedroom.

The next day, Mum said that we had no choice but to accept what had happened. She said that sometimes life is unfair. I know she felt bad saying this to me, because she didn't get mad when I trashed my room – she just sat on my bed and cried as she watched me do it, and then she hugged me and told me that we should be grateful that Slick had come into our lives, and that it would get easier in time. It hasn't.

Three months after Slick died – I say died because that's what it feels like – Vito showed up at my house to tell me he had come up with an idea. It wasn't what I had promised Slick, but it was better than anything we'd managed to think of so far. Vito, Ethan and I worked on it every hour we could find between school and work until finally, after two weeks, we figured out how to do it.

On the night of 11th April, Vito uploaded Slick's data to *Land X*. I typed in the coordinates for Bertie's Castle and waited as the map of *Land X* opened up, then zoomed down, through the clouds and past the turrets of the home Slick and I had built together, until my avatar was standing at the entrance of our fortress.

There, waiting by the tall wooden doors – just as we had hoped – was Slick. Nobody said anything. Just because his avatar was there, it didn't mean it had actually worked.

I put my fingers over my keyboard and pressed control-C.
The chat box opened up.

I began to type.

Hi Slick. Are you there?

We waited a few seconds.
And a few more.
And then...

BALTIC_SLICK: Danny?! Is that really you?

ACKNOWLEDGEMENTS

There are too many people to thank by name here. How lucky I am to have so many friends and family who helped, supported and offered advice while I was writing this. I will thank each and every one of you in person.

A special thanks, however, to:

My agents Stephanie Thwaites (Curtis Brown Literary Agency) and Tina Dubois (ICM Talent) – who were there for me every step of the way. Michael Lesinski for knowing how to fake-code anger. Elisabetta Minervini and the brilliant team at Alma Books, especially my UK editor, Will Dady, for his endless patience, enthusiasm and words of encouragement. Thank you.

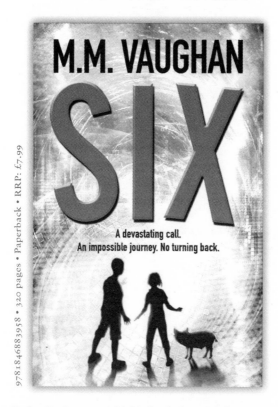

9781846883958 • 320 pages • Paperback • RRP: £7.99

When Parker Banks moves with his family from London to New York, he struggles to adapt to his new school and environment. His scientist dad is constantly at work on a top-secret technological venture for a major corporation, when one day he is kidnapped. It is up to Parker, along with his deaf sister Emma, their friend Michael and the pet pig their father left behind, to find and rescue him. They have at their disposal the E.F.E. device that their dad has invented to allow the family members to communicate with one another through telepathy.

As their search progresses, it becomes clear that SIX, the project that Parker's father has been involved in against his will, is a sinister enterprise that poses a threat not only to the Banks family, but to the world at large.

SHORTLISTED FOR THE ESSEX BOOK AWARDS AND
STOCKTON CHILDREN'S BOOK OF THE YEAR AWARD